IT ENDS AT THE WALL

LISSY PORTER

Copyright © 2025 by Lissy Porter

All rights reserved.

No part of this book may be reproduced in any form or by any electronic or mechanical means, including information storage and retrieval systems, without written permission from the author, except for the use of brief quotations in a book review.

Previously published as The Wall.

Cover design by Story Graphix Plus

ISBN 9781917374972 (paperback)

ISBN 9781917374996 (ebook)

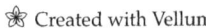 Created with Vellum

CONTENTS

England – The Year 2049	5
1. Harra	17
2. The Night Before Stage 1	32
3. Stage 1	48
4. Stage 2	57
5. Stage 3	71
6. Stage 4	92
7. Stage 5	109
8. Stage 6	123
9. Stage 7	154
10. Stage 8	175
11. Stage 9	189
12. Stage 10	208
13. Rest Day & Stage 11	219
14. Stage 12	249
15. Stage 13	256
16. Stage 14, 15 & 16	272
17. It Ends at The Wall	288
18. 2017	295
2030, 19 Years Earlier	301
About the Author	305

ENGLAND – THE YEAR 2049

THE FLOOR WAS COLD, slick with the icy flow that percolated through the stones above his head. Clenching his teeth shut, he tried not to moan out loud, while he prayed for the night to pass.

Over two weeks of travelling had brought him to this moment, and despite all those perils, only now did his nerve fail him.

He was alone, completely, in the darkened hole he'd been instructed to use. He wasn't sure what he'd expected. But it wasn't this.

For the entire length of his journey, sneaking his way ever further north, he'd worried about meeting the deadline. Now, as he shivered and shook, he wished he hadn't lingered for one of those past days. He'd not have arrived in the middle of the sodden downpour. It might have covered his covert movements, the black sky seeming to hang too low, tendrils of the heavy clouds reaching out to personally soak him with elongated fingers that threatened to hold him back from his final actions. Better to have taken chances when the sky was clear, if only to prevent the pain and discomfort now.

It hurt to clench his fingers. It hurt to unclench his fists. His feet were an agony, even moving his toes painful. His nose ran without ceasing, his wet hair allowing twin runnels to flow down his back, and pool in the waistband of his trousers, which had been clean on only last night.

A sudden shaking and a need to cough had him covering his mouth with the soggy remains of the only item he had with him, an old back-pack, the blood-red design dulled to the russet of scabs.

The noise, in the enclosed space, echoed ominously and he winced against it, praying and hoping, all at the same time that he'd not be overheard.

The Border Drones, powered through some form of magic, unknown to all, had no compassion. They'd been meticulously programmed, an eon ago, and none could undo that programming. So they continued, as instructed, to kill all who trespassed beyond the cave onto the unsheltered land that lay between the last rocky outcrop of English hills and The Wall, a glimmering haze in the near distance. An object so vast it could only truly be appreciated from a distance.

He scowled and held his breath for the tell-tale whirl of the rota blades of the drones. But the rain fell too heavily, the noise drowning out everything apart from itself. He hoped that was a good sign as he shuffled deeper into the cave, pale eyes peering painfully at the high entrance point that marked the only way into, and out of, the cave. If the Border Drones came, he'd be done for. There were no other means of escape other than through that slant that allowed the rain to pour inside his supposed shelter.

When he heard nothing but the thrum of the rain, his back relaxed, just a little, a low whimper frothing from his lips. He'd walked for three straight weeks, through all types of terrain, mostly in the dark, and now he found it painful to stop, although he'd dreamed of little else throughout his journey.

His body was young but tired, and lacking any decent food throughout his childhood, he was below height and weight. None would have taken him for the seventeen-year-old he was. None.

His head lolled backwards, smashing into the damp rocks, as he mumbled awake. He dare not sleep. Not now. Not when it was so close. He couldn't sleep through his moment. Not after all his family had endured to bring him to this place, now. To give him the chance that they would all literally die for.

Seeking to distract himself, he reached into his sodden bag and pulled forth the bedraggled piece of paper that was all he had to guide him now.

He read the sixteen stages he'd been instructed to follow by the use of a low torch, flickering intermittently, the connections bad in the battery compartment because the batteries were old, seeking the reassurance that all had been done as it should.

He checked Stage 15 and Stage 16, running his hand over the gloopy bag that had been his to protect for the last few weeks.

It was imperative that everything was timed, as it should be.

A battered wristwatch, only half of the digital marks still working, rested on his thin wrist, pulled tight to the very closest notch and still it turned uncomfortably on his wrist with every movement. By the watch he must judge the right time to pierce the gloopy bag, and then, to make his dash for freedom, no matter the rainstorm that lashed the landscape.

Everything that his family had laboured for came down to his actions in the next ten or so minutes. Or so he thought.

Shaking his head, and his wrist at the same time, he peered at the lines on the watch.

02:08

Stage 15 instructed, only at 02:08 was he to pierce the bag with the sharp needle, the transparent tube already primed and ready to enter his arm, the other needle on its far end just waiting in his arm, an unpleasant sensation, but not painful.

The final transfer would take no more than five minutes, or so Stage 15 further stated. After that five minutes, he would stand, ensure the way was clear from his damp sanctuary, and begin the sprint across the wasteland, populated by little but rabbits and hares running wild on the largest piece of grassland he'd seen in his entire life.

The animals then were free from the ravages of the Border Drones. Somehow, the Drones found the animals unworthy of their attention.

His watch read 01:59, he checked, making sure the digits were as complete as they could be. He didn't want to mistake 02:00 for 02:08 and venture forth eight minutes too early, for the Border Drones would still be flying then. Only at 02:16 did they go offline, and only then for three minutes.

He had little time to reach The Wall, and it must all be done as the instructions in his hands demanded. Stage 16 was most adamant, as was Stage 1, which had begun the enterprise. The paper had been pressed into his hands, along with his gloopy bag, just over two weeks ago. It had been creased and worn then, the splatter of red gore on it, no sign of hope, and yet, it had been his family's choice, and he'd leapt at the prospect of freedom. A way out of the hellhole of England.

Away from the smog that always hovered over his home, away from the constant and perpetual violence, away from the endless hunger and the continual self-hatred. None were immune from it. But he'd been gifted with a chance of another life.

He checked his watch, swallowing hard against the horror of seeing 02:00 only without the left-hand bottom line of the 0.

Did it say 02:08 already? Was he too late? The number ticked over to 02:01 and he allowed a nervous laugh for his fears.

Seven minutes yet. Seven minutes in which he could change his mind, or be captured, or just end it all here. Either way, there was no going back, and there was no way his family would ever know the truth about what had befallen him.

They might live life hoping he was safe and warm and well-fed, while his bones rotted in the dank little cave, a waste of so much hope and promise, hard-work, black-market dealings and the further impoverishment of his family.

02:02

His breath was even more ragged, his hands shaking so much he feared he'd been unable to pierce the gloopy bag when the time came. Fear and cold consumed him, and he slumped to his side, eyes open, damp hair resting in a pool of water.

He couldn't do this. There was no chance. Terror engulfed him, as he trembled, tears of dismay obscuring his vision, just like the rainstorm outside had done.

02:04

He forced himself upright, his hands to unclench, and his body to stillness.

It didn't matter if he wanted to do this or not. There was no decision, not any more.

As per Stage 15, he squeezed the gloopy bag in his hands. It said to warm it slightly, but there was no chance of that in the frigid cave, his hands blue from the cold. Instead, he slunk it between his folded knees and his belly, hoping that he had some residual body heat available.

Grimacing at the feeling, reminiscent of the cold pottage his family lived on, he thought of warmth and heat, but the concept was too strange for him. He'd never known heat, or warmth in any significant amount.

02:06

Nearly time, but he kept the gloopy bag against his stomach. Any heat would aid the process, or he'd spend more than the allotted five minutes on the task. He licked his dry lips. He wanted to drink, the irony of being somewhere filled with water, and yet unable to savour any of it.

He'd vomit soon enough as it was. Better it be on an empty stomach.

02:07

He flexed his arm, feeling the waiting needle pushing against his vein, but needing to ensure his body was warm as well when the time came. He peered at his watch, counting in his head, as he'd been taught as a child. One elephant, two elephants, three elephants, and still the time dragged.

His eyes threatened to close, exhaustion overcoming him even though he was so close to the final act, to completing Stage 15 and going onto Stage 16.

02:08

Finally, the numbers glared at him, the dull green adding an eerie glow to his labours.

He sprang into action. The gloopy bag against his stomach remaining there as he pierced it with the other needle, and watched, in the glow of the flickering torch, as the liquid eased its way along the only available line of escape. But it was slow, far too slow.

Irritated with himself, he remembered that the bag needed to be higher than his arm, and he released it from its warm shelter against his skin. Now, entangled as he was, it was almost impossible to move without dislodging either end of the perilous needles, bag and arm combination.

Tears of frustration welled in his eyes as his wristwatch showed 02:09 and still he'd not felt the cold flow of the new blood entering his body.

'Damn,' he growled, using his other arm to hold the gloopy bag high, while he lay below it. This was it. This was all he could do. He only hoped it was enough.

With a gasp of shock, as his watch flashed 02:09 still, balefully declaring his actions too late and too slow, the first slither of the precious liquid entered his body, glowing black and insidious in the green and orange light of the ancient torch and even more archaic digital watch.

Growling with pain, he felt his eyes flicker against the invasion once more. Any more of this and his body would reject it, once and for all. The last time, just before he'd left, he'd passed out, having to be revived by the cold hands of his father. A shimmer of anger in those hard, steel eyes, had told him he was a disappointment and unlikely to succeed now.

He would prove them wrong. Even if they never knew.

02:10

His shaking from the cold had been replaced by a juddering from the infusion going into his arm. The gloopy bag, while draining at an adequate speed now, was heavy in his outstretched arm as it shook with exertion, dangling above his prostrate body.

He gritted his teeth. 02:11, or so he hoped, the bottom line again missing. 02:12, or so he prayed, the bottom and the middle line missing on the 2. The missing digits were never the same, as though the watch mocked him for trying to use something older than his grandparents.

His one hand was growing lighter, the other ever heavier. He knew it was working, but it was little consolation, as he felt his eyelids growing heavy as his body spiralled into shock.

02:13

And he fought for consciousness, throwing the two-thirds empty gloopy bag to one side, the needle splashing from it so that the precious contents sheeted across the floor in a black ink of corruption. The smell made him gag, as he yanked the needle from his arm, sending it the way of the gloopy bag as well.

Hastily, he bound his arm, dabbing the salve onto the needlepoint mark that would heal it instantly, belying what he'd been up to.

He reached for the sodden cave wall, his torch in one hand, flickering over the mess he'd leave behind and dismissing it as he fought to stay upright. He clawed The Wall with the other, nails cracking with the pressure of his grip.

He fought nausea.

02:14

Staggering he peered upwards. The exit seemed suddenly far away, the noise from the rain receding as well, as though he were suddenly far away from his shelter and the elements outside.

He stood, and he breathed shallowly through his nose, trying not to inhale any more of the bloody mess.

02:15

He needed to go. There was no more time. A faint electronic beep came from his watch, and he cursed, fumbling for the too tiny button on the side to silence the watch, an alarm he'd set weeks ago, and thought to never use. A useless endeavour that threatened to reveal him now.

02:16

On legs grown rubbery, he followed his thrown backpack up the three steep and jagged rocks that formed a natural stairway.

02:17

He burst outside, no thought for any of the Border Drones that might still be about their business. But the night had grown silent, even the heavy rain falling without ceasing, seeming to do so without the noise of impact. A curtain to mask his actions provided he remained quiet.

He squinted upward, shielding his eyes from the deluge, assuring himself of just where he needed to head, and he ran straight downhill.

The path was steep, or rather, the hillside was steep, and there was no path, but only an expanse of rutted stones and grass, punctuated here and there with a precarious rabbit hole.

His breath was ragged in his throat, his legs pumping beneath him, and his arms flailing as he tried to keep his balance, his backpack thudding against his sodden waistband.

The torch jostled in and out of usefulness as his arms pumped to aid him.

Stage 16. There were only three minutes to make this perilous journey. Three minutes and the drones would once more be about their duty. They needed precious little time to recharge and reboot. But still, three minutes could be a long time, as he'd discovered in the cave.

His feet splashed through wet grass, his calves, wet already, drenched before the terrain levelled out. With a quick glance upwards, he checked he was still on course, The Wall seeming to beckon him, and he redoubled his efforts. His watch flashed in time with his shaking torch, but luckily, the glow was too feeble for him to be able to see in the strange gloom. For the first time in weeks, the count had no meaning for him.

Abruptly the terrain changed, no more slick grasslands, but rather the smoothness of concrete, the white of the beacon of hope, causing him to pull up short and forget his headlong dash forwards.

He was where he needed to be.

Still the clouds hung too low for him to see the moon. The rain sheeted, falling with the softness of snow, as he slapped his hand onto the faintly glowing control pad.

This was it. The moment of truth.

He'd come all this way. He'd taken all these risks.

And now, well now he'd know the truth.

Only him, and him alone, for none would witness what befell him now. Not even the drones, which were still recharging.

The control panel sprang to life, a too-bright blue in the bleakest of nights, no doubt visible from miles around.

Words appeared, instructions he'd been told about, although how anyone could know had baffled him and still did. Who would come all this way only to retreat and return south? Swiftly he placed his hand into the chasm that opened beneath the control pad and felt the sting of needles penetrating all four of his fingers and his thumb on his left hand.

A wave of nausea once more threatened to engulf, but he breathed deeply through his nose, willing himself not to look at the watch on his right arm, or to strain to hear the return of the drones.

Long moments passed in which he willed his heart to slow, his fear to subside, but he knew he was out of time. There had been far too many 'elephants' muttered in his head, in place of seconds.

More instructions appeared on the screen before him, as he withdrew his hand.

He glanced at the words.

'Legal agreement.'

'Terms and conditions.'

'Please acknowledge and accept.'

And his heart leapt with joy. This was it. He'd made it.

He fumbled his finger to the control panel, devoid of rain, but fogged by lack of use, and he ran his finger over the top, marvelling as a green line traced where his hand had been, his acceptance of the rabidly spooling words.

He didn't have the time to read them. No one did.

Hastily, he shrugged his backpack free from its place and threw it to one side.

He'd not be needing that now. Never again.

A rumble, like thunder, but more ominous, filled his ears and a grin finally stained his cheeks.

This was it. Freedom.

And then the screech of an alarm began.

CHAPTER 1
HARRA

SHE HUDDLED, cold and tired, as always, on the slight mattress through which she could feel the ancient bed springs every time she dared twist or turn.

She pulled the thin blanket tighter to her chin, knowing it was useless, but doing so all the same.

Cold. She'd always been cold. It was the overriding memory knifing through every childhood remembrance. No matter what, she'd never felt warm.

Money was scarce, she knew, but of late it had been even scarcer, and she wished her belly were fuller so the chill would bite less deeply.

She'd thought with her cousin's disappearance there might have been some respite in the strict controls exercised over everyone's diet, over how much was set aside for heating. But no, if anything, while the family grieved her missing cousin, they grew even more tight-fisted.

'Harra,' her name was called softly but insistently, as she complainingly threw back her spartan covers, and placed tepid feet on the freezing slabs of her bedroom floor.

'Coming,' she called, just as softly, a hint of annoyance making her voice sound whiny.

Down the stairs, lit only by one spluttering candle, and she was shocked by the sight that greeted her.

Before her, arrayed around the family table, sat not only her mother but also her aunt and uncle, parents to her missing cousin. Not that there was anything unusual in that, rather it was that they'd rolled her aged grandmother out as well. The old dear was so feeble Harra feared to touch her, half thinking she'd turn to dust beneath her fingers and crumble away to nothing.

Questioning eyes flickered between her mother and her uncle, but their faces were expressionless, stony even.

'Sit child,' her grandmother's voice was old and ragged, croaky from lack of use, and always tinged with sorrow.

Harra did as she was told, her compliance a given.

She shivered, wishing she'd brought her scratchy blanket with her, but too intrigued to ask to go back for it.

She waited, her eyes on her grandmother, wondering what all this was about.

'Your cousin is gone,' her grandmother eventually said. Unsure how to respond, Harra looked from her aunt to her uncle and swallowed heavily.

'I know, grandmother. I understand.'

No real explanation had been given for what had happened to her cousin, but then, it wasn't rare for family members to just disappear. Death stalked the lives of all. Harra had assumed whatever had happened to him was just too terrifying to tell her. She was grateful for that. Better to imagine him having a peaceful death than knowing the truth of the situation.

'We've arranged for you to leave as well.' Now her grandmother's eyes held the flint that brokered no argument.

'What? Leave?' burst from her mouth in shock. Where had her cousin gone? How had they managed to ensure he left?

'Listen, don't interrupt.' The huskiness of her grandmother's voice had disappeared. Now she spoke as one used to being listening to and obeyed.

A hundred thoughts shot through Harra's mind, the most pertinent, that no one leaves. It's forbidden, impossible, and anyway, if her family could have left, they would have done so, long ago. Before The Wall. But they were forever stained. Forever. Blood doesn't lie.

'There's a way, if the rules are followed. We'll begin tonight. It'll be a secret, no one must ever know. You'll have three months to prepare yourself to never see your family again, apart from your cousin. Perhaps.' Her grandmother ended with a twist to her too thin lips. Harra didn't know her well enough to appreciate if it was a sign of grief or joy.

Harra's mouth opened, but no question rushed through her trembling lips. Never see her family again? No, that was impossible. No matter her gripes about the cold and the lack of food, she couldn't abandon her family, not here, never.

'You'll not want to go. The future is suddenly filled with terror. I understand,' her grandmother tried to eject some softness into her tone, but it utterly failed. She had always been implacable, offering no comfort for scraped knees when Harra had been a child. Always an assertion that it was 'nothing to cry about.'

'It's too late for the rest of us. But you, there's still hope, and we'll give it to you.'

As her grandmother spoke, and Harra tried to deny the words, firm hands gripped her arm, a sharp poke causing her to hiss through suddenly clenched teeth, but whatever was happening, her head was held firmly in place so she couldn't witness what her aunt and uncle were doing. No, she could only see the tears falling from her ragged mother's eyes, eyes she loved, and which her grandmother had just told her, she'd never see again after three months time.

'It's best you don't know any details. We'll call you here, every week for three months, and only then, if successful, will you be instructed on how to proceed.'

Harra thought back to the last few months with her cousin, as she fought for composure. Had he been keeping a secret from her? Was this even possible or were they really doing something else? Perhaps they would kill her too? Then there would be more food for all to eat.

'Don't question, and don't ask. No one will speak to you of what must happen in this household, and you must not mention it to any of your friends. They will tell their parents or guardians, and people will come knocking on our door, to take us away, for treason. Heed my words.'

As her grandmother continued to prattle, Harra felt her head begin to swim, nausea forcing her to breathe through her nostrils to keep the sick feeling at bay.

Yet, even this had been anticipated, as her mother finally stood and silently reached for a bucket, to place beneath her retching head. Holding the bucket with one hand, and pulling back Harra's long and tattered hair with the other while Harra repeatedly vomited.

'Keep her conscious,' the barked instructions of her grandmother.

Harra cried as she vomited what little had been in her stomach, and then as her eyes fluttered closed, the sharp slap of a hand on her cheek awoke her.

Her mother watched her, horror on her tired and lined face at what she'd done, but firm resolve as well.

Harra cried, even more, the tears falling freely down her face, as her arm slumped onto her lap. What had her uncle done to her, with the help of her aunt? What had they done to her cousin?

'Good, take her back to her bed. Perhaps in the morning she'll think it all a dream. Until the next time.' As Harra was supported to her feet by her mother, her eyes sought out her grandmother, but the old woman had already turned her back on her granddaughter and was painstakingly wheeling herself back to her bed on the ground floor, the stairs long ago proving too much for her weakened body.

Harra bit back her sobs of horror. She couldn't leave her mother. And yet, it seemed her grandmother's decision was final. Bewildered and confused, she allowed her mother to guide her back up the rickety stairs to her slight mattress, and even thinner blanket barely conscious.

As she slipped onto the bed, too tired to even fight the bedspring that always cut into her back, her mother dipped low and kissed her forehead.

'It's for the best. You're stronger than your cousin. This will be easier on you. Now sleep.'

The arm her uncle or aunt had seized trembled as it lay on the bed, all but useless, her mouth hollow with the taste of vomit, as her mother stood and left the room.

Harra thought she'd cry, but instead, her eyes snapped shut, and she slept.

———

Three weeks later Harra was woken in the night by a soft call. Déjà vu engulfed her as she trembled her way down the stairs, to face the stony faces of her mother, aunt and uncle sitting, as always, beside the kitchen table.

She felt certain this had happened before, and yet she couldn't quite grasp the true memories of when.

'Good evening,' her mother offered. 'It's time, once more. It'll be quick. You're doing well.'

If the words were supposed to comfort, Harra didn't feel

them, instead, and without her noticing, her aunt and uncle had stood from their seats, and now one of them grabbed her arm, only for her to feel a sharp sting.

'What?' Harra cried, the familiar feeling of nausea immediately swooping down on her.

'Now isn't the time for questions,' her mother cautioned, her tone devoid of all empathy, standing, a bucket in her hand. Harra swallowed heavily, breathing through her nose, as her blood ran icy cold through her aching body.

She didn't know what was happening but knew then that it had happened before. But why, or when, she couldn't remember.

Over the last few weeks, she'd begun to feel ill on many occasions. The food she ate tasted wrong, and what little she'd once wolfed down, now sat in the bowl and slowly congealed. She never felt any warmth any more, never, not even beneath her blanket and wearing all of her clothes.

At work, she was lackadaisical and had been reprimanded only that day by her supervisor for her inability to perform the simple data input tasks she'd been given. She'd stayed silent when asked about her day at work by her family. It had taken much persuasion for her to be granted the job at the Government Agency. Her mother would be angry if she lost the job. The money was too eagerly needed. And yet. Well, perhaps it wasn't her fault after all.

Tears ran down her face as the queasiness built and she knew her mother was experienced with the bucket and would know when to act.

'It's only been three weeks,' her Aunt said, pride in her voice. 'She's managing remarkably well.'

'She's better suited to it,' her Uncle replied, his voice tight with displeasure.

She wanted to ask what she was better suited to, but at that moment, vomit began to flow, as she heaved into her mother's bucket.

The smell was rancid, and once more, she wondered why her sick was always tinged with bits of orange. It wasn't as though she ever ate anything that was orange. No, her diet was bland, consisting of the same everyone else ate, the ubiquitous pottage.

There was no variety to the grey sludge they ate for breakfast and dinner, and there was certainly nothing orange to be had.

In fact, she only knew the colour orange because of a single, solitary flower she'd once found as a child, growing beneath the shade of the coal store. She'd watched the flower all afternoon long transfixed by its delicate colour, and wondering just where it might have come from.

Even now, she'd never seen anything quite like it, although she'd looked, whenever she'd passed the coal store, hoping it was something that would be repeated.

It had shone, brighter than anything she'd ever experienced beneath the smog-filled sky. Some spoke of the sun, but she had only patchy recollections of it. She knew, from her brief education, that the sun and the moon were responsible for day following night, but she'd never seen the moon either. Only ever the impenetrable black of night, and the olive haze of the smog during the day.

'Come on, back to bed.' Her mother's eyes were kind as she placed the bucket to one side, and slung Harra's other arm around her shoulder.

'Goodness me, you're getting light,' there was a flint edge of worry in her mother's voice, but Harra could think of nothing but her bed, and sleep. And so she walked, carefully, wobbling from side to side, back up the steep, bold staircase, the wood bowed in places, screeching against the action.

One day, her mother had warned, the staircase would give way entirely, and then they'd have to rely on the ladder to get up and down the stairs. Harra had worried about that when she was so small it was a stretch to reach one step after another. Now, she knew she'd never be able to mount a ladder. Not the way she felt.

So she stepped carefully, avoiding the soggiest pieces of wood, relieved when she could collapse on her bed.

'Sleep well, my love,' her mother's lips on her brow were warm and reminiscent of a time when she was little more than a babe in arms. Indeed, her mother hadn't kissed her in such a way for years. Or had she?

———

Eight weeks later, Harra peered bleary-eyed at her mother, aunt and uncle; surprised her grandmother was also part of this strange ritual.

Her eyes were unfocused, and she'd since lost her job. Surprisingly her mother had been understanding, her aunt and uncle as well. And even though she lounged around all day at home, she was still receiving the same food portions as before, and no one begrudged her for adding fuel to the fire to drive the constant chill from her body from being still for so much of the daytime.

She struggled to remember how she'd once filled her days in the Government Agency, marvelling at how quickly the clock now ticked around each day, seeming to gobble the hours between her family going to work, all except her grandmother, and then returning later that day.

If they expected food to be prepared for them, now that Harra was home all day, there was never any anger if she'd merely watched the clock all day, tick-tick-ticking, forgetting what it meant when the large hand pointed at the twelve and the small one at the five.

That day she'd managed to cook the evening meal, and it had tasted divine, even to her own lips. And yet even that was a haze to her now.

Some elements of her day were so vibrantly real, while others seemed to fade into nothingness. She'd never felt more alive, and yet also, more confused, more perplexed about what it was that she actually did day after day.

Now she shook her head, her eyes slowly focusing on more than just the shape of her family. Her beloved family, devoid now of her cousin.

Her grandmother watched her with something like fervour, her mother with quiet pride, while her aunt and uncle whispered one to another, as though she weren't in the room.

'It's time you knew the truth,' her grandmother dictated. 'You've done well, and I'm proud of you, but now is the most difficult part of your escape.'

More and more she'd begun to think of another life to the one she knew, and the use of the word 'escape' jarred her, so closely mirroring her own thoughts.

'We've prepared you, but now you must master a few pertinent skills, and then it will be time to say goodbye.' The finality in those words caused her mother to judder, but her grandmother covered her mother's shaking hand, that rested on the table, with her own. A display of comfort Harra had never witnessed before. Her grandmother had always been a hard woman. Never one to run to with scraped knees and bruised fingers. Never one to wipe away tears and snot.

'Your mother, aunt and uncle will help you now, and in a week, your adventure will begin. It will be dangerous, and fraught with peril. But you'll succeed. You'll make me proud.' Those words, sharp-edged and icy, forced Harra's vision to clear. As she peered at her grandmother, sudden understanding came to her.

This woman had once performed a careless act out of ignorance, nothing more, and she'd been punished and humiliated all her life because of it. She'd sentenced her children to this stark existence, and in turn, her own grandchildren.

Whatever Harra was about to be told, she knew, without having to ask, that her grandmother had been instrumental in enacting it.

Her grandmother lapsed into silence then, still and expectant. It was her Uncle who took the lead.

Onto the table before them he lifted a small bag, burgundy in colour, although it seemed to be ice cold, gently steaming in the air around them.

'This is the final one of these, and we'll inject it into your arm now.' At the words, her right hand fisted and then released, a memory that this had been done before.

'It contains all you need to change you, as is needed. But there'll be another for you, at the end. And you'll need to administer it yourself. It's a little different, but the technique's the same.'

As he spoke, her uncle lifted other equipment onto the table. A needle, and a thread of what looked to be see-through tubing. Her aunt hesitated only a moment and then stood. Circling behind Harra, she reached out and gently patted her arm, on the inside of her elbow.

'To insert the needle, you first have to make the veins show, you pat them until the blue shows clearly.'

Warm hands on her skin were a shock for Harra, and she almost recoiled but instead concentrated on her aunt's dexterous fingers.

Harra had always admired her aunt's soft hands, so unlike everyone else's. She made her living in a beauty salon, for those with the resources to afford such luxury. For her, it was unacceptable to show the ravages of the hard life she lived.

Now Harra watched those hands and delicately manicured nails.

'When the vein is up, you insert the needle, which will be attached to the tube.'

Her Uncle had joined his wife now, the maroon bag in his hand.

'You have to manipulate the bag a bit, warm it if you can, but if not, at least break up the ice, or it will not flow into you, no matter what.'

Harra nodded, trying not to show her revulsion. She wanted to ask where the blood came from, why she needed it in her veins, but her grandmother watched on, her expression forbidding. Harra held her tongue.

'The most important thing is to ensure the tube is inserted into this end of the bag. There's another needle for that, see, here.' And he showed her, and she tried not to wince at the size of the other needle, or at the strange smell of the maroon bag.

'It's also imperative you hold the bag up high, to aid the flow of the fluid.' Now, as the needle penetrated her arm, she watched her uncle hoist the chilled bag high in the air, as she felt the cold fluid enter her arm.

She grimaced and shivered, a wave of memory and nausea sweeping over her.

'And it's important not to be sick,' she also muttered, and her mother laughed, a strained sound, but one Harra thought showed her pride.

'And to remain conscious at all times,' her uncle commented dourly, trying not to show any satisfaction in a lesson well learnt, but still respect filled his voice.

'It won't be easy, or so I imagine it. If possible, lie flat and hold the bag above you, or use a stone, or a ledge to keep it higher. It should be quick, no more than five minutes.'

Momentarily, Harra's head span, and she bit back the taste of bile.

She wouldn't be sick. Not again, and not for many weeks

now. Harra was surprised by her returning memories. How had she been able to forget her strange nighttime meetings?

While the fluid flowed inside her, a piece of paper was laid on the table before her.

'These are your instructions. They must be followed, or you'll not succeed. Read them, learn them, memorise them and ask what questions you must. We'll answer as we can. There'll be no one else you can ask.'

Harra found her eyes drawn to the list. It was too far away to make out all the words, but she could tell that it was crammed with small words, perhaps typed, onto an old and stained piece of paper.

Paper, how she'd longed for it as a child, to scribble on and draw pretty pictures. But there had been little enough of it then, and even less now. Wood was too valuable to waste on making paper, especially when there were homes to heat throughout the long winter months.

'You can't lose your instructions. You'll fail if you do, and there's no replacement. Each set of instructions is particular.'

Harra nodded.

'My cousin, he managed to do this, and so shall I.' She didn't miss the sharp inhalation of her aunt. Unsure what it meant she continued to fill her gaze with her grandmother's face.

'Tomorrow you'll consider what you need to take with you. Nothing big, and nothing that will serve as a reminder of your family. You'll leave everything behind, just before.' The sentence hung unfinished. Harra didn't push her grandmother for further information but relieved of her aunt and uncle's attention, she reached out with her left hand for the piece of paper.

It was rough beneath her hands, and, as she'd thought, filled with small, neat typed letters, although some of the lines weren't quite straight so the tops and bottoms of some words merged into those above or below them. From a typewriter, an ancient one, but then, everything was old these days, industry a thing of the past.

'Stage 1,'

she read, her lips moving with the words. Her stomach clenched with fear as she read, silently, each point seeming to drive her further and further from her home and all she'd ever known, despite the fact she sat still.

'Stage 2,'

she continued, understanding the depth of the instructions, and running her eyes to the bottom of the page. It went all the way to Stage 13, but she didn't think that was the end, but neither could she turn over to check, not when her grandmother was watching her so intently.

Instead, she read as quickly as she could, point after point, after point, until she reached the end of the page, and was finally able to turn over. Scanning down the list, she was relieved to see it ended at Stage 16 and that it didn't fill the page, as on the other side.

Each stage raised questions she needed answers for, but she held her tongue, in the flickering of the single, bare light bulb, just above her head, that illuminated the immaculate, if decrepit kitchen of her childhood. She understood now why her chair had been placed as it had been, the windows carefully covered by the heavy, drab curtains, that had always been there and which were routinely beaten free of the dust from the coal fires.

'I understand,' Harra announced when she'd finished reading. Clearly, this task was not easy to accomplish. Some of the points filled her heart with fear. But she'd do what she was being commanded to do. It seemed there was no turning back, not now.

'Good,' her grandmother spoke with finality. 'It's agreed that you'll leave in six days. Prepare yourself well.'

With the pronouncement made, her grandmother struggled to her feet, a stick held in each shaky hand. The movements were slow, almost painful to watch to Harra's suddenly too alert mind. She could have stood and run around the room fifteen times before her grandmother finally swayed upright on unsteady legs.

No one watched her grandmother leave, other than her. No one saw, other than Harra, when her grandmother stopped just before entering her room and allowed her tight shoulders to deflate. Harra swallowed.

Her grandmother had never apologised for anything in her life, had never been less than entirely sure of every action she took. To see her weak, in such a way, was sobering.

Her grandmother wouldn't live forever, but it seemed Harra was to be deprived of those final few years with her. Just what would her mother do then? She had no one but her mother and her daughter, and soon, Harra wouldn't be there any more.

Who would care for her in her old age? Who would provide food and heating when she was as weak and tired as her grandmother?

In being forced to leave by her grandmother, her mother was being consigned to no future worth anything. Her family would never be able to pay for the care of those too old to work. The thought gnawed at Harra, but she turned bright eyes toward her mother, aunt and uncle.

'You have my heartfelt thanks for this opportunity,' Harra managed to force past tight lips, tears falling unshed down her cheeks, a stream with no visible source and no apparent end.

'It's the least we could do,' her mother murmured.

'Restitution,' her uncle confirmed. But Harra shook her head.

'It's not yours to make restitution for,' she said tenderly, understanding in her voice. 'You had no voice. You were too young.'

'The sins of the father,' her aunt said, her green eyes filled with pleading for the painful conversation to end. Harra bowed her head and let the conversation die away into silence.

Sins, what a stupid word to use, Harra thought bitterly. But really, what other way was there of describing what had happened?

CHAPTER 2
THE NIGHT BEFORE STAGE 1

HARRA WAITED until the house stilled into the silence of dead sleep before she stood.

She felt both unsteady on her feet and filled with confidence she'd accomplish all that was expected of her. But before she could leave, tomorrow, there was something she had to do. And her grandmother wouldn't approve of it. No chance.

On silent feet, she crept down the ancient stairs, avoiding at all costs the creaking steps that would give away her movements and ultimate intentions.

At the front door, she held her breath, just listening. She needed to be sure her grandmother didn't hear her illicit journey. While Harra knew after tomorrow she'd never see her grandmother again, still she didn't wish to disappoint her and leave under a cloud of silent anger.

The door was old and noisier than the stairs, but Harra had taken the opportunity, earlier in the week, to work some forgotten-about-oil into the stubborn hinges, and now she turned the key and eased the door open as silently as it was possible to be.

She heard, or imagined she did, the suck of the enclosed air shooting out of the door, to be replaced with the choking smog, as she stepped outside, naked feet encountering the concrete of the front step.

Sooner to creep out the front door, as far from her grandmother as possible than risk the back door, with its more used and pleasant entranceway.

Outside no light shone, apart from the faint glow from her newest possession, a Casio wristwatch her mother had wrapped around her wrist as though conveying a gift of the most significant import only that day.

To know the time, all the time, was a luxury long-denied her, reliant only on the clock in her place of work, and the chimes of the church bells. They still rang, provided someone attended to them. More often than not, no two church bells agreed with each other, leading to confusion which meant it was best to ignore the sporadic attempts.

Pushing the door closed behind her, she reached for her boots, hidden hours earlier behind the food bin, and slipped them onto her feet.

The smog of night enveloped her, but Harra would have known her way to the shoulder-high front gate, blindfolded and gagged. This, after all, was the only home she'd ever known, and the connection was intimate and conditioned by years of association.

The front gates, more closely guarded than the front door to the house, were another obstacle Harra had considered much earlier in the week. The hound, which typically ran wild during the day, was chained at night but trained to wake at the slightest noise. Her grandmother said the hound was worth the cost of feeding it and ensuring it remained healthy. No one had ever managed to sneak beyond the animal.

Until now.

The hound slept solidly, a full belly to thank for that, and also a spattering of a sleeping herb her mother used. Harra had worried about injuring the animal by medicating it, but she needed to accomplish her covert task, and so had conceded to the necessity of it all.

Now, she snuck past the hound's cage, and to the array of locks and bolts that secured them from the outside world. Again, Harra had greased all of the sliding locks in preparation, and she opened them quickly and without allowing failure to worry her.

She'd grown confident of late. Otherwise, she'd never have attempted this.

Pulling the gate open, only so much as needed to slip outside, Harra reached her hand over, hooking the top bolt, and sliding it home.

Only then did she spare a glance up and down the street. It seemed deserted, but it was impossible to tell in the strange olive glow of the smog-drenched night, the moon unable to permeate the layers of clouds above her head.

Not that it mattered. If there was anyone to question her, she was under no obligation to answer, and they too would have been breaking the strictly enforced night-time curfew as well. More likely, any fellow night-time wanderer would have ignored her, as she would have done them.

Free now, she turned right and took to her heels. She had a long way to travel that night, and only her willpower and feet to get her there.

Looking only ever in front of her, hoping the murk would be just enough to offer her pointers on the landmarks she'd known all her life, Harra made good time.

Barely glancing at the statue of some long-forgotten man, festooned with the muck of ages, or at the Church tower, where the soft chimes of the bells could be heard, even throughout the long night, she rushed ever onwards.

The only shop in town flew past her, and then the building where she'd once worked, and then through the overgrown parkland, where her mother assured her, children had once climbed the tangled wreck of iron and splintered wood that made the area look as though it was presided over by a twisted spider. Still, she ran onwards.

This was a pilgrimage, one that would take her almost to the outskirts of their benighted settlement.

She heard no other sound as she ran, apart from her breathing, and the ticking and striking of the clocks on all public buildings. Neither did she see any other living creature. And why would she? It was said gangs of the dispossessed and desperate roamed at night, always keen to take what they could from those with little more than themselves.

The prospect of any sort of encounter didn't unsettle her. Not with her heightened senses.

Eventually, her rapid pace slowed, and she bent double, resting her hands on her slightly bent thighs, just catching her breath and thinking about the next steps.

The desire to get here had driven her thinking all week. What she'd do on arrival had not concerned her. Not until now.

How best could she do this?

The abandoned church rose up before her, a behemoth that had for centuries before been a significant landmark. It had long since fallen into ruin when the leaded roof had collapsed in on itself, injuring no one, but leaving everything inside exposed to the outside. Decay had soon set in, and yet, this was where her father lay, in eternal slumber, and it was to him, she must say farewell. And it had been his choice to be buried here.

The graveyard rose before her. A mismatched collection of standing stones cast in inky shadow, appearing to ooze green smog.

She shivered, but just the once. If the eerie scene put her off, she'd never have the chance to make this pilgrimage again.

Straightening her shoulders, Harra ran down the moss-encrusted steps, and through the mangled remains of the black iron fence, without thinking about what she did.

In all the years since her father's death, she'd never since been allowed to visit the dilapidated site. Her grandmother had forbidden it, as was all conversation about her father. It had been hard to grow up without ever speaking of her father again. No photographs had been allowed in the house. Her grandmother had forbidden his name to be mentioned.

Harra cursed softly, slipping on mounds of piled leaves and abandoned rubbish. The pathways through the graveyard were cracked and overgrown, weeds and grasses causing trip hazards, and she had to rely on her memories of over ten years ago to hunt her father's grave down.

Harra had always pitied her mother the life she'd been forced to lead, both when her father was ill, and also afterwards, when her grandmother had tried to erase him.

But Harra had never forgotten him. Not his laughing eyes, and fabulous stories, and not his gentle love that had made her earliest years the happiest of her life.

Her grandmother's attitude toward her father's death had been too harsh, and unjustifiable. As though it had somehow been his fault cancer had engulfed his body, the treatments far outside the reach of his mother's meagre wages.

That he'd died, from a disease that could have been cured had the money only been available, never ceased to sadden Harra. If he'd been ill before the event, his treatment would have been free, and his health recoverable. His death had been the result of politics, nothing else, and she could never forgive that.

Now, Harra wondered, if what she was about to endure was her grandmother's long overdue way of making reparations, for everything that had happened to Harra in her short life.

Certainly, this was Harra's way of saying goodbye to all that had gone before.

Clinging weeds rubbed at her legs while thin spider web trails ran between the prominent gravestones, No matter how often she swiped at her face she couldn't stop her shoulder blades from itching, or the threads from coating her. In the glow of her watch, the green gloom only intensified.

Twice she walked down the wrong path, and twice she realised and turned herself around. On the second attempt, her eyes inadvertently caught the flashing numbers on her watch, and she knew time was quickly running out. She needed to find the grave, or she'd have to risk either being discovered or not finding it at all.

Worry redoubled her speed, and she tripped and skidded her way down yet another path. This one seemed to be clearer than the others, and that gave her hope. Perhaps she wasn't the only one to have sought out the more recent graves. The church might be disregarded but people died with dizzying regularity, and the churchyard was still used, even if not all of the burials were sanctioned.

Life was expensive; death was as well, and with it came the inconvenience of having to dispose of the physical body of the deceased. Harra grimaced at her dark thoughts, but she wasn't alone. Only having one parent was a similar story to many. Her aunt and uncle were a rarity, still being together, and still having each other, after so many years.

Her grandmother was even rarer, living to a grand old age in relatively good health. She might not be able to go to work, but neither was she a burden on her family. Few others of her age could say the same.

Finally, Harra stopped before a short, squat gravestone. She remembered this well. On that fateful day, when her father's cheap coffin had been lowered six feet into the earth, the small stone had struck Harra, lying ready to be placed on the sealed grave.

It had been so much smaller than all the others, with merely her father's name on it, and no dates or special messages, unlike that to either side. Yet, it had cost her mother all of the savings she'd had, and Harra knew she'd been proud of it.

In the murky light, it was impossible to read her father's name, but she bent and traced the engraving with her fingers, all the same, forcing away the moss that had tried to fill the expensive lettering.

Tears filled her eyes, and so did the longing to have a father. But, and she considered this carefully, would her life have been much different if her father had lived? What would he have been able to do to enhance her life, to even free her from the hopelessness of the future that had been hers ever since she'd been old enough to understand her options?

All talk of the future had once filled her with nothing but the dragging sense of futility. Her family had now given her the opportunity for something else. But had it only been because of her father's death?

On her knees, she bowed her head low. No prayers came to mind and no entreaty to God. England had once professed to Christianity, but in the face of the pointlessness of it all, no one believed any more.

Instead, she spoke to her father, soft words, wrenched from deep inside her, where they'd been hidden for over a decade.

She told him of the events in her life she wished he'd seen, of trivial matters that meant nothing to anyone but herself, and she sobbed for all that was irreplaceable and so very precious, but gone, out of reach, for all times.

Only then, cried out and exhausted beyond any ability to stand, did Harra throw her head back. Here, she cried for her old life and lost chances. For she had hope now, and so, her voice a little lighter, she spoke of escape, of new opportunities, and how she wished her father had only benefited from the same.

Only when she was dry inside did she stand, a hand trailing along the tangled vines atop the gravestone. She wished she could pull all of the weeds free, remove the moss and lichen, but that would mark her path too easily. No, she would have to leave it as it was, but that was almost too painful.

It already felt as though her father had been forgotten about. When she left, it would be like she'd abandoned him as well. Or would it? The memories of her father she stored in her mind would travel with her. She'd not lose him, or her mother, aunt, uncle and grandmother. Rather she'd take shadows of them, always a part of her, if never seen by anyone else.

That thought and that thought alone enabled her to finally walk away from her father's grave.

Her face was dry of all tears, a fierce determination that somehow, when she was free, she'd be able to take some action to ensure he was never forgotten, somewhat like the yearly celebrations which once marked those who'd fought in England's wars to keep her free from oppression.

It hadn't taken long for that celebration to fall to abeyance once The Wall was built. After all, there was no point in celebrating those who'd only prolonged England's interference in Europe, against the wishes of the surviving English population.

On her wrist, the faint numbers of her watch's digital display caught her eye. She'd lingered too long.

Taking to a sprint, Harra rushed through the graveyard and back to the tangled fence and gate. They rose out of the gloom like long-limbed spiders, and she shuddered at her over-active imagination that foresaw those iron spiders crawling through the graveside, feeding on whatever they could find.

Trying to touch nothing that would stain her clothes with the all-pervading green lichen, Harra erupted onto the eerie street. It was still some time until dawn, and in any eventuality, the vaporous smog would obscure the sun no matter what. Yet the flashing digits on her watch and the distant chime of old church bells forced her to rush.

She wanted to return home before her grandmother woke. Her mother might not admonish her, or her aunt and uncle. But her grandmother would. Harra didn't want to leave on a sour note. She was beginning to appreciate just how much the treatments she'd been receiving must have cost her family, and more, Harra was convinced it had been at her grandmother's instigation.

Harra rushed through the silent roads, even her shoes raising no sound, sparing no energy to look around her.

Now she knew this would be the last time she saw any of the landmarks of her childhood, it was impossible to care about them. Now there was only the future. Not the past.

Harra only stopped on reaching the gateway to her home. Listening carefully, and sensing the hound still slept on, she reached over and fumbled the bolt on the gate, only to stifle a scream. A hand slapped away hers, and with a pounding heart, Harra waited. She'd been discovered, but by who?

'Who is it?' her mother whispered, and Harra collapsed in relief.

'It's me.'

'What?' her mother gasped, pushing the gate open just enough to see the truth of the words.

'Where have you been? Did you do this to the poor bloody hound?'

'Yes,' Harra whispered, matching her mother's tone. 'I had, I had to go somewhere before I left.'

Closing the gateway quickly behind her, having rushed her inside, Harra's mother silently and carefully replaced all of the bolts and locks before turning to face her daughter. Harra was unsure what her mother's reaction would be to the night-time excursion.

'You should have asked me,' her mother grunted, not the reaction Harra had been expecting. Not at all.

'There are always means and ways,' her mother continued, 'that don't involve knocking the watchdog out. If your grandmother had woken,' her mother shook her head as she bent to nuzzle the dog's pointed nose, her tone sharp. It was evident he was beginning to rouse from his long sleep, and night of dereliction of duty.

'I don't wish to know where you've been. I can imagine well enough. Now, get in the house, and pretend you've been asleep all night.'

'Thank you,' Harra said, turning to grip her mother's hand. 'Thank you,' she repeated more softly when rebellion flared in her mother's troubled eyes.

Her mother nodded, a waiver of tension running through her hand so she gripped Harra tightly.

'Go,' her mother hissed again, and Harra ran to the front door, and let herself inside, scarcely breathing as she tried to float up the stairs, boots in one hand.

Only when she settled on her lumpy bed did she consider the task complete, and only then did she allow her eyes to close.

Moments later, a firm shake on her shoulder woke her. Her mother. She looked tired, and drained, last night's jaunt having taken a heavy toll on her.

'Come on. You've slept nearly all day.'

The knowledge sent a flutter of panic through Harra.

'But, but, you should have woken me,' she said, again grasping her mother's hand. 'I wanted to spend today with you,' a whine had entered Harra's voice, and her mother's reply was not kind.

'Instead you spent your final night with a dead man, and now I will have to say goodbye to you with many things left unsaid as well.' The edge in her mother's voice almost provoked an angry retort from Harra, but instead, she settled herself.

'I'm sorry,' she managed. 'I thought I'd be able to survive on a few hours' sleep.'

'Well you were wrong,' her mother said, heat still in her voice. 'I hope you'll remember this disappointment when you embark on your journey. It's best to do as your instructed, not as you wish, if you're to succeed.'

Harra nodded sadly. She didn't want to leave with an argument.

Abruptly she threw her arms around her mother's neck and clung to her.

Hesitantly, her mother returned the embrace, but the contact was over too quickly, as her mother pulled away, patting at her clothes as though she could wipe away all traces of the physical contact. Harra kept the hurt from her face, just.

'Come on, there's little time. Gather your possessions.'

Clearly not keen to allow Harra any time for anything but the essentials, her mother watched her scramble for what she needed, gathering the gifted backpack to herself, and stuffing it with incidentals.

Harra had taken to heart what she'd been told about not taking anything that couldn't easily be discarded, and yet it hurt all the same to leave behind what faint reminders she had of her childhood. A single picture had always adhered to her wall, bright with the colours of a summer Harra had never experienced. The soft blues, yellows and greens of the tree leaves, cloudless sky and gentle sun, had infected many of Harra's dreams, only to always wake to the same olive smoggy gloom.

Harra gazed at it one final time.

'Your father's, when he was a boy,' her mother explained curtly, having never shared that with Harra before.

'On his wall, when he grew up?' Harra asked, suddenly filled with hundreds of questions about her father that would never be answered. Not now.

'Yes, but come, hurry.'

'You'll keep it, here, forever?' Harra demanded, desperate to know her mother hadn't forgotten the man she'd once loved.

'There's nowhere else for it to go,' her mother replied, but her eyes slid from the image without seeming to see it. Perhaps, the picture was too much of a reminder for her mother.

'You could put it in your room,' Harra offered quickly, wondering if that was the problem, but her mother shook her head.

'No, it was yours. It will stay here. With the rest of your things.'

Those things amounted to very little, and still, Harra hesitated. Could she do this after all? Could she just forget about her family and move on? The hopes of last night, shared with her father's grave, suddenly seemed too far-fetched, too impossible, and Harra turned to her bed, convinced she should merely crawl under the threadbare blanket and sleep away the dream of the future.

'Now is not the time for second thoughts,' her mother admonished. All trace of softness gone from her voice.

'Come, now,' the command, a whip down Harra's back, caused her to speed up, despite not wanting to. With a final glance at the reminder of what a summer's day must once have been like, before, Harra sped down the stairs. This time she little cared to avoid the creaks and groans, instead purposefully stepping in the 'wrong' places, the better to fix even that small memory in her mind.

In the kitchen, she could already see her Aunt and Uncle waiting for her. But not her grandmother. That concerned her, but her open mouth closed abruptly when her Aunt shook her head.

Now, it seemed, was not the time for questions.

On the kitchen table, an assortment of items waited for Harra to place in her backpack.

As she'd been instructed, there was a bag containing the gloopy looking substance, and the tubing she'd need to complete the final transfusion. There was also the list of instructions, the letters too small to make out in any great detail where she stood over them. Harra had memorised the words, all the same.

There was also a small bundle of food, stuff that would last a few days at most, after which she'd need to forage or survive on only her wits, the instructions only told her to take food for a handful of days. There was also a flask, and a bottle of water. Both were heavy as she hefted them in her hands, but also imperative to the success of her endeavour.

There was also one final item; one Harra hadn't been expecting to see. As she carefully wrapped the gloopy bag inside a jumper, cushioning it from all snags and tears, she tried not to focus on the small journal. She knew what it was, but was amazed it still existed.

Was this a gift from her grandmother, or her mother?

Folding the sheet of instructions into four, she pocketed it down the inside of her backpack, within easy reach but hidden from a cursory examination, should she encounter anyone who questioned what she was doing. Not that it was her greatest worry.

No, the politicians cared only for the area around the border, ensuring no one ever had the chance to escape because of the Border Drones, whereas other people, the beleaguered of

England, were too miserable, tired and exhausted to consider what others did around them.

The days of the mass rallying cries were long past.

The outrage and demands for fair treatment for all had fallen on deaf ears, and few could even consider a change now. England was doomed. It had always been condemned, since that fateful day.

Her mother's hand covered the small journal just before Harra reached for it.

'Remember, you must discard it before you make the crossing. Remember, and make me that promise.' Her mother's voice was hard once more, any trace of fondness evaporated in the fierceness of her request.

'I give you this to take, only so you will know more, as you should have done all along. Don't attempt to take it with you. It would endanger all of us if news of this reached the Government of England.'

Harra tried to hide her offended feelings but knew she'd failed when her Aunt once more shook her head as a warning not to try and argue. All this time, her mother had kept the survival of her father's journal a secret, and now she'd only be able to hold it for a few weeks before she'd have to leave it behind once more. The unjustness of her mother's actions outraged her. Was she, after all, just as callous as her grandmother?

However, Harra bit her lip and held her tongue. She needed to be grateful for what time she did have with her father's words.

'You have my word,' Harra muttered softly, succeeding, just about in keeping the anger from her voice.

'Then you may take it,' her mother's voice was gentle now, happy with Harra's words, and with only a brief moment of hesitation, her mother lifted her own hand from the journal and allowed Harra to claim it as her own.

The journal smelt of her childhood, and her father. Tears threatened to stream down her face. Harra remained resolute, as she forced herself to place it inside her backpack without even flicking to the first page to see what was written there, or perhaps drawn. Her father had never been without a pen, either to write or draw. He'd been most content when his hand had been busy.

She'd have been the same, if only they could have afforded the copious amounts of paper she'd craved since childhood.

Harra hefted her bag onto her shoulder. The instructions for Stage 1 were concise and to the point, and it was time to go, without a fuss and without tears or sorrow. That, she knew, would be difficult to accomplish.

Once more she glanced toward the closed door of her grandmother's room, but there was no sign of the door opening. Instead, she turned to her Aunt and kissed her soft cheek, and then hugged her Uncle. When she was small, she'd thought him the tallest man ever, but under her hands, he felt frail, and she was almost as tall as he.

Finally, and without further words, she turned to her mother.

Her mother's face was glacial, no expression showing and Harra swallowed thickly.

Her mother had kept the secret of last night's excursion, had finally explained the origin of the picture in her room, and had gifted her with her father's journal. Her mother must love her, and yet there was precious little to show that was the case in her silent presence.

With a lump in her throat, Harra stepped toward her mother and embraced her one final time.

Her mother returned the hug, although it was a tepid thing compared to the embrace they'd shared in her room. Harra was again struck by her mother's frailty. Not yet forty years old, she seemed insubstantial, a wisp. How much longer would she live when Harra was gone?

'Goodbye,' Harra whispered. 'I love you.'

And with those words spoken, she turned and walked out of the front door, to the gate, guarded by the dopey looking hound. Through the gate, her uncle rushing to swing it closed after her, and then she was on the street, in the olive gloom of night, and she knew turning back was fruitless, but did so anyway.

The future beckoned her, and she must complete Stage 1 of the instructions if she were to succeed.

CHAPTER 3
STAGE 1
'BE READY TO LEAVE AT 00:00 HOURS.'

WITH A PAINED EXPRESSION, Harra took a swift, final glance at her home, unsurprised none watched her departure, biting her lip as she did so.

Stage 1, was, of course, the most challenging part of the endeavour, and should she get this wrong, none of the following stages would be possible.

And yet, whoever had provided her family with the list of instructions, had been intentionally vague. For all that, Harra had scoured the list, rereading it and then rereading it again, before memorising it all. But she had found no names on the list of instructions, none at all.

Stage 1 read,

> 'Be ready to leave at 00:00 hours. Head west for eleven miles. You will know when to stop. Bring food and drink to last for at least three days.'

And so the subsequent stages also read, until the final two were encountered.

But, or so Harra worried at her nail, what if she went the

wrong way from the very first steps. Her understanding of east, west, north and south were compromised because she'd never used them before. Her uncle had said they used to be able to tell where east and west were by the rising and setting of the sun, but with the smog layer absolute above her head, it was impossible to detect the sun's rising, even if it hadn't been night time.

All of her travelling was to be done at night, that much was clear.

Her uncle had read that first instruction and nodded as he saw it.

'Just turn left as soon as you leave the safety of the gateway.' He'd sounded assured and confident, and Harra had seen that reflected in his sharp nod to the left when they'd parted, but all the same, she worried even now, with only three or four steps taken, she'd made a mistake.

The fear gnawed at her.

Harra followed many of her steps from the previous night, undertaking Stage 1 of her instructions. This part was all about getting away from the more built-up area of her home and finding the ancient roadways that would lead her ever north, or so she supposed.

The thought both terrified, and thrilled her.

She'd never left her hometown, ever. It just wasn't done. No one had the money, or the means of transport to move around a great deal. At school, she'd been taught about the transport network that had once allowed England to thrive, the roads and railways, the ferries and airports. All had long fallen into disuse.

Harra had wondered what it must be like to just jump into a car, and travel hundreds of miles. She'd never been able to imagine it, and in all honesty, still couldn't. Now that she was finally going to leave, it would be her feet that took her places, nothing else.

Not that she didn't agree it would have been nice to drive north, to have sat in a car and watched the world pass her by.

Abruptly, Harra came to a joining of roads. This, she realised, was where she needed to leave behind all she'd known before and step out into unknown territory. Around her, she could feel the empty void of space she must travel along, and terror temporarily stopped her progressing.

All of her life she'd known about this road but had never walked on it. As far as she knew, no one had. There was no point.

No one knew precisely where it led, other than west. And no one from the west had ever come from the road. The assumption had been made that there was nothing there. And now. Well, now she needed to take those first steps, illuminated in the faintest yellow glow of a nearby church clock.

Trying to clear her mind, she considered what it would have been like to drive a car down the short incline, pointing ever westwards. And then she squared her shoulders and did just as she imagined the car doing, placing one foot in front of the other, and taking the first monumental steps to freedom. Only then she felt relieved to walk instead of driving in a car. It was difficult enough to just walk on the Western Road without tripping let alone try and drive a car across the uneven and broken surface.

Not that she could see a great deal, but she was sure the vast expanse of pitted tarmac before her had once been smooth and flat, before being abandoned. Wildlife along the roadside was regaining a footing, plants snaking across her path, trip hazards all around her.

Harra bent, running her hand over the vastness before her. She could just see, in the olive gloom, that plants and grasses covered much of the originally flat landscape.

Harra wished she could see better, but was too worried about following the instructions to indulge her curiosity by straying too far from the road. Instead, she told herself she could look later, when the eleven miles were completed.

Placing one foot in front of the other, Harra marched forward, trying to banish the fears that she travelled east instead of west. She warred with herself. She'd been walking west as her uncle had shown her. He had no reason to lie to her. Everything he'd said to her, about where she'd encounter the road, was right. Why wouldn't she be going the correct direction?

Yet, as the wind buffeted her face, making it hard to breathe against its force, she couldn't help worrying.

Arguing, she resolutely tried to banish her fears, her thoughts only on how long it would take to travel eleven miles on foot. On her wrist, the watch glowed hauntingly, the time, according to her watch 01:17. She'd left home precisely when the watch had recorded 00:00, as instructed.

Should it have taken her so long to reach the Western Road? Would she have time to complete her eleven miles before the new day began? Not that she'd have any clues, other than the silent passage of time on her watch.

Two hours later, sweat beaded her face and worry still fretted at her resolve to walk the eleven miles, but she'd seen something, in the dank light that had caught her curiosity and which she couldn't ignore, not this time.

She'd seen a number of posts, stuck haphazardly out of the ground at odd angles, but now there was one hinting at greater knowledge.

Despite her intentions to remain firmly in the middle of the Western Road, she found her feet sliding ever closer to the left-hand side, and eventually allowed herself to follow them.

Emerging from the murkiness, a post held a piece of metal aloft. The roadside vegetation had reclaimed it, and yet, as Harra tugged at a piece of trailing vine, it fell away easily, revealing a much battered and beaten sign.

Harra yelled in delight, the sound echoing in the thick murkiness. At the top of the sign, almost out of sight, it read 'The North.' And that was all Harra needed to see to redouble her speed, and accept she was heading the correct way.

She could also decipher the names of places she'd never heard of, but she ignored them. All she needed to see was 'The North' to believe she was completing Stage 1 as she should.

With more speed now, her watch continuing to show the advance of the night hours, Harra rushed onwards. She kept a careful eye on the ground before her, as well as for more signs telling her which way was north.

She had no clue how quickly she could walk eleven miles, not with the fierce wind, and yet Stage 1 ran out after eleven miles, and Stage 2 began only with the instructions for the next night's journeying. She would know when to stop, that was all it said for the end of Stage 1. With no way of calculating when she'd walked the required eleven miles, wasn't it possible she'd miss her stop for the night?

Worry once more drove her ever onwards despite her curiosity about the sign.

On her wrist, the green letters glowed 03:58 and Harra grumbled in frustration.

How quickly could she walk eleven miles? How fast could she walk just one mile? She'd never done a great deal of exercise. Few did. It was deemed better to be somnolent than risk any form of a cough caused by the smog, and there was no quicker way of catching an infection than by breathing too deeply, and too often of the contaminated air. Rushing anywhere was frowned upon.

Her foot kicked something, and her arms windmilled to keep upright. Peering down she could see nothing to cause her to trip, and bent ever lower, closer to the ground. With her hand, she reached down and felt a bump in the surface. Whatever it was felt hard and well in-bedded. With a shrug, Harra stepped to the side and continued her walk.

On her wrist the green numbers glowed 04:13 and Harra veered once more to the side of the road, to peer upwards at another of the large poles, only half a sign still attached to it. Pulling on yet another vine, Harra cleared enough of the foliage to see that it read, 'The North.' She also noticed there were numbers next to the names she'd never heard before. Only most of the names were missing, so a useless list of numbers, gaining in size as she went down the list, glared at her.

Frustrated, and growing too tired to keep up her steady pace, Harra stumbled back to the middle of the road. Glancing subconsciously to what she now knew was the east, she was convinced sunrise must be close. She was certain an easing in the shadows of night was taking place. Now more grey-green than black-green. She stifled a sob of impatience.

Harra needed to be off the road before daybreak, but she had no idea how much further she needed to go.

Then, in the distance, her eyes caught a flicker of something, a flashing or some such, and Harra increased her pace, excitement building inside her.

Could this be the sign she'd been waiting for to indicate she should stop for the day?

Ahead, the road seemed to veer upwards, and Harra followed it, drawn by the flickering light that showed every three or four steps even through the blackness of the night. Harra felt sure this must be her destination. Why else would there be flickering lights in the middle of nowhere?

Heading upwards, Harra considered finding her torch to illuminate the ground beneath her feet and what lay ahead, but she stopped herself. She mustn't draw attention to herself, no matter the desperation. Such had been made clear to her.

Not that she'd seen or heard anyone since leaving her home.

But, with the flickering light, it was possible there'd be more people, perhaps men and women who scratched a living from the wild grasslands encroaching over the abandoned road.

A scratching sound startled her, and she stopped, mid-step, her heartbeat racing.

The sound came again, closer. Harra wished she could see better, the murk impenetrable, other than when illuminated by the flickering light before her.

She hesitated. Was it just her imagination playing games with her? For so much of the night, she'd heard nothing but the sound of her breathing and footsteps.

Her eyes were drawn to the iridescent light once more. The shape was slowly coming into view, and a small smile touched her tired lips. It was an arrow. She was sure of it. An arrow telling her where to go.

Ignoring the scratching noise, which came once more, she completed her halted step, and then the next one. Slowly, the arrow came into clear sight, and she giggled with delight. She'd been worrying how she'd know when to stop, but now she did. As the green dial on her watch flickered to 04:27, Harra stopped in front of the arrow sign.

It was so bright it burnt her eyes, but below it was a doorway. It was metal and pitted with age, and yet the handle gleamed brightly, as though someone had just polished it.

Reaching out, Harra gripped the handle and pulled it downward. With an ear-piercing screech, the metal door opened inwards, and Harra stepped inside.

There was a small lamp, emitting a glow to reveal a small, single bed, neatly made with a single pillow. There was nothing else, as far as she could see.

'Hello,' she said softly, her words barely above a whisper. And then, when she received no response, she spoke again, this time, more loudly.

Still, there was no response. But, pulling the door close behind her and stepping closer to the lamp and the table it rested on, she saw a piece of paper wedged under the light. She bent to read it.

'Rest,' it said, in large printed letters written by hand, in black ink, on a piece of ancient and rubbed paper. 'You'll be woken when it's time to move on.'

'Oh,' she huffed. This then was her sanctuary for the day, but she was alone within it. For a moment, she felt strange, but then her exhaustion won. Sitting heavily on the bed, which bowed only slightly beneath her weight, she dug into her backpack and pulled forth the bundle of food, and bottle of water she'd carried with her.

Drinking deeply, she turned her attention to the sandwich her mother had made. Pausing, for this would be one of the last times she ate anything her mother had made for her, something landed on her foot. Reaching down she picked up the journal she'd also been gifted.

Too hungry to be sentimental about a sandwich, Harra bit deeply, and turned the journal over in her hand.

The cover was well worn, soft and pliable.

The sandwich tasted delicious, perhaps the best sandwich she'd ever had, but she ate with distraction.

Now she held her father's journal, she was almost loath to open it.

She had only childhood memories of her father. What might she discover hidden inside the pages that chronicled his life?

With a deep sigh, she peeled open the cover, a gasp escaping her mouth at what she found.

The pencil drawing could have been of her, and yet she knew it was her mother when she'd been little older than Harra now.

The sparkling eyes seemed to shine from the page, the laughter peeling free of the paper prison.

Tears clouded her vision, the sandwich drying like glue in her mouth.

Harra had never imagined her mother as young. Now the thought brought a sad smile to her tired lips. Of course, she'd been young once. How silly had she been to never consider it?

The image held her rapt attention as she sniffed her sorrow, returning to her sandwich because she was ravenous.

Just how long had her father known her mother?

With difficulty, she turned the first page. Scrawled letters in black pencil greeted her. Her father's words. Again, tears poured from her eyes, and she held the journal away from her, not wanting to cry on it and damage this most precious link to him.

Only with her tears dry, and her sandwich eaten, did Harra return to the journal. Her eyes were trying to close, but she held them open, just to read the first page, just to hear her father's words in her mind.

'This journal belongs to Harry. If found, please return to 31 Oxford Street, York.'

Harra jerked at the words. She'd lived at 31 all of her life, but she'd never known it had a road name, or even that the place she called home was called York. Why had she never known that? She shrugged. It was because the names of places just weren't relevant to people who never left home.

But she could read no more. Her eyes closed, and she slumped in sleep over the small, solitary bed, the light blazing throughout the day.

CHAPTER 4
STAGE 2

'LEAVE AT PRECISELY 20:03 HOURS.'

A SCREECHING alarm woke her hours later. Her watch glowed balefully at her. 18:20. She'd slept for hours and hours, and she needed to relieve herself and eat. Her tongue was stuck to the roof of her mouth, and she'd slept in her clothes, although not her boots. She felt grimy and dirty already.

'Ah,' she shouted when the alarm seemed to show no sign of ceasing. At her cry, the alarm faltered and then stopped altogether, as she rubbed her face, sitting on the side of the bed.

Looking around, she noticed another area illuminated by a stark white bulb. She was convinced it hadn't been there the night before.

Now she stumbled to it, curious.

A metal tub sat just off the ground, curved legs reflecting in the single lamplight, and a sheen of steam shimmered from its surface. Two towels were laid out as well, and more importantly, a toilet could be seen just to the right of the tub.

Glancing around, just to be sure, Harra made a beeline for the toilet, and then, quickly stripped out of her clothes, and dipped a toe into the water.

She hissed at the heat. She dipped her foot fully in, before adding her second foot.

Quickly she ducked down and immersed herself into the water. She'd never had a bath so deep in her entire life.

She giggled, despite the strangeness of the situation. Had someone been inside the room while she'd slept? It was a creepy feeling, but she tried to banish it. The water was so soothing on aching feet she hoped she'd never have to rise from the bath.

Resting her head on the back of the metal tub, wondering why the metal didn't burn her with the heat of the water, Harra closed her eyes, breathing in the flowery scent of the water.

Whoever had arranged this for her, she was deeply grateful. This was luxury she'd never known.

Time passed, the digits on her watch passing. Only when the water was finally losing its heat did she scrub her body with the provided soap and cloth and then step free from the bath.

Immediately the water began to drain out of the bottom.Harra almost wished she hadn't stepped free of the bath. She could have stayed there all night.

Drying herself on the fragrant towels, she padded to her backpack and pulled forth clean socks and underwear, and then dressed quickly.

Only then did she stuff her dirty underwear and socks deep into the bottom of the backpack, checking as she did so, that the precious oozy bag was intact and safe. She also pulled out another of her mother's sandwiches and devoured it.

Her hand strayed over her father's journal, but instead, she reached for the sheet of paper and read Stage 2 once more.

> 'Leave at precisely 20:03 hours and find the Northern Road. Travel North for ten miles.'

She'd been warned there'd be hills to climb the further she went and they'd prove arduous. The stage only instructing her to travel 3 miles in a day was the one worrying her the most. This one, she hoped, would be relatively easy going, once she'd found the Northern Road. Still, she was reassured of her route, having seen the signs the previous day.

Glancing at her watch, she saw it was only 19:47. She had time yet, and her hand ached to touch her father's journal, although she didn't want to miss her precise departure time. Instead, she drank more water and then ensured her backpack was packed and closed tightly. She didn't wish to lose any of her few possessions.

Glancing back at her watch, the time read 20:01. Close enough, she thought, tugging on her boots, and striding toward the door. Yet, although the single light flickered off as soon as she moved away from last night's bed, the door she'd stepped through refused to open. She tugged on it, turning the handle first one way and then the next, in case she was doing it wrong, but still, nothing happened.

With a huff of annoyance, she glanced at her watch, and as the time changed over to 20:03 a metallic clang sounded, and the door opened.

'Amazing,' she muttered to herself, stepping outside quickly, and then hesitating. Leaning back inside, she called, 'Thank you,' before pulling the door closed. Her grandmother had always chastised her for having terrible manners. Now was the time to prove her wrong.

Somehow she'd forgotten what would greet her when she was outside.

The olive gloom of the smog came as a surprise, and she grimaced unhappily, coughing a little after spending the day sleeping in purified air. Would she ever see a sunrise and sunset as it appeared to the rest of the world?

The rest of the world? That was a strange concept. The rest

of the world had ceased to exist on that fateful day in 2030. For those older than her, it had been a huge change, for her, it meant almost nothing. She hadn't even known she'd lived in York, or even the name of the street she'd lived on. It had always been 'home' to her.

Even in school, she'd never been asked for her address, or when she'd been at work. What was the point in knowing such things when social interactions were few and far between, and all monetary transactions took place with coins and barter?

Quickly, she glanced around, searching for the Northern Road. For a moment she faltered, only seeing the road she'd travelled on the day before, but then she took ten steps away from the building she'd slept inside, turning her head all around.

There, she could just make out something to the left of her.

On unsure feet, she followed the discarded pathway and allowed a howl of triumph to wrench from her tight lips when she saw what was needed. Another road ran beneath her feet, the bridge she stood on hinting at options and possibilities she was unused to having.

Here, the Western Road continued ever westwards, but there was also the possibility of travelling east, back the way she'd come, and if there was a Northern Road, then it must also go south.

Harra allowed herself to smile. For all the secrecy of what she was doing, she was filled with a spark of joy and freedom, something she'd never had before. Turning to face north she glanced back the way she'd come. The building she'd spent the day inside was invisible, the bright arrow no longer flashing. Truly it had been only for her. The thought cheered her. What would the next day bring?

Quickly she made her way to the incline that headed to the Northern Road, content she was going the correct direction, and more importantly, doing the right thing.

Time passed slowly, as she stayed close to the centre of the road, veering only ever to read the signs, where they'd survived, and to make sure they still read, 'The North.' She found her need for constant reassurance childish, and yet, this was it. With this act of defiance, she was saying goodbye to her childhood.

If she were successful, she'd have no family, and no one to care for her. She'd be an adult, and the future would be hers to decide.

Reminded of her father's journal entry, Harra considered what he must have thought at her age. Born before the cataclysmic events of 2016, he'd been too young to have any say in what had been decided, even though it had been his life that had been destroyed.

Had he comprehended what was about to happen? Had he understood, or had his concerns been more mundane. Perhaps, matters of the heart, as the drawing of her young mother indicated.

She smiled through her sadness.

But even thinking of her father couldn't dispel her boredom. There was nothing to see, and almost no change to the road, other than the odd dip and rise, and quickly, when her watch read 22:14 she knew she was both bored and flagging in her speed.

That first night it had been easy to walk, the experience new and fresh. Now, after her bath, she could feel aches in her calves, and her feet were starting to hurt as well.

Pausing, she took a swig from her water bottle and returned it to her backpack. How could she amuse herself? Was there a way of making the journey go quicker?

There was complete and utter silence all around her. It was as though she walked alone, through a world of olive dankness, and she was the only living thing within it. She shivered at the thought. Better to be alone than worrying she was being followed.

Her uncle had assured her the only place she'd risk being apprehended on her journey was on the final stage. Only there could any attempt be made to stop her from reaching The Wall by the Border Drones.

She began to hum softly under her breath, a song she couldn't remember the words to, but one of which she knew the tune well enough.

23:32 flicked on her watch, and she knew she still had a distance to go, despite trying to walk quickly and keep a constant speed.

It had taken her over five hours to walk the required distance last night, and tonight it would be similar, although she had set off earlier, no doubt because there was no one to witness her movements.

She thought there must still be at least an hour of walking to go, perhaps more. Stifling a moan of frustration, she redoubled her efforts. Better to get there as soon as possible. Then she'd be able to sleep for longer. Already she was dreaming of a hot bath come the morning, and a warm and comfortable bed. She peered into the distance as though a flickering arrow were about to come into view once more, indicating she should stop.

Yet it didn't. Not this time. Instead, as her watch read 00:37 the road she was following came to an abrupt end. Was this her destination?

Glancing around she looked for some sign indicating where she should sleep, but there was nothing. Instead, the road reached an end, with no indication as to what she should do.

'What the?' she complained, tired and dismayed there'd be no bath.

She thought back over the instructions for Stage 2. These had been some of the simpler ones to remember. But there'd been no indication what she should do at the end of the ten miles. Stage 3 began only with instructions to continue along the Northern Road. Yet it had, to all intents and purposes, stopped.

She turned and looked around her, peering into the olive gloom. What should she do? Where should she go?

'You're early,' a petulant voice spoke close to her ear, and she screamed and turned in shock.

Before her, illuminated by a single candle, sheltered from any wind by a hand cupping it, stood a woman of indeterminate age.

'Follow me,' the woman said. 'Tread carefully and quietly.'

Of all the things Harra had been expecting, it wasn't the sight of another person. Indeed, she'd thought she'd reach The Wall without speaking to anyone.

She was lead, by the single light, down a slight depression, and then along a tight track way that wound its ways between two buildings, or through a tunnel, it was hard to tell in the scanty light.

By now her feet were pulsing with pain. She thought she'd cry if she couldn't rest soon. Abruptly, the woman stopped, and wrenched open a metal door, similar to the one the night before. This one opened silently.

Stepping inside, Harra saw a scene much as last night, a small bed waiting for her, a single lamp illuminating it, and little else.

'This is where you'll spend the rest of the night and the day,' the woman said. 'When I leave, I'll lock you in. I'll come and release you when it's time.'

'So we won't be spending any time together, other than this?' Harra asked, peering into the far reaches of the room in the hope of finding an inviting bath.

'No, I've work that must be done, and you must rest. The facilities are basic, nothing fancy, but the sheets are clean.

There's a cold-water tap, but no warm one. But don't drink from the cold tap. I've pre-boiled water in those four jugs, and you can drink that but wash in the tap water.'

Harra suppressed a sigh of disappointment, as she looked to where the woman had pointed. She'd been looking forward to a soak in the bath, like earlier.

Hidden behind the candle's flames, Harra could see almost nothing of the woman, other than a vaguely human shape.

'You can walk around in here, but don't touch anything. The place is filled with rusting equipment no one knows how to use any more. No one will come running if you get stuck.'

Harra had a sudden feeling the woman cautioned her because some problem had occurred in the past. She dutifully nodded her understanding. She couldn't see what the equipment was but thought she'd explore all the same. Despite the instruction not to do so.

'I'll leave you with the lamp,' the woman nodded her head toward it. 'I need the candle,' and without another word, she turned and left Harra, pulling the door closed silently behind her without a backward glance.

Harra shuffled to the side of the bed, sitting heavily on its protesting springs, and tugging her boots from her feet.

She wrinkled her nose at the sudden aroma of sweaty foot, and forced the boots as far from her as she could with her toes, removing her socks, and tossing them after the boots.

Removing her jacket as well, slinging it on the end of the bed, she lowered herself to lie fully stretched.

Her feet still tingled, her mouth felt dry, and yet she also wanted to see just where she was spending her time. She tried to counsel herself to get some sleep, or at least to eat one of her remaining sandwiches, but the tug of the shadowed recesses called to her.

With an aggrieved sigh, she sat back up and reached for her backpack.

The single point of light, the small lamp, couldn't be moved because it had a power cord attached to operate it. If Harra was going to see what rested around her, she was going to need her precious torch, with its limited supply of batteries. She'd been advised to use it as little as possible, which is why she'd relied only on the brief light of the dank smog to guide her steps so far.

Reaching into the bag, her watch glowing at her, as though rebuking her for not sleeping, she pulled out the long metal tube and turned the button so a stark beam of light joined that of the single lamp.

Satisfied, she reached for her boots, but then changed her mind. Her feet were sore enough from wearing them and walking over twenty miles in two days, not to mention her excursion of the preceding night to visit her father's grave. She'd risk being barefoot.

Standing, she shone the torch before her, trying to gain an idea of how large the room was where her bed for the night had been set up. It seemed vast, every shuffling step she took echoing loudly, and taking time to die away to silence.

The beam of the torch picked out strange shapes, all sharp edges and occasional curves, and reaching for one of the sandwiches, she stuffed some of it in her mouth and set out toward the rusting equipment.

The ground beneath her feet was cold, to begin with, her toes, being deprived hot water, enjoying the coldness, but when it turned from swept clean to dusty, Harra hesitated, and returned for her boots, finding yet another fresh pair of socks first.

Socks had been on the list. Her mother had stuffed about thirty pairs at her. Harra hadn't seen the need for so many, but now she was grateful and understood. If she was to walk her way to freedom, her feet needed to be kept free of blisters.

She set out once more, her feet aching at being returned to

her boots. At least she'd not stub her toe or step on something painful, or have itchy, dirty feet.

With the torch in her left hand and her half-eaten sandwich in her right, she swept the light before her. The flashlight was powerful, but even it couldn't penetrate to the back of the building. Harra realised not only was it a massive room, but the the ceiling was a long way away. Whatever this room had been used for, it had been built to accommodate something massive.

Drawing ever closer, Harra saw metal shimmering brightly in the luminosity of the torch. Not everything was rusting, not to shine as it did. Stopping abruptly, Harra ran her hands around a circular shape she knew was called a tyre. It had long since gone flat where it touched the ground, but remained round along the top free from the ground.

The black tyre led her eyes to look ever higher, and she gasped in surprise, as letters formed before her, black on a yellow background. 'Highways Maintenance,' it read, the letters still complete. Reaching out, she traced the shape of the metal from one end to the other, and then back around to what she thought must be the front.

'A car?' she breathed. 'Or perhaps a truck or a lorry.' All three had disappeared from England's streets before she was born, and now she scanned the torch around her. The entire place seemed filled with vehicles of all shapes and sizes, and she ran from one to the other marvelling at their various shapes and sizes. They all carried the same lettering on their sides, 'Highways Maintenance.'

'This must be a storage facility,' she said aloud, just to hear the comfort of a voice. 'But I thought they'd all broken down, been unable to run any more.'

That was what she'd been told whenever she'd asked about flickering lights flashing red, orange and green along the streets they walked to go to school, work or to the single shop.

Her mother had explained they'd been used to regulate traffic but Harra hadn't truly comprehended what she'd meant.

How much easier would it be to just drive one of the vehicles north? Surely it would save her feet.

Becoming ever bolder, Harra searched for and found what she thought must be a door into one of the machines.

This one had huge tyres, flat to the ground, with deep ridges on the tyres, unlike the smoother ones she'd seen on the first vehicle. There was a massive step up to the door, and as her hand slipped under the handle, or so she took it to be, she lifted her leg to add some heft to the action.

But the door opened smoothly in her hands, no hint of even a groan of protest, and Harra swung into the vehicle.

Her torch flashed over a seat, alone and positioned behind a wheel shining blackly under the glare of her flashlight. For a moment she stopped, and then laughed a little. What harm could it do?

She settled herself in the chair, her free hand, now devoid of her sandwich, taking hold of the wheel. Harra sat there, imagining what it must have been like to be able to move a machine so large using the power of petrol and oil.

Her feet kicked out and hit pieces of metal below the steering wheel, and she leaned over, her torch in her hand, peering at what she'd encountered.

Three pedals appeared from the gloom, as her forehead creased. What had been the purpose of those?

There was a not entirely unpleasant smell inside the vehicle, as she straightened herself and looked out, over the top of the wheel, and through a glass front. She shone her torch forward, but the light reflected back at her rather than penetrating the glass, and she moaned with frustration.

But there were knobs and buttons to either side of the wheel, and she reached out, hands eager to turn and twiddle all of them. Most did nothing, and she thought the vehicle probably needed to be turned on to make them work only she didn't know how to do that. Then she twirled one of the knobs and a beam of light shot from the front of the truck.

Her jaw dropped open as the strong lights revealed row after row of neatly parked vehicles, all nose to tail, as close together as it was possible to be, apart from the one she'd chosen. This one was instead close to a huge pillar that rose to meet the ceiling, high above her head, and Harra could see that it couldn't have fit between the pillar and the vehicle directly to the left of it. As such, it had been left with more room around it.

'How many?' she whispered, leaving the switch turned on, but jumping back to the concrete floor. How many of the things had they once used? And what had they used them for?

Laughing with delight, she ran down the aisle floodlit by the lights, peering up at the silent creatures, and considering what all of them had done, for few were alike. The basic shape on most was the same, most having four wheels and a bulbous carriage where the driver sat, but some seemed to have giant spades attached to their fronts, others had sharp spikes and yet other had long, long metal tubes.

The only thing the same was the colour of them all. Even in the shaft of light, she could tell that they were all the same yellow, or at least once had been. On some, the paint was peeling away, revealing a darker colour beneath, the difference between the two shades, when she reached out to touch them, going from smooth to jagged. She had no idea why.

All of the machines also had the same words on them, 'Highways Maintenance,' and she laughed again. She would have liked to sit in one of the behemoths and drive up and down the gently undulating concrete strip of road outside. For that's what they must have been for. Perhaps they'd kept the concrete free from the advancing undergrowth, or perhaps kept it flat. That was the only reason she could see for the lorry she found, with a giant roller attached to the front.

Abruptly, the light from the truck went out, and Harra was cast into darkness.

'What?' she stopped walking forward, her hand resting on one of the vehicles, as she looked about in confusion. In her delight, she'd left the torch inside the lorry with the lights, now she had no way of finding it.

'Shit,' she muttered, turning in what she hoped was the right direction.

She'd run and skipped her way along many vehicles, and now wished she'd taken more care, remembering where she'd come from.

She needed the torch, and she needed to find it, quickly. But why had the lights gone out? Had someone turned them off? Knowing a brief spark of worry, and with hands stretched out to either side to prevent her walking into anything, the hulk of the machines acting as a deterrent as well, even in the pitch black, Harra began to stumble back the way she'd come.

Had she left the torch on? Would there be a small pinprick of light for her to follow when she got closer? She couldn't remember and instead relied on her memory of those moments of enjoyment. Her watch still flicked at her, its green gloom the brightest she'd ever seen it. That was all the light she had with which to see.

With a great deal of effort, Harra kept calm, ignoring her aching feet. As she passed the sleeping vehicles, she was aware of the faint glow of the single lamp by her bed for the night, and was tempted to just fight her way back to it, but knew if she did, she'd never find her torch. And she needed it. Of that she was sure. Indeed, she knew if she moved away from the row she was on, she'd never find it again.

So taking her time, she wound her way back down the endlessly queuing vehicles, feeling her way along the metal bodies of them, wondering just how far she'd walked. A mounting sense of panic made her jumpy, and by the time she found the torch, still on, and with the door of the truck hanging open, she was almost sobbing.

'Bloody fool,' she berated herself, jumping back up to try and see why the lights had gone out. She twiddled the knob that had made the lights come on, but nothing happened.

'Strange,' she said, but grabbing her torch jumped down, closing the door behind her. She'd done more than enough exploring for one night. Quickly, she walked her way back to the solitary lamp, slumping onto the bed, and finally feeling tired.

Removing her boots for a second time, she wiggled her toes, and then lay down, pulling the blanket over her. Sleep immediately claimed her, and only as she drifted, did she realise her father's journal was waiting for her to read.

CHAPTER 5
STAGE 3

'LEAVE AT PRECISELY 18:00 HOURS.'

SHE WAS WOKEN by a buzzing sound, many, many hours later, and fought to rouse herself from a deep sleep. Her watch showed 16:00, but as she'd not checked her watch last night, she had no idea how long she'd actually slept.

Her bladder was uncomfortably full, and even though she knew there was no bath, she still ached to be clean.

Standing, she meandered to the jugs of water, and also found a small toilet cubicle. She made hasty use of the amenities, and stripped quickly, sloshing as much water over herself as she could. Her nose wrinkled at her sweaty odour, as she dreamed of yesterday's soap and deep bath. Perhaps tonight, or so she bribed herself, as the chilly water touched her skin time and time again.

Using the towel that had been left for her, soft but thin, she quickly changed her underwear and donned the clothes she'd been wearing for two days. Her stomach growled angrily, as she returned to the bed, and she reached into her backpack, pulling out the remaining food and also her father's journal.

Her watch read 16:16 so she ate hungrily, opening the journal to the second page.

'23rd June 2016,' it read on the top line, a date forever ingrained in Harra's brain. Her curiosity pricked, she read on.

> 'She said her name was Rebecca. She smiled at me, and all I could see were her blue eyes and very white teeth. I've never met her before, I'm sure of it, but she laughed at me when I said that. She says that we went to the same primary school together, but that she's since moved away. I don't know whether to believe her or not. I came home, determined to find the old photographs, but Mum and Dad were embroiled in some heated debate, and so I left them to it. Now I'm in my room, trying to remember her, but I just don't.'

Harra laughed aloud at her father's complaints. It wasn't at all what she was hoping to read, but then, her father had been her age on the day of the referendum that had begun England's descent into its current state of neglect and total rejection by every other country in the world. What would he have cared about anything?

Quickly she turned the page, keen to see what happened next.

> '24th June 2016. Everyone at school was talking about what happened yesterday, but I didn't really want to listen to people just repeating what their parents had said. Rebecca said the same. She said her parents had voted a week ago,

> using postal votes, because they were still registered at their house in the Midlands. I nodded as though I knew what she was talking about, but I just wanted to stare at her. She's so beautiful.'

Again, Harra laughed. It seemed her father had held no interest in the referendum, and in fact, as she flicked through page after page, the dates going from June to December 2016, she realised her father's only concern had been her mother. The thought cheered her. She'd often wondered what life had been like before the building of The Wall in 2030. It seemed it had been one of careless childhood, and not at all what she'd expected. The chaos had come later than she'd believed. Her father then had enjoyed some years of childhood in the fourteen years after the fateful vote. That pleased her more than she expected.

Her father's life had been cut so short, she was inordinately pleased to know he'd enjoyed these years.

As she turned to the next page, the dates flashed over to 2017, and her father's tone changed from that of a lovesick puppy to that of a frustrated teenager.

> '17th January 2017. The bloody newspapers and the news channels are filled with bloody Brexit crap. It's so tedious and terrifying. What the hell did people think they were doing when they voted for it? My Mum and Dad argue about the consequences all the time, my Aunt and Uncle are no longer speaking to my Dad, and I'm just

bloody angry. Rebecca says that I shouldn't get so upset about it all, but it's just all so fucking stupid.'

She wanted to read on. This was what she'd always been so desperate to know, but the watch read 17:56 and she suddenly remembered the instructions for Stage 3. She needed to be ready for 18:00. Quickly, flustered, she hastily repacked her bag, having to dash back to the small toilet cubicle to pick up her discarded underwear and socks.

Just as she grabbed for her father's journal and placed it on her stock of clean clothes, and the gloopy bag of fluid, the door opened without a sound.

'Are you ready?' the woman barked, perhaps surprised to see Harra wasn't waiting impatiently at the door.

'Yes, yes, apologies, I am.' With a quick look behind her, Harra walked smartly to the door, wishing she'd tied her boots tighter.

'Do you have a coat?' the woman asked dispassionately. 'It's been raining all day and will probably continue all night.'

Harra suddenly became aware of the hammering of hard rain on the concrete outside and nodded quickly.

'Yes, yes, it's in my backpack,' she fumbled once more at the ties on the bag, eventually kneeling down so that she could find her raincoat.

It was a piece of light material, yet her mother had assured her it would keep her dry, no matter what.

'Be careful,' the woman warned, sounding dismayed at Harra's rough handling of all she had to ensure her journey was a success.

'Okay,' Harra sighed, making sure everything was repacked, as it should be.

'Did you refill your water bottle and flask from the jugs?' the woman further admonished, and Harra shook her head.

'Quickly, do it. Otherwise, you'll be thirsty, and you can't drink any water you find on your way.'

Harra rushed to carry out the instructions, annoyed with herself for getting caught up in her father's journal.

When she returned, the woman was watching her with a strange expression on her face. Harra opened her mouth to speak but quickly shut it again. On her wrist the watch read 18:02 and she knew she needed to be on her way.

Yet, she took a moment longer. Bending, she felt through her backpack, feeling for the items she couldn't journey without. The list of instructions, the gloopy bag, the torch and spare batteries, her clothes, her other bottle and also the tube she'd need when she made it to The Wall. She also reached for and touched her father's journal. Everything seemed to be as it should be.

Still, she breathed deeply in and out another five times, just to clear her mind and make sure she had all that was essential.

'I'm ready,' she said, the rustle of the jacket drowning out the sound of the rain briefly. Her backpack back in place, she turned back to the woman, finally able to see her because the candlelight was to the side of her face.

She was an older woman, perhaps the age of her mother, and she had the same pinched expression of constant want and poor health, her clothes tired and well worn. Harra swallowed against her cry of surprise.

There was a hunger on the woman's face, and Harra worried. Did the woman wish to take her supplies? Did she want to make a run for The Wall?

'Good. Hurry up. It'll be a long night for you if the rain persists.'

'My thanks,' Harra muttered, before stepping outside.

The sound of the rain was loud in her ears, and she

grimaced at the thought of walking through the oily substance all night long.

The woman shut the door quickly and began to march back the way they'd come the night before.

Harra rushed to keep up. Quickly, the tunnel above her head disappeared, and the rain covered her. Puddles had already formed on the concrete surface, and Harra skipped to avoid them. She had her coat to keep her clothes dry, but nothing for her boots.

'Good luck,' the woman said, returning to the place where she'd found Harra.

'Just follow the instructions, as you've done so far.'

'Goodbye,' Harra called, but the woman was already disappearing into the olive gloom, Harra forgotten about.

Stage 3. What had it said again?

> 'Follow the Northern Road for fifteen miles, heading north.'

It was after this stage that the instructions became more complicated. For now, Harra banished them from her mind, concerned more with trying to avoid as many of the puddles as possible, and with avoiding the slippery undergrowth, drenched by the downpour, and seeming to ooze across the old and broken concrete.

It was sure to slow down her progress. But, her watch only showed 18:16. Harra was sure she'd accomplish all that was needed before daybreak lightened some of the perpetual olive gloom from the sky above her head.

Yet those long miles were so slow as to be almost unbearable. The first time she tripped into a muddy pool she persuaded herself she'd been daydreaming as she walked, and not paying enough attention.

But by the time she banged her knees for the tenth time, she knew it was the conditions and not her own fault. Her watch read 19:01 and she was convinced, if she squinted, the shape of the building she'd slept within during the daytime was still vaguely visible, as well as another building, an odd shaped one with a curving roof. Whatever it had been used for, Harra wished she couldn't still see it.

Fear rolled in her stomach, quickly turning to rage.

Why was she even doing this? Would it not have been more productive to just wait until the following day when the rain stopped? Surely she'd have been able to make up a single day's travelling over the space of two? But the instructions had been clear. Everything must happen as they said. There was no room for delays and equally, arriving early was not encouraged.

Heaving herself back to her feet, and out of yet another pool of icy standing water, Harra staggered onward. Torch in her hand, a decision taken to try and keep her boots dry, she used it to highlight the area just in front of her, checking for pooling water and snaking greenery. Her knees were aching, and her hand when she looked at it in the light of the torch, was grazed and dirty. Grimacing, she forced an image of a bath filled with hot water into her mind, and with only that as her objective, she redoubled her efforts.

By the time her watch had moved to 21:47 she knew the rain wasn't going to stop, but she'd also made up valuable time.

Only then the unexpected happened. Her road, as she'd come to think of it, suddenly offered more than one option to follow. Shaking her head and dislodging water over her shoulders as she did so, Harra stared at the strange sight before her in the yellow of the torchlight. Here there were two roads, one stretching before her, and also another one, at a slight angle to it, and on a slight bend. A bit like the road during Stage 2, only she'd been aware of the pending decision. Now she was flummoxed.

Moodily, she kicked at a stray rock in her path, wincing when it was heavier than she'd thought it would be, and her cold foot hurt from the impact.

Angrily Harra gazed upwards, her eyes filling with rain, as though looking for some sort of help, a sign that said, 'The North' like before, but instead, a faintly glowing red light flickered. Only for it to change to dull orange, and then to green.

A traffic light. This was something she'd encountered already, and it was also something her uncle had mentioned to her.

'At busy times of the day, roads had traffic lights to help with the flow of the traffic. It allowed some cars to go while others waited.' She'd frowned at his words. To him, it had all seemed so sensible but had seemed bizarre to her.

'Why not just build the other road somewhere else, so t the two roads never needed to meet?'

Her uncle had shrugged at her question. 'I didn't build them,' he'd said with a soft laugh. 'I've no idea why they were put there. They just were.'

Shining the torch forward, Harra could pick out a raised area before her, and also something else, appearing out of the gloom.

Under the sporadically flickering light, Harra walked to the raised area. Here, the undergrowth had completely swamped whatever had once stood there, and she kicked something as she drew level with it. Peering down, her torch before her, she realised that this was some sort of raised curb. How strange, she thought, to build something in the middle of the road?

For a moment she considered climbing over the top of the knee-high weeds and vegetation, but the rain still fell, and in the flicker of the torch, she could see how wet and damp the whole place was.

Instead, and keeping the raised curb to her right, she followed it in a circle.

Flashing her torch from side to side, her head high, despite the rain pooling down her exposed nose and cheeks, another road sign was quickly illuminated. It too was festooned with greenery and dirty streaks, but she laughed because it did say, 'The North,' and more, grimy white lines were depicting what she assumed must be the right way to go.

Feeling more confident, she doubled her pace, keen to find the correct road. Immediately her steps quickly faltered, as her torch flickered over something slumped in the road.

Without having to peer too close, she knew exactly what it was.

'Hello,' she called, unsure whether she wanted to get a response or not.

In the glow of her light, which she swept from the head of the slumped form to the feet sticking out at the other end, Harra considered whether the person slept or was dead.

'Hello,' she swallowed again, a little louder so the sound pushed passed the noisy rain.

'Hello, are you okay?' she tried one last time. She looked around her, but there was, of course, no one else there. Just her, and the body, or sleeping person, but she knew it was a body.

She shook her head. No one would choose to sleep in the middle of the road, even if no cars or vehicles had driven on it for over a decade or two, if not longer. The person had to be dead.

Resolutely, she walked past the body, her torch firmly trying to pick out where she needed to place her feet next, and yet her traitorous body swung around, when the object was still in sight, and she stifled a scream.

Unseeing eyes followed her every move in a face white and pallid. Nausea swelled in her throat, and yet still she looked.

The face, while dead, looked too young to die, although age

no longer seemed to be a significant factor in people's life expectancy.

Was this another of the people trying to reach The Wall? Was this someone who'd failed?

At her strangled scream, the right arm of the body started to jerk, and she screamed again, the sound piercing despite the rain. Surely not?

'Hello,' she called again, her feet firmly rooted in position. There was no way she was getting any closer. In fact, she didn't understand why she lingered, but then, just as she was about to walk away, something slunk free from the body.

She screamed again, the sound echoing in the close atmosphere, but two glowing yellow eyes greeted her own, and now she understood. An animal. It was nothing more than a scavenger. And yet that surprised her as well.

The smog coating England had long extinguished much of the wildlife population, or so she'd been taught. Those that had survived tended to live in close proximity to people and were not precisely wild any more. Where then had this creature come from?

Still, it watched her, yellow eyes flashing in the dankness, and Harra found she'd dropped to her knees to see it better.

At her action, the creature shot toward her, and she fell backwards in her desperate attempt to escape. She'd not expected the animal to dart her way. Before she could regain her feet, the creature was upon her.

A nose insisted she open her hand, and rather than screaming and running, Harra remained still. A snuffling noise accompanied the nose, the yellow eyes almost pleading.

'Hello,' she said again. 'Who are you?' At her voice, the creature stilled, wary once more. She was at a loss as to what to do. Hesitantly, her other hand hovered over the creature's head. It seemed to wait for her, and with a final deep breath,

Harra placed her hand on the head, rubbing between two ears that dripped with water.

'Hi,' she said. 'I'm Harra.'

Unable to answer, the creature, Harra thought it was probably a dog, licked her other wrist, warm breath touching her wrist as it did so.

'Well hello,' she said again. 'What are you doing out here?' the dog, she'd decided it must be one, remained silent, obviously, as Harra laughed at herself for even asking the question.

'I'm going that way,' she pointed to where she hoped the road was. 'Do you want to come with me?'

She continued to stroke the dog's head, struggling to stand as she did so. Her clothes were soaked through, her boots as well, but she had miles to walk yet. She shouldn't linger any longer.

Her watch read 23:59.

'You can come, if you want, or you can stay,' she said, taking the first step to walk away from the dog. It remained sitting on its back legs, tongue sticking out between its upper and lower jaw. Perversely, she didn't want to leave the dog behind. Not now.

'Come on then,' she said brightly, hoping the dog would follow, but as she took ten steps, the dog remained sitting where it was, a low whine coming from its mouth.

'Come on then,' she said again, indicating with her arm where she wanted to go. The dog stayed where it was.

Unsure what to do, feeling precious time was being lost, Harra walked back to the dog and reached out to stroke once more.

'Come on, we need to go, if you're coming with me.' Still, the dog made no movement, and Harra huffed in annoyance.

'Fine, stay here. Some of us have got places to be.' Resolved to leave, she set out walking again. The dog had survived for this long alone; it would just have to continue to do so.

For all that, as she returned to the curb in the middle of the road, looking for the way she needed to follow, she felt lonely and bereft. Just another victim of her hopes of a future where she wasn't alone.

The rain seemed to be falling ever harder, her torch only just able to pick out the opposite side of the road in the strangled olive and yellow light of the smog and the torch. Still, she flashed her torch higher, higher, hoping for a sign to show her the way, but there was nothing but vacant posts. Whatever signs had once been in place were long gone, ripped down or taken away to be put to better use.

She stopped. Had she missed the right road the initial sign had told her to take?

She was loath to return to the body and the dog, but perhaps that had been where the road had been. Maybe the person had died right where she should have been walking.

Grimacing, she turned around, keeping the curb to her left now. As she did so, she heard a faint tip-tapping sound and jumped.

'Who's there?' she called, unsurprised when she again received no response.

Wishing she could see better, she stepped quicker. There was nowhere to hide out here. The only safety was in movement.

A shape flashed in and out of shadow, and she screamed, and then laughed at herself. It seemed the dog had chosen to follow her, after all, only at least twenty steps behind her.

'Which way is it?' she asked the animal, just to hear something, her voice a whine of annoyance. Holding the torch high, she searched for the roadway on the far right, or a sign, squealing with delight when she detected a break in the road on the far side. She turned smartly right, only for her foot to encounter an object.

She shrieked again. Her scream too loud, so that she stuffed her hand in her mouth to stop herself from doing it again. She'd screamed far too much in a short space of time. If there were anyone out there, they'd know precisely where she was.

Sightless white eyes watched her, and she swallowed around the bile in her throat. The body.

She was right. It had blocked the correct turning.

Quickly, she jumped clear of the reaching arm and unseeing eyes and strode to the road.

Bloody hell, she thought as she again heard the tip-tip-tapping of the dog following behind her, she'd come very close to going the wrong way.

Damn that body. She must take more care.

Her watch showed 00:13 and she almost broke into a run. She still had to walk many miles, and each step was a squelchy agony. Her feet sloshed in her boots, and her hair was so wet where it poked free from her hood, it was glued to her face in cold streaks.

Grumbling at the weather and the delays, Harra swept her torch over the dog trailing in her wake.

It looked as miserable as she felt.

'Well, you may as well walk with me, as behind me. That way we can be glum together, as opposed to separately.'

This time, the animal understood her instructions, and sidled up to her, even coming close enough to rub its saturated coat against her leg. Harra scowled as the dampness caused her trousers to stick to her clammy skin, but then shrugged. She was wet already. What harm could a bit more water really do?

The concrete beneath her feet angled sharply down, before levelling out. Harra sensed this part of the road was somehow better maintained than the one she'd been walking on. The concrete felt smoother, and there were fewer eruptions of greenery through the abandoned road surface.

The thought surprised her. Why would this section of the

Northern Road be less derelict? It was impossible anyone still used it. There was no fuel for traditional combustion engines, and even less electricity to try and power the last generation of electric cars. England survived on coal from its once-abandoned coalmines, and from what small reserves of gas it had. There was never enough, even for the small population.

Indeed, even wood was in short supply. Pity, she thought, that they couldn't convert all the greenery on the road into some form of fuel. It wasn't as though there wasn't enough to go round.

At her side, the dog walked confidently, tongue lolling from an open mouth, and Harra smiled. Having some company in the dreariness was nice. Even with the rain continuing to fall, she felt as though she was making better time on the second stretch of the journey.

The woman at last night's stopover had implied this part of the journey would be more difficult by wishing Harra luck, and yet she was finding it far more manageable. The road was smoother, and fewer puddles had formed despite the terrible storm. She sensed the road itself was smaller. She'd not yet ventured to the edge of the road on the right-hand side, but the gaping emptiness over there somehow felt 'less'. It was an odd feeling to explain.

Almost running, so fast was her speed, Harra sped down the road. By the time her watch read 02:42 she knew she couldn't have much further to go.

And then a worry struck her. What should she do with the dog? It was happy to follow her, and indeed, she'd encouraged it. But would her custodian for the night allow her to keep the dog with her? She couldn't very well abandon it. Not now.

Worry slowed her steps, and the animal eventually turned and looked at her, as though perplexed at this reversal in their behaviour. What should she do?

At that moment, a too bright light illuminated her, and she gasped in shock.

'About time,' a male voice called, as Harra squinted, unable to see who spoke, or even where the sound came from.

'Come on. Let's get you two out of the rain.' The voice sounded kind, and as it included the dog as well, Harra walked toward where she thought the sound had come from. At her approach, the light dimmed a little, and then she heard the sound of a metal door opening, and a fainter light poured onto too wet concrete as the larger light was extinguished.

Trying to slap the rain from her boots, and from her clothes, she stepped inside, still blinded, even by the softer light.

'A rotten night,' a deep voice offered, a towel being provided from behind the lamp, so a white arm appeared, displaced from any body.

'Bloody wet,' she agreed. Already she could feel herself starting to shiver.

'There's a warm bath for you in the far corner,' the voice continued. 'And I've made hot food as well. Hopefully, it'll keep a chill from forming.'

Now an older man walked into the light. He was short, really short, and Harra was surprised to look down rather than up.

'I'm Peter,' he offered, holding out his hand to greet her.

She mirrored his action, and she felt old, creased skin, but warm, enveloping her own.

'I'm less secretive than the other buggers on the road,' he offered, by way of an explanation. 'I've lived a long life, and I don't much care who sees my face and knows what I do. Now, go, be quick. Close the door. There's a bolt, for privacy, but it tends to stick. Don't panic if it does, just lean against the door, and it opens eventually.'

Peter walked away then, a pronounced limp to his left leg, and the dog she's found, followed him, as though they knew each other. Which begged the question as to whether they did or not.

But her entire body was starting to shake, and so, clamping her teeth shut, she made a beeline for the bathroom, and quickly closed the door behind her, as Peter had suggested.

The small room was warm, the bath steaming with hot water, two gleaming taps holding the promise of more heat to come. Stripping out of her clothes was an ordeal that took forever. Her coat was stuck on her, the zip seizing halfway down her front, so she had to struggle from it by pulling it over her head. Of course, as soon as the coat was off, the zip opened all the way under her hand, and she swore, 'bloody thing,' before turning to place it over a thin, but tall radiator in the bathroom.

She did the same with the rest of her clothes, placing her boots under the source of the heat. Naked, but already warmer, she took the opportunity to run hot water over her soaking socks and underwear in the small sink next to the toilet, adding plentiful soap as she went. It would be good to have cleanish clothes to add to her rapidly depleting collection of clean clothes. Not, that she suddenly realised, any of it would be dry.

Reaching for her backpack, she fiddled with the damp ties until they came open, and then pulled out a spare pair of trousers, a top and a fresh set of underwear and socks. They weren't too sodden, but it would be uncomfortable to put them on from a hot bath. Quickly, she moved all of her sodden clothes down the vertical radiator and lay her cleaner clothes to warm through on the higher bars.

Only then did she allow herself to leap into the bath.

The smell of the water was enticing, fresh and clean, and the warmth, as she settled into the bath, quickly worked its way through her frozen flesh. If she'd been sodden when arriving at the previous day's accommodation, Harra doubted she'd ever have gotten warm, but here it was completely different.

A bar of soap and something soft and squidgy had been left for her to wash her body with, and she set to work, keen to remove the stink of sweat and damp from herself, even going so far as to dunk her head below the water and scrub at her hair.

Her hair had never been very long. It had never grown as she might have wished it to. Now she was pleased. It took her only a moment to run the soap through her dull brown hair, and then to squeeze the water and soap from it.

Unsure how long she'd wallowed in the bath, her watch discarded on her backpack, and out of sight, she reached for a welcoming towel, fluffy and shockingly pink, and wrapped herself up tight inside it. This is what she imagined freedom to be like.

Drying herself, she reached for the warm clothes and hastily put them on. Her stomach was grumbling loudly, and the smell of warm food was making it hard for her to concentrate. She'd eaten nothing warm since the day before she'd left her home.

Leaving the bathroom a mess, she worked the bolt, as Peter had advised, and stumbled into the expanse beyond. In the far corner, a few lamps illuminated an area with seats, and a stove, with Peter engrossed in conversation with the dog, settled at his feet.

'How do I get rid of the water?' she called, embarrassed by the dirty skin of filth layering it.

'Press down on the nob between the two taps,' Peter responded, as though he'd been waiting for the question.

She did as he advised and then set about returning the bathroom to some semblance of order. The water drained quickly, and she swished the dirty marks from the side and rearranged her wet things so the pink towel could also fit onto the radiator.

Only then did she leave the bathroom, and make her way toward Peter and her new companion.

'You look much restored,' the older man said, from his place by the stove.'Now eat, and then you can rest. Your bed for the night is over there.' As he spoke, he pointed back toward the bathroom, and Harra could see another lamp behind it, a small bed showing in the faint light.

'My thanks,' she offered, eagerly claiming a bowl from him, a spoon as well.

'Just a stew,' he offered. 'More vegetables than meat, but it'll warm you all the same.'

She ate hungrily, the warmth of the food hitting her stomach and flooding her inside with the heat her outside already benefitted from.

'I was expecting you two days ago,' Peter offered returning to his chair, his own bowl resting on the table.

The news stilled Harra's frantic eating, and she shook her head.

'Not me, but I did find someone,' and here she paused. 'Dead on the way here. The dog was with the body.' A sudden sadness filled Peter's face, but he shook it off quickly.

'A sorrow,' he said. 'But it isn't the first time, and it won't be the last. Not everyone can manage the rigours of the Northern Road.'

'The dog followed me. I'm not sure what to do with him.'

'He is a she, and her name is Jessy.' At her name, the dog's tail wagged on the hard floor, and she looked at Peter in adoration, as he also placed a bowl of food before her on the floor.

'You know her,' Harra asked in surprise, but Peter shook his head, laughing at Jessy's ravenous hunger.

'No, she was included on the information I received, when

someone is coming this way. It helps me know what food to prepare.'

The knowledge surprised Harra.

'So you know my name as well?'

'Well, I thought I did, but now I think you must be Harra and not Jessy's owner. I thought I might have three for dinner this morning, but alas, only the two of you have made it.'

'And what else do you know about me?' Harra asked, unsure that she liked this friendly man after all. At least with her other two custodians, the one never seen at all, she'd not felt exposed.

'Nothing, just your name, and your time of arrival. See,' and the man held up a small piece of paper, something printed on it. Harra squinted in the pale lights, but could just make out her name and the number 01:56 beside it.

'It's all very precise,' she commented.

'Precision is the way the scheme works. Precision and secrecy.'

'So I wasn't too late then?' she asked, remembering the worry the rain would slow her down.

'No, well within expected parameters. Not like Jessy's owner. Poor soul. I will have to remove the body.'

'What do you do here?' Harra asked, curious, but Peter shook his head.

'I can show my face, and offer small talk, but nothing of significance. The entire network is a secret. I don't know who you met last night, and who you'll meet tomorrow night. All I know is your name, and that you'd meet me today.'

She nodded. It made perfect sense to her.

'Then can I ask why the road to here is so much better maintained than the first one I was on? This casserole is excellent,' she finished. The food was amazing. Perhaps the best she'd ever tasted.

At this Peter's face creased, and then he nodded.

'I don't see why I can't tell you that. These roads are still used, occasionally. They're important. Further south, no one bothers with the roads any more.'

'What are they used for? Do you still have cars here, petrol, diesel?'

Peter shook his head.

'No, we have some that are powered by electricity, nothing as exotic as petrol and diesel.'

Still, the thought amazed her.

'Can I see one of them?' she asked, excited at the thought of actually seeing a car move. But Peter laughed.

'You're here when no one else is. There's a reason for that.'

'Ah, of course, secrecy,' Harra confirmed. Still, she was disappointed all the same.

'Have you finished eating. You should really sleep. It was a rough night for you, and I have work to be getting on with.'

'Of course, yes, and thank you for answering my questions.'

Peter chuckled as he took her bowl away.

'I hardly answered your questions, but you're welcome all the same. Now, good night,' he said, humour in his voice, as he turned his back on her and walked toward a small sink, already piled high with another plate and whatever instruments he'd used to prepare her meal.

She lingered, for just a moment, but then yawned wildly, and knew she should rest. It had been difficult going in the rain, Peter was right.

'Leave everything in the bathroom. No one else will come in here, once I leave. The door will be locked, and I'll return at 18:00. You can finish the casserole, if you want, and there's also a sandwich and water if you're hungry or thirsty when you wake.'

'My thanks,' she said, walking away. The dog, Jessy,

seemed content to stay with Peter and so she left her. What use did she have for a dog anyway?

CHAPTER 6
STAGE 4

'RETURN TO THE NORTHERN
ROAD AT 18:00 HOURS.'

WHEN SHE WOKE, later, she was too comfortable to consider getting out of bed.

She'd never slept on a bed quite so soft, or with so many blankets. From her toes to her nose, she felt suffused with warmth and snuggled even tighter into the blankets having checked her glowing watch display. It read 15:45 and so she lingered in the bed.

She had over two hours before Peter returned for her and she began the next stage of her journey.

She closed her eyes and recited the instructions. They were simple, and she worried that they were too simple.

> 'Stage 4 – Return to the Northern Road at
> 18:00 hours and walk North for 10 miles. Food
> will be provided from now on. Take plenty of
> water.'

She was as perplexed by the idea food would be given to her as she was by the simpleness of just walking 10 miles. Why would they suddenly give her food when they hadn't before now?

She'd asked her aunt, but she'd shaken her head. 'I don't know. Probably because you can't carry enough food for the length of the journey and everything else you need as well.' The logical answer had soothed Harra then, but now she wasn't quite so sure. Why would there suddenly be extra food available?

No one ever shared their resources, and certainly not with total strangers. Apart from Peter, last night, and she'd thought it extremely generous at the time, and perhaps had only occurred because she'd been so cold, wet and damp from the storm.

But the thought of food caused her stomach to rumble, loudly, and she knew she'd get no more sleep. Sliding from the bed, she was surprised to discover the floor felt warm beneath her feet, not cold. A strange sensation, so odd she bent down and ran her hand over the smooth surface. Yes, it was definitely warm.

She really wanted to know how it was possible but was distracted by both a rumbling belly and a full bladder. Hastily, she returned to the bathroom, saw to her needs and dressed, removing the crisply dry underwear and socks from the radiator. They smelled about as clean as she could get them, the soapy fragrance pleasant in her nostrils. She bundled them together and stuffed them back into her rucksack, amongst the cleaner clothes. For a moment she considered turfing out the dirty things but realised it would take too long to dry them all.

'I should have done that last night,' she moaned to herself, before hearing a tip-tapping sound on the floor. Opening the bathroom door, she was greeted by the inquisitive nose of Jessy.

'Hi girl,' she said, surprisingly overjoyed to see the dog. 'I thought you'd gone with Peter?' Not expecting an answer, Harra made her way back to the kitchen area.

A bowl of last night's food had been left out for her, the

edges surprisingly warm, and beside it, there was another plate, filled with small pieces of meat. Harra was surprised by Peter's generosity towards the dog.

'For you, I assume,' she offered, laying the plate on the floor, where Jessy immediately started work on it.

Taking a spoon, Harra returned to the chair she'd occupied yesterday, keen to settle her demanding stomach. She thought she'd never been so hungry in all her life.

As eagerly as Jessy, Harra ate the food, savouring the few pieces of rich meat and many vegetables. Back home, she would have done anything for a meal quite this tasty. Peter was certainly a good cook. Yet, he'd also roused her curiosity in the strange, secretive ways allowing her to escape from England's broken future.

He'd left the piece of paper he'd shown her last night on his own chair, and she reached for it.

The paper was smooth, soft, beneath her fingers, not like anything she'd ever felt before.

What she'd taken to be hand-written words, were actually too regular to have been written by a human hand. They had the look of the digits on her watch about them. But where had they come from?

Other than her name, and the time, the sheet of paper was entirely blank. So how had he been sent it?

Gnawing at her lip, she considered what possibilities there were. There were surprisingly few. Her mother had told her about the internet, and emails, and how, by using computer screens, electricity and something called broadband, people had once been able to communicate simultaneously with each other, from one side of the world to the other, as though in the same room together.

The lack of mains electricity made that venture impossible now, but perhaps there were older ways, which Harra knew nothing about, which Peter could access. Just like her old watch, was Peter able to make use of technologies once thought obsolete but which were viable again?

Jessy came and rested her head on Harra's knee, soft brown eyes watching her.

'Hey there,' Harra said, running her hand through the fur above Jessy's eyes, and behind her ears. She didn't know what sort of dog Jessy was, just that she was one, as her tail wagged excitedly from side to side under Harra's ministrations.

Jessy's eyes were deep chestnut, her fur a mixture of black and white splodges, and soft to the touch. She was certainly in better condition than when Harra had found her.

'Has Peter been smartening you up?' Harra asked, laughing at the slight whine her question occasioned, which she took to be affirmative.

'Where did you spend the night?' she'd thought Peter had taken Jessy with him, but now she wasn't so sure. Maybe Peter had taken her for a while and then brought her back to sleep once he'd combed her fur.

Settling back in the chair, Harra kept her hand on Jessy's head, pleased to have some company, the piece of paper forgotten about in her other hand. Her stomach was sated, and the thought of going back to sleep for a bit was suddenly appealing. Her eyes rolled closed, just a little, but then opened wide in shock, Jessy's weight suddenly landing fully on her lap.

'What?' Harra asked breathlessly, but she too had felt a rumble echoing through the building. The sound came again, as Harra clutched Jessy to her side, both of them whimpering in horror.

'What?' Harra said again, only for the same rumble to happen once more, followed by a strange whining noise far louder than anything Jessy or Harra could have managed.

'What's that?' Harra finally managed to say when no further rumbles happened for long minutes, and she allowed herself to relax. Jessy slid from her lap, something like embarrassment on her face, but Harra had enjoyed being terrified with her. Far better than being alone.

She checked her watch. It only read 17:02. She had nearly an hour until she needed to begin Stage 4, and little to occupy her time. Yet, not wanting to be caught out, as she had been the evening before, Harra carefully pulled the instructions from her backpack, ignoring her father's journal as she did so. It had been that which had distracted her yesterday, and she had no intention of delving back into its contents.

Her hand brushed her water bottle and flask as she did so, and mindful of the instructions, she grabbed them both and took them to the taps over the sink.

All the cooking implements of the day before had been cleared away, and Harra reached for one of the taps, trying to determine which was hot and which cold, as neither of them showed any sign of being different.

She emptied the remnants of yesterday's water from the bottle, and then refilled it, pleased the water was clear in the lamplight and it remained cold. Hastily, she did the same with the flask, shimmering silver in the solitary bulb, and then returned to her seat. Her coat was draped over the back of her chair, ready, should she need it, meaning there was more room than usual in her backpack. She placed the bottle and flask inside, drying any stray drips from their sides first, forcing her father's journal as far from them as possible. She also hunted until she found the small container her mother had given her, and which had contained all the sandwiches she'd since eaten.

She stood, opening the container as she went, and placed the sandwich Peter had left out on the table for her inside the box. 'Food will be provided,' Stage 4 read, but she wasn't sure if this was it, or not. Not content to take any chances, Harra took the two sandwiches, all the same, admiring the thick brown bread as she did so. They'd be tasty, when she was hungry enough to eat again. She sniffed at the fillings but was undecided as to what it was. Certainly not the ubiquitous meat paste she'd been eating all her life.

She doubted there was any meat in the paste, but had refused to question it, too worried it would revolt her and she'd never eat it again.

With that done, she smoothed out her list of instructions, and reread Stage 4, just to be sure.

It hadn't changed, obviously, so she settled to wait for Peter's return. She tried her boots, they were just about dry after yesterday's downpour, and she thought they'd be okay to continue the journey in. Not that she had any choice. One pair of boots had been allotted to her, and she'd not thought to bring a second pair of shoes. There just hadn't been room in her backpack.

Her eyes wondered to Stage 5, considering what the next day would bring, but before she could finish reading, there was a loud banging noise, startling Harra, and causing Jessy to whine once more.

It seemed to be coming from the doorway, but Harra was rooted to the spot. Peter would have no need to knock. He had the key to the door. Whoever was on the other side wasn't someone who knew about Harra, or Jessy, and she quaked. It wasn't yet 18:00.

The banging continued, louder, always louder, reverberating through the almost empty building, and Harra cowered, reaching for Jessy, unsure what to do. Harra stayed silent, but Jessy, with eyes showing wild fright, was whining softly.

'Shh,' Harra said as gently as she could, trying to get the dog to look at her, and not at the door. But Jessy shivered just out of reach of Harra's hands.

'Shh,' she said once more, hoping Jessy would understand, but the dog was terrified, despite Harra's efforts to comfort her

Not liking it, but feeling she had no choice, Harra snuck her hands around Jesse's nose, hoping to at least prevent her from barking. It would be disastrous if their presence were discovered.

Just heard over the sound of the thumping, were raised voices, none of which Harra recognised. She was hoping for Peter's voice, but whether she couldn't recognize it over the shouting, or whether he wasn't there, she couldn't determine. Reaching forward, and just to be on the safe side, she flicked the lamp off, and sat with Jessy between her legs, one hand around the dog's nose, the other stroking her comfortingly. But the dog quivered, and if Harra was honest with herself, she was almost as terrified, tears sheeting down her face.

To have come so far and face discovery now wasn't something she could truly comprehend.

Long moments went by with no light other than from her watch display. Painfully slowly the digits moved from 17:07 to 17:11 and abruptly the hammering stopped, the shouting as well.

Yet she still sat on the floor, in total darkness, her hand slowly releasing Jessy's nose so she could turn her calmer eyes on Harra and lick her face, as though in thanks.

They remained together, not wanting to tempt fate and have the noise start again. Indeed, only when her watch showed 17:57 did Harra shakily reach for the lamp, to turn it back on, and then quickly gather her possessions. Working swiftly and concisely, she made sure she had all that was needed in her backpack, ready for a quick escape, should it prove necessary.

She double-checked her instructions for the coming night, everything having been driven from her head in fright, even the straightforward instructions.

Pleased she knew what she was doing, Harra waited by her coat, anticipating returning it to her back. But the time on her watch read 18:01 by now and a new fear took her.

What if Peter had been detained? What if he wasn't able to come and release her from the room? Then she wouldn't be able to continue, and the careful plans would be ruined.

Timing was everything. Why else provide the watch?

By 18:05 her stomach had turned to a writhing mass of worry and fury, which Jessy had picked up on. Harra was pacing, Jessy winding her way unhelpfully between her legs when at 18:12 the door finally opened.

A small figure hurried inside, and Harra was overjoyed to see Peter, but he didn't mirror her relief.

'There's a problem,' he said, filled with agitation, constantly looking over his shoulder as though the door he'd locked behind him on entering might shoot open at any moment. 'You can leave here, but it'll have to be done quickly and without alerting the attention of the men and women who've chosen tonight of all nights to spend their evening here. They, well, it's not important you know who they are, simply that you aren't seen by them. It could ruin everything, and certainly, they'll be too many questions.'

Anxiety consumed Harra. This was her worst worry, realised.

'Take the dog. I'd keep her, but they'll ask questions I can't answer in any way to satisfy them. Take her, and follow the instructions. No one will come after you, not once you're back on the Northern Road. No one ventures out after dark, not when the smog comes down as thick as it is tonight. I'm just pleased I moved the body yesterday.'

The words were far from reassuring, and for a moment Harra wanted to argue and refuse to move, but time was pressing, and punctuality was vital to the success of her escape.

'My thanks,' she managed to say, her mouth dry. 'For the risks and your help. I'll not forget your assistance.'

'And you have my thanks as well, for not panicking and opening the door when they shouted for entry. You kept your head, and I'm grateful to you. Now come, quickly. They're busy elsewhere, and none will look here, not now they believe the building is derelict.'

Far from reassured, but knowing it was past time to be gone, Harra grabbed her coat, her backpack and beckoned to Jessy to follow her, as she trailed in Peter's wake.

He paused for a moment, his ear cocked to the door, and only then did he turn the key, peering outside and then beckoning Harra and Jessy onwards.

Outside it was as gloomy as ever, if anything the olive smog seeming to pulse thicker than usual. Harra took a final gulp of the filtered air inside her accommodation before stepping outside.

At least it wasn't raining. Although it hadn't been long since the rain had stopped because the ground was covered in deep puddles. Harra grimaced, vowing to keep her boots dry, as she followed Peter back down the slight incline.

Once there, he turned to walk away, his finger pressed to his lips, asking for silence. She held her tongue, but smiled her thanks and walked away without looking back.

Quickly, the smog closed around her, stifling all sound, and she rushed for the first thirty minutes, keen to be as far away as possible from the possibility of discovery.

At her side, Jessy kept close, and as the watch showed 19:04 Harra finally paused and gave herself a two-minute respite. Her breath was running harsh; Jessy's as well, but the better-maintained road was worrying her more than her breathlessness.

Peter had said the roadway was still used, and there were people at his home that night. But where they had come from, and what their job was, were unknown to her. She simply hoped she'd done enough to outrun them.

Jessy came to her side then, tongue lolling, with bright eyes. All traces of fear were gone, and Harra tried to mirror the dog's calmness. But it was hard. Her heart raced, and she wished herself off the road and long gone from the Northern Road altogether. There was only one way to do that, and so she straightened her body and set out once more. She had many miles to go yet, and she'd do them as quickly as possible, if only to outrun anyone who might make use of the road during the daylight hours.

An hour later, Harra wheezed on her hands and knees. She might have been trying to speed her way to the next stop off point, but for some reason, her body was far from receptive. Her legs ached, her mouth dry, no matter how much she drank, and breathing was becoming ever more difficult.

She coughed, swallowed water and then spat it, her throat feeling clogged, as she concentrated on breathing in and out through her nose.

Around her, the olive smog pulsed thicker than before, and fear took shape inside her. Was it the insidious smog causing her difficulties? Was it somehow more deadly to her? Was its clumpy texture even more dangerous to her, than the haze she'd endured all her life?

This was her fourth night of walking all night and sleeping all day. Her night-time hours were spent in the impenetrable smog, something everyone tried to avoid as they went about their lives. Her daytime was spent in a room where the air was filtered to remove as many impurities as possible. Could the difference in air quality be compromising her ability to breath?

She'd asked no questions about the instructions demanding she travels at night even though no one travelled at night when the smog was at its most treacherous. No one. However, she'd done that, for four straight nights in a row, and really, it had been five nights if she counted the trip to her father's gravesite. Was it that which now affected her, or was it just sheer exhaustion?

She had ten miles to travel. In the first hour, she'd walked as fast as possible, practically running, and calculated she'd covered three miles at least. Since then her pace had dramatically dipped. So she thought she still had five miles to go, but how could she, barely able to stand?

The thought of the filtered air inside the daytime shelters abruptly gave her an idea. She pulled her coat clear from her body, and removed her jumper. Rushing back into the coat, her skin clammy against the gummy material, she held the jumper against her mouth and nose, already convinced she could breathe more deeply.

The concerned eyes of Jessy met hers, but the dog seemed none the worst for her continuing exposure to the smog.

'Come on then,' Harra confirmed. 'Let's get this done. Perhaps there'll be something to help me at the next stage.' The thought cheered her flagging steps, and the next two hours passed far more easily.

At her side, Jessy let out a low growl, and Harra startled in fear.

'What is it girl?' she called softly, voice muffled by her jumper, but it was a human voice that answered.

'Harra? Follow my voice.' Doing as instructed, although sound was muted in the gloomy night, Harra found herself facing what she took to be a young woman from her voice, although a facemask covered her so it was hard to tell. Harra didn't miss the look of concern flashing through her troubled eyes when Harra appeared before her.

'Hurry,' was the harsh instruction. Harra rushed to keep up with the suddenly vigorous steps of the woman striding away, Jessy at her side.

Hastily Harra scaled a steep decline, and then a light burnt in the near distance, an odd blue glow as the yellow of the light mixed with the olive of the smog. Just as Harra began to stagger and cough once more, her jumper barrier seeming to lose its effectiveness with every step, she came to a sudden stop below the light.

The woman eyed her with concern, but opened a metal door and led her inside.

Once there, Harra removed the jumper from around her mouth and coughed more and more, horrified at the black muck coming from her mouth with each deep cough. Whatever left her body made it more and more difficult to stop hacking, and Harra had a distinct feeling the dispassionate eyes had experienced this many times before.

The woman watched her with indifference, waiting for the coughing to pass, handing her a beaker containing an orange coloured liquid as soon as Harra could master two breaths without resorting to coughing.

'Drink it, it'll clear your tubes,' the woman offered, a smile of reassurance, as she removed her facemask. Harra sniffed at the liquid, which smelt clean, and then gulped it quickly. Immediately she felt her chest loosen and the constant urge to cough die away.

'Did you lose your mask?' the woman asked, hand outstretched for the empty beaker, looking at Harra with worry. Now her mask was removed, Harra could see the woman was indeed young, although her face was crisscrossed with scars running from cheek to cheek and chin to forehead. The woman had suffered in some way, perhaps from a disease, or a terrible beating. Harra held her tongue not wishing to be rude.

'I never had a mask,' Harra spoke, her words tight for all felt much better. Jessy circled the small space they were within, a corridor of some sort, as though she sought something out, nose to the floor, tail tight between her back legs.

'The previous custodian should have given it to you,' the woman explained, perplexed, only then walking down the corridor leading off the doorway, the beaker returned to a low shelf. 'I have one for the next stage of the journey, but you should have had one anyway. I'm amazed you made it this far.'

The words chilled Harra, and yet she couldn't be angry with Peter. He'd been fearful of detection when he'd released her from the building. It was no surprise he'd forgotten to hand her the facemask.

Another door appeared at the end of the corridor. As Harra followed the woman, she paused just before it, and typed something into a glowing dial beside the door. It opened with a whoosh of air. She offered an explanation as the door fully extended.

'We have to go through an airlock. It doesn't hurt. Don't worry. Just do what I do.'

Harra did as told, Jessy at her side, perplexed by what was happening. The door behind them clanged shut. A loud whining noise filled the room. At the same time, Harra could feel air rushing over her, as though water, and then another door opened before them.

'Come on in,' the woman smiled, the scars hidden by shadows. Harra walked into a room similar in all ways to the stopovers she'd already experienced, apart from the airlock.

'The outside air is too toxic for people to breathe. Inside, the air is filtered to remove as much of the bad stuff as possible.'

'So I shouldn't have just been walking around in it then?' Harra queried, just to be sure, and the woman shook her head.

'Not at all. As I said. You're lucky. You're strong. A lot of the others are weak by the time they make it this far. They wouldn't have been able to survive as you did. Good thinking with the jumper. Give me all of your clothes, and I'll get them cleaned for tomorrow. It'll also remove any of the bad stuff that might cause welts to form on your skin.' As she spoke, she beckoned at her own face, and Harra nodded with understanding.

'There's a bathroom over there, clean night clothes for you, and also food for you, although you'll have to share with your friend. I wasn't expecting the dog.'

Harra felt she should explain, despite the stern tone.

'I found her. With a body, not last night, but the night before.'

'Ah, I feared as much,' the woman said, but with only a slight softening to her tone. 'It happens, sadly,' she continued, but the words were just those, words. Harra heard no real compassion. It was hard to feel pity for others when life itself was such a struggle.

'I have a mask for the dog, if you plan on taking her with you. If not, she can remain here. If you want. We can make use of healthy dogs.' Leaving the conversation hanging, and Harra reaching out to grab Jessy possessively, the woman waited impatiently, as though expecting an answer.

'Go, change. I've much to be doing. I'll return this evening, at 20:00.'

Hastily, Harra went to the bathroom and stripped off all her clothes, stuffing them into a bag that seemed to be waiting for them. It was black, but with bright yellow warning signs she was sure meant her clothes had become hazardous to human touch

She also opened her backpack and pulled out the remainder of the clothes she'd worn, being careful not to mix up any of her other possessions in the soft bulk. Laying the gloopy bag to one side, the tube and needles, as well as the torch and her father's journal and the list of instructions, she handed over almost everything else, apart from the clothes she'd not yet worn.

'Here you go,' she called, and a hand snaked through the gap in the door to claim the bag.

'Enjoy your bath,' the woman called, a hint of impatience to her voice. Harra waited for the sound of footsteps to recede, and for the airlock to swallow up the woman before she allowed herself to relax. Peter had been very friendly the night before. Tonight's custodian was far from that, and yet she seemed efficient and unperturbed by the death of one of the potential escapees. Perhaps it was preferred to being too friendly. After all, Peter had nearly killed her with his oversight during his panic to have her gone.

Her head aching from what she assumed was the abrupt change from the smog to the clean air, she lowered her naked body into the waiting bath. The bathroom was more inviting than the previous two, the surroundings almost luxurious, yet the supplies left out for her were harshly coloured in yellow and black, and she assumed they were to clean her hair, body and skin of any further toxins.

Leaning over the bath, she met the eyes of Jessy. The dog seemed fine, and yet Harra was suddenly concerned about her safety as well.

'A bath for you, I think,' she announced, while Jessy whined, but first Harra set to work making use of the astringent smelling soap to clean herself, paying particular attention to her hair and any exposed skin during her night-time travels, especially on her face. The custodian's face was a warning as to how damaging the fog could be.

Harra rubbed so hard, her skin felt raw and only then did she feel able to rise from the bath and wrap herself in the waiting fluffy towel, warmed from the radiator. It was dark blue, a sensible colour. Drying herself, she turned to Jessy.

'Your turn,' she said, bending to pick Jessy up. She thought the dog would refuse to enter the water, and yet, with half of the water drained away, Jessy stood in it, her tongue sticking out, seeming to smile at Harra. Jessy even lay down in the water, covering her entire body and waiting patiently for whatever came next.

Harra laughed. A dog that wanted a bath!

Harra quickly worked the soap into her hands and massaged the dog's fur, disturbed when it felt as though handfuls of the stuff were coming loose. She thought of her own hair. Had much of it fallen out? She'd not considered it when she'd washed her hair.

Still, Jessy seemed content no matter the fur, so Harra continued her work, ensuring no inch of her wasn't cleaned of whatever it was that so terrified the custodian.

Only when Jessy finally lost patience, standing and shaking soap all over Harra, did she stop and pick Jessy up and dry her on the towel she'd already used.

Harra wrinkled her nose slightly. The smell of damp dog was not the most pleasant. As she rubbed her companion dry, she paid careful attention to any clumps of fur loosened by the water and scrubbing but found none. Reassured, Harra stood and leant over the bath to empty it of the scummy water. Here, her own hair and Jessy's fur layered the water, and Harra felt sick at the sight of it all.

Little of it made its ways down the plughole, and Harra was forced to lean in and remove a wad of matted hair so she could rinse the bath entirely clean. Unsure what to do with it all, and with no bin in sight, Harra flushed the hair away, down the toilet, shaking with disgust as she did so.

Whatever had coated her and Jessy, as they'd walked that day, it wasn't pleasant. Not at all.

Only now did the pair of them leave the bathroom and make their way to the small kitchen area. Food had been left out for them, well for Harra, another meaty but really vegetable casserole with grains that bubbled a little on a small stove. Harra searched for, and found a spare plate and ladled some of the chunks onto it for Jessy, and then set to her own food with relish.

She was starving. Harra also drank deeply from the nearby water jug. She'd drunk all of her water as she'd walked. She'd not done that before. She pondered the effects of the smog on her body. Last night she'd struggled to breathe freely, what would happen as she went ever further north?

The custodian had made it clear she needed to use a breathing mask when she left the next day. Harra could only hope the whole north of the country wasn't swamped with damaging pollutants. She didn't like the thought of being dependent on the breathing mask, and also, of what damage just being in contact with the smog might be doing to Jessy and herself.

When Jessy had licked her plate clean, Harra found a small bowl and sloshed water into it as well. She'd managed to squeeze some water into Jessy's mouth during the walk, but the way she lapped up the liquid now, made Harra aware she'd been just as thirsty as Harra during their journey.

Settling back on the softly cushioned chair, Jessy resting below her fingers, Harra allowed her eyes to close. She was exhausted.

Her watch glowed with the time. 02:54. But Harra was already asleep.

CHAPTER 7
STAGE 5

'RETURN TO THE NORTHERN ROAD AND WALK NORTH FOR FIVE MILES.'

WHEN SHE WOKE, hours and hours later, her neck was stiff with having fallen asleep in the chair, and there was a dull ticking noise forcing her to wakefulness.

Bleary-eyed, she turned to her watch, amazed to find it read 16:36.

She'd slept for a long time. Now she was thirsty, had the beginnings of a headache forming, and needed to use the bathroom.

Standing, swaying a little on her feet, Harra opted for the bathroom first; water afterwards and then, hopefully, some more food.

Jessy eyed her with curiosity as she stood, and was still waiting for her when she returned from the bathroom.

'You okay, girl?' she asked, bending to add more water to the bowl as the dog lapped at the water noisily.

There was a pile of clothes waiting for her, on another of the chairs, and the smell of cooking food also filled the space. Only then did she notice a blanket had been wrapped around her shoulders when she'd woken, discarded now on the chair.

Clearly, the custodian wasn't quite as uncaring as she'd appeared.

Sniffing appreciatively at the food warming on the stove, Harra saw a further covered bowl and quickly decided it had been left for Jessy. It was meaty and gelatinous, but perhaps not the meat she'd want to eat. It was everything a dog needed.

Jessy ate hungrily and then whined a little so Harra poured yet more water for the dog, before diving into her own food.

It wasn't a casserole, as the night before, but a meal of oats, sweetened with some honey. Harra enjoyed each and every mouthful, sitting back to pat her full stomach.

She didn't think she'd ever eaten quite so well.

But she allowed herself only a few minutes to savour the food. She needed to dress, refill her water bottles, and discover what provisions she had for the coming day. She also wanted to spend some time with her father's journal. She'd neglected it of late, and the weight of time passing her by was starting to worry her. Would she make it to the end of the journal before she reached The Wall?

Only when she'd accomplished all her tasks, did she allow herself to settle at the table once more, her father's journal before her. With eager eyes, she found the place she'd left off but saw little to truly enthrall her.

Her father had become alert to the perilous predicament his country found itself in, and there were pages and pages filled with clippings from old newspapers. Harra ran her hands over each and every one of the headlines, marvelling at how two different newspapers could report exactly the same news. Even as she read now, so many decades later, she could feel a slow rage smouldering away inside her.

If only she could go back in time and tell them all what it was really like to no longer be a part of Europe, or indeed, of the united kingdom.

But really, Harra was searching for mention of her mother. After the first few pages, however, she rarely appeared. Harra wondered if they'd perhaps not always been friends during those years. Either that or her father had shared his more personal thoughts elsewhere. The journal had become a scrapbook for the events taking place within England, almost to the exclusion of everything else.

One set of newspaper headlines really stumped her, and she peered at the colour images of poppies and gravestones.

The UK had marked the one hundred anniversary of the end of World War One with great solemnity. Some of the headlines moved her to tears, and yet she shook her head, not in sorrow, but in anger. 'For your tomorrow,' one of the papers read. 'Their past is our future,' read another, images of sorrowing individuals covering the large sheets of paper she delicately unfolded to read, one after another.

Another three decades had passed since then, and still, politicians played fast and loose with people's lives. What point those sacrifices when England was so weak and sick now? So far from the world power, she'd been told it had once been.

England, as it was now, had its own army, but it was a poor thing, without enough men and women, or machinery. It was a joke. Should an attack come, as unlikely as it sounded for who would want such a desolate and deprived place, Harra was sure any enemy would quickly overpower the English army.

England could never be called into a conflict again because England would be unable to protect itself.

On she went, checking her watch to make sure she still had time, and then turning to the actual moment the UK had left the European Union on March 29th 2019. Again, her father had cultivated a collection of newspaper headlines and images, smiling faces, and solemn ones, and once more, Harra read with a dizzy sense of disbelief the lies and untruths foisted on the people of what had then been the United Kingdom.

How little they'd all known. How little, and much of what they had 'known' had been utter bollocks.

Dismayed, she slammed the journal shut, her breathing a little too quick. There was little she'd not known beforehand, and yet to see it all, laid out in her father's journal as it had happened, sickened her. To appreciate what it must have been like to live through such times, to know it would be utterly reprehensible to follow through with the half-ass ideas of leaving the European Union, and be powerless to act because it was unconstitutional to go against less than a quarter of the United Kingdom's population who had voted for the actions!

Such bloody fools. All of them.

Glancing at her watch, she read 19:34 and decided it was time to make preparations to leave.

She ensured her rucksack was packed, as usual, stuffing her father's journal far to the bottom, out of sight of prying eyes, and then she reached for Stage 5 of her instructions.

These instructions hadn't worried her before, but now they did.

It had all seemed too brief, but now she understood why. Five miles might not be far to walk in a day, but if it were through noxious smog, she'd have to take her time, exert herself as little as possible. And make sure she didn't remove her facemask, when she was given it, and she'd make sure she received one. This time.

Jessy sidled up to her, perhaps aware they were about to go outside once more. Harra rubbed her hand over the dog's fur, keen to see if it was coming away in tufts in her hand, relieved when it wasn't. She hoped the bath had merely been an accumulation of the days spent travelling, and probably, neglect before that as well. Few could afford to keep an animal, and certainly not one needing food a human could eat.

'You ready?' she asked Jessy, and intelligent eyes met her own.

Stage 5. That was all. She still had many more to go, and only her own feet to take her where she needed to go. Harra sank into melancholy, only rousing from it when the custodian opened the metal door with a rush of air and stepped inside.

She greeted Harra with a small smile.

'You look better,' she offered and then turned to glance at Jessy.

'And so do you. Here, I've got one for you, and a spare for your backpack. I hope this one will help the dog.'

As she handed over the two masks, Harra saw the third mask had been remodelled for Jessy with a longer nose shape. Slipping the spare mask into her backpack, Harra tried hers for comfort, adjusting it so that none of the elastic nipped or tucked around her ears and her mouth.

Then she bent to Jessy, a smile on her face, and beckoned the dog closer.

'You need one of these as well,' she explained, as Jessy sat, tail flapping on the floor. 'Will you let me put it on you?'

At first, it seemed Jessy wouldn't, jerking her head out of the way a few times, but then, having sniffed the contraption, she allowed Harra to pass it over her head, and tie it in place.

Jessy looked strange with the mask on, clamping her jaw almost closed with its catches and tags, but Harra patted the dog and called her a good girl. It would make it easier for her if Jessy weren't taken ill on the journey.

Standing, she faced the custodian, surprised to find some hesitancy in her actions. As the time on her watch advanced, the woman seemed unprepared to let them go.

'I'm not meant to offer advice, but I must. From here, the road north is dangerous, the smog as thick as butter. You must take care and never remove your facemasks, no matter what. I think many have failed to get beyond this stage of the journey, but I understand, the smog will begin to lift, in a day or two with a change in wind direction, and so I caution you to be careful but also determined.'

Harra nodded, relieved to know as much.

'Come then,' the woman said, finally turning back toward the closed door.

'My thanks for your hospitality and warnings,' Harra offered, but the woman either didn't hear or chose to ignore her. She fiddled with the door instead, indicating Harra and Jessy should step inside so the airlock could do its work. They moved quickly down the corridor and outside once more.

The sound of the wind greeted Harra as soon as the door was opened, and she shivered at the abrupt drop in temperature.

A cold night, then, and one where she'd have to move slowly to protect herself. She doubted this was going to be pleasant.

The woman led the way, back to where they'd first met, and then pointed in the direction Harra needed to take. Peering into the distance, Harra could already tell the smog was thick and visibility much reduced. She turned back to say a further thank you but the woman was gone, and Jessy and Harra were alone once more on the tarmac of the Northern Road.

Harra glanced down at Jessy, suppressing a wry smirk for how strange she looked with the breathing mask on. She wondered what Jessy thought of her own mask.

'Come on then, girl. Let's get started.'

Initially, Jessy walked at the speed they'd started out at yesterday, and no matter how many times, Harra called her back, Jessy still set off too fast again.

'We need to go slower,' Harra cautioned Jessy, but she didn't understand the huffed words, leaving Harra with a problem. The cloud was so thick she feared to lose Jessy. That made her walk too fast as well. Already she could feel an ache in her throat, despite the oxygen mask. Jessy was nearly on the point of disappearing out of the restricted beam of the torch Harra had been forced to use to light the path.

'Shit,' Harra muttered, rushing to catch up with Jessy once more. 'Come here,' she demanded, pointing at her side. Jessy tilted her head to one side, not understanding the command at all. Harra thought hard. The dog had seemed well trained when she'd first found her. Maybe it wasn't Jessy's fault. Maybe Harra was using the wrong commands.

'Heel,' Harra tried, after considering all she knew about dogs. She was surprised and pleased when Jessy immediately settled at the side of her leg.

'Good girl,' Harra complimented the dog, rubbing a hand over the dog's fur. Together they set off at a much steadier pace, and the ache in Harra's throat eased slightly. She dreaded to think what they walked through, and what made the smog so thick it felt like a living breathing thing. They walked in and out of thicker sections of smog, some reducing visibility to mere feet in front of them, others allowing her to see far into the distance.

When she'd been at school, the problem of the smog had been explained to them, something to do with burning too many fossil fuels, particles already in the atmosphere and the heat of the sun. Harra had found it ironic the sun they so rarely saw could be the cause of its own elimination from their lives.

Of course, the smog hadn't been presented as the fault of the English, but instead of the Europeans, who refused to trade cleaner energy supplies with the English. That Harra remembered all too clearly from her teacher.

Skin cancer, once a significant problem, back when they'd been a health care system, had been replaced as a problem by other, less pleasant cancers that ate away at people's brains if they were exposed for too long to the smog.

As Harra walked, she tried not to flinch at the trick of the light, the smog feeling like hands on her arms and back, but she grew more and more alert as time went on. She might well be walking at a slower pace than before, but her heart hammered in her chest and her breathing was jagged.

Harra reached for Jessy, to find the solace of another warm body, but where Jessy had been, there was now nothing.

'Jessy,' she called, her voice thick from the mask, and frightened so she doubted her voice carried far beyond the stretch of her torch.

'Jessy, heel,' she tried again, endeavouring to project her voice further. Yet the dog didn't materialise. Abruptly she stopped, unsure. Should she go on and hope the dog found her? Or should she go back, or even stop precisely where she was?

'Jessy, heel,' she repeated, listening to her voice echo in the strange atmosphere. This time, she was sure she heard a whine of response.

'Jessy, heel,' she called, her voice catching between one word and the next, straining to hear, trying to determine where the answering cry came from. With the torch in her hand, she flashed it into the olive murk, hoping to penetrate it and find Jessy watching her.

Harra saw nothing but was confident enough to take more steps toward the left. Harra didn't like to deviate from the path she'd chosen, but neither was she about to abandon the dog, who cried for her.

Five steps she took, counting carefully, but still, nothing appeared out of the gloom.

Another five and her heart was beating too fast once more. Swinging the torch back the way she'd come, she was dismayed to already feel herself losing her way. Yet she pressed on. She must find Jessy.

After another five steps, the flicker of yellow eyes reflected in the beam of the torch, and Harra cried out in alarm.

'Jessy, what are you doing?'

Jessy was quivering where she stood, a low whine coming from her mouth.

'What is it?' Harra asked, rushing to run her hands over the dog, making sure she was uninjured.

Under her hands. Harra could feel Jessy settle, just a little, but still, the dog didn't move.

Resting back on her heels, Harra slowly turned the torch all around them. What was it that had attracted Jessy's interest but then terrified her so much?

Harra could see nothing, nothing at all, and then there was a movement, in the smog, and Harra screamed, the sound too loud in her ears, constrained by the facemask. Immediately the mask fogged.

There was something out there, and it growled, just as Jessy whined.

'What the?' Harra said, hastily turning the torch on to the animal.

It flinched in the harsh beam but made no effort to move. Wild eyes watched her once more, and Harra held herself as still as possible.

'What are you?' Harra asked, feeling foolish. Was this another stray, just like Jessy? Another animal abandoned on the way to the north, or was it a wild animal, somehow surviving alone in the wildlands?

Jessy's whimper intensified, but Harra made no move to calm her down, or even to approach the animal. When she'd met Jessy, Harra had simply walked away, and Jessy had followed. Would the same tactic work here? Would the animal attack them, or just leave?

Harra hesitated, and then made a decision. She had to get on, walk her five miles for the day and reach the next staging post.

Reaching for Jessy's neck, she turned to walk away. Jessy

resisted, still quaking, but then she capitulated, finally doing as Harra asked her. Harra didn't look behind her as they walked away. She didn't want to risk meeting the eyes of the animal that might turn wild, hunting them down.

Instead, she walked away, slowly, Jessy at her side, hoping the other animal would leave them well alone. She couldn't have run, not even if she'd tried. Just walking was effort enough.

Too terrified to look behind, Harra went only forward, Jessy's head under her hand, so she knew the dog hadn't run off again. It was impossible to tell if the other animal followed her or not, because of Jessy's claws tap-tapped on the concrete, masking any sound of pursuit, and even then, that noise was only just audible above her frantic breathing.

Harra thought hard about what the animal could be, or where it might have come from. Was it possible it lived in the wild, even in the noxious smog? Had the animal evolved so it could survive as it did?

Distracting herself with the thought, Harra pressed on, not too fast, but not too slow either, making slow, but steady progress.

When her watch glowed faintly 02:39, she realised on other night's she'd long since have arrived at her destination, but not tonight. She felt as though there was still a distance to travel, and fatigue was warring within her.

Every so often, she was half convinced more than Jessy's claws journeyed with her, but Harra refused to shine the torch behind her, to see if the animal hunted them.

The road, as had been the case for the last few nights, was reasonably smooth, and maintained in a better condition than the first few nights of travel. Harra considered that it might be because the noxious smog kept all growth at bay, and as such, the tarmac and concrete hadn't been ruptured.

However, as the road began to climb higher, she quickly reconsidered her thoughts.

Here, the road was littered with upturned chunks of concrete, greenery and other dead and reaching plants, forcing their growths through the once uniform surface. No, here at least, the road was poorly maintained.

Puffing heavily, the road steep beneath her feet, Harra ground to a stop, Jessy with her. Only now was she sure they didn't walk the road alone. Already out of breath from the climb, Harra felt her pulse quicken once more, and tears squeezed from her eyes.

She'd tried to forget the glare of the animal, the bestial look on its face. But it seemed out of sight, didn't mean it was genuinely out of mind.

Jessy whined softly, her fur sticking on edge. Harra felt the hair on the back of her neck standing tall. Surely, surely, they'd walked the required number of miles?

Walking once more, as quickly as she dared, Harra began to peer further into the olive cloud, hoping for the sight of a custodian or the building where she'd shelter for the rest of the night, and the coming day.

She could see nothing, even when she shone her torch in a wide arc in front of her. The road just seemed to get steeper and steeper, and she knew her pace was steadily slowing, her legs growing heavy, her knees protesting the exertion.

Worry drove her, Jessy still intermittently crying at her side.

'Come on, girl,' Harra said, her voice high and breathless, the encouragement more for her ears.

Abruptly, the path she could see in front of her seemed to disappear, and she stopped, perplexed. Where had the road gone? Gingerly, Harra stepped forward, one foot at a time. Had the road fallen away overnight? Or was it there, but out of sight?

Jessy moved with her, and Harra noted the dog was braver than she was, looking behind, her whining increasing in tone.

Still, Harra could see nothing in front of her, and fear deadened her legs. Her fight or flee instinct was lacking. All she wanted to do was sit down and cry; hoping whatever stalked her would stop.

Hesitantly, she reached out with her hand, almost on her hands and knees, allowing her fingers to roam forward, seeking the concrete. They reached a cliff edge, or so it seemed, but still, she quested forward and down, hoping, hoping she'd find something.

Buffeted by a gentle breeze, Harra shrieked with relief when her hand hit the rough surface of the road, lower than she might have thought, but there all the same. It was as though the road had cracked on reaching the peak, and now dipped lower and lower, always lower, as it quested to reach ground level.

Content the road was there, and passable, if at a slightly alarming decline, Harra stood, and clutching Jessy tightly, moved to step over the edge. For a moment, she faltered, her foot encountering nothing but air, only for it to eventually hit the concrete she'd felt with her hand with a heavy thud.

'Come on, girl,' Harra encouraged, again more for herself. 'It can't be far from here.'

Reassured, Harra and Jessy set off, the pace increasing as the torch lit the way forward. Not that the smog had noticeably thinned, instead, Harra just felt as though she could see further, and rising out of the dank darkness, despite the broken road, she could see what she hoped was the end of that night's journey.

A small, dull red light flashed through the olive haze, and Harra began to track closer to it. Ignoring Jessy's crying, Harra thought only of having a door to close on the beast following them. By the time she could clearly see both the red light and the long-hoped for metal doorway into a flat-roofed structure, as shown by the glow from above it, Harra was almost running.

She rushed at the door, fumbling with the handle, almost having to bang for entry, when it swung open before her. She and Jessy tumbled inside. As she wrenched the door closed, swinging the locking mechanism into place as she did so, she was convinced amber eyes emerged from the haze.

Leaning heavily on the door with her back, Harra wrenched the mask from her face, and just concentrated on breathing deeply, clearing her body and her mind from the fears stalking her all night long.

Only then did she realise no one had come to claim her on the road.

'Hello,' she called, the facility boasting a corridor and airlock facility like the night before.

'Hello,' echoed back to her, and she shivered. Was she in the right place because she wasn't going outside again?

Making her way to the airlock door marking the entry into the inner sanctum of the building, Harra wrenched it open. The suck of air leaving the room greeted her ears, and she stepped in, leaving the door open, to peer through the hatch on the other side.

Harra could see through the scratched porthole, the room beyond was set up for her. A small lamp illuminated a kitchen area, and another the bedroom, and yet another, the bathroom.

Harra banged on the door, hoping to attract the attention of whoever her custodian was for the night. But no one came. She reached for the handle, trying to open the door, but as she did an alarm sounded in her ears, the sound piercing and too high. Clamping her hands over her ears, Harra tried to dim the sound, while Jessy whined once more.

'Damn,' Harra muttered, only then seeing a red light over the door she'd tried to open, and an amber one flashing over the door still hanging open. Hastily, she pulled the open door shut, the whoosh of air leaving the room assuring her she was doing what needed to be done.

Immediately, the alarm stopped, and she waited impatiently for the red light above the door to turn to green.

Only then did the door into the inner room allow her to open it, and she did so, again calling, 'hello.' But her voice echoed back to her. It seemed there was no one there to greet her, not this time. Yet, everything had been left for her, as on previous nights.

The smell of cooked food reached her nostrils, as her stomach growled, but still, she felt uncomfortable.

'Hello,' she tried once more, giving up when she heard nothing but the echo of her voice in what must be a cavernous room.

'Come on Jessy,' she instructed. 'We may as well bathe and eat. Looks like we're on our own tonight.' Her thoughts returned to the tap-tap-tapping sound of the beast beyond the doors, as she sunk into her steaming bath. Would it still be there when she left? She'd hoped to ask the custodian about it, but that was now impossible. If it were still there, what would she do? She couldn't remain inside for the rest of her life, hoping to ignore it.

Eating the warm broth left for her, Harra tried to relax and not think about what awaited her the next day, and yet, as she settled in her bed, a howling noise started up, muted, but there, all the same, causing the damp hair on the back of her neck to stand on end.

Whatever was out there hadn't given up.

She swallowed heavily, fear making her turn to Jessy and bury her face in the comfort of the dog's freshly cleaned fur.

What would she do?

CHAPTER 8
STAGE 6

'LEAVE AT PRECISELY 19:00 HOURS.'

DESPITE HER WORRIES, Harra slept, waking with an urgent need to visit the bathroom, and a groan of dismay at what greeted her. Of all the things she didn't need, it was an upset stomach. Whether caused by the food, the water, or even the constant inhalation of whatever lay within the smog, she didn't know.

Her head thudded, as she groaned and cried tears of anger and pain, combined.

Her watch showed only 08:19. She'd slept, but just a little.

Staggering from the bathroom, half an hour later, Harra looked longingly at her bed and sleeping Jessy, but instead stumbled her way to the kitchen. She was thirsty, and her mouth tasted disgusting.

In the kitchen, clear after last night's meal, which surprised Harra, as she'd heard no one while she'd slept, there was a small white box waiting for her on the table.

'Take two tablets, with water, and go back to bed.'

Somewhat relieved to see her desperate need had been anticipated, Harra hastily swallowed the pills without even considering what they might be. Instantly, she felt sleepy, and hastened back to her bed, burping foul air as she went.

She tumbled to the bed, only to wake an hour later, the need to use the bathroom again urgent.

Harra dashed to the bathroom, wrinkling her nose at her own smell.

Exhausted, she once more returned to her bed, cursing whatever had been in those tablets.

Yet, when she woke again, at 15:19, she felt better, even her headache all gone, and only the rumblings of an empty belly to remind her of the previous affliction.

Still, she wrinkled her nose at herself, concerned by the lingering smell, and returned to the bathroom.

She ran the hot water until the bath was almost too full for her to risk getting in without sloshing the water all over the tile floor. She added to it a packet of something, left out for her, and with a label on it that read, 'add to bath,' in an exotic curving script.

These little instructions reminded her of a story she'd read, long ago, and that comforted her, as the slightly odd smell of the now yellowish bath filled her nostrils.

Only the whining of Jessy forced her from the bath, the dog refusing to come to her side even when she called to her.

'What is it?' Harra asked, a rough edge of annoyance to her voice. She clutched a towel around her body, and let out a surprised yelp when she finally caught sight of her custodian. It was clear Jessy wasn't keen on whoever the person was.

'Hello?' Jessy called again, but the straight back of the person didn't move, even when Jessy huffed with annoyance. What was this?

Hastening into her clothes, Harra marched to the kitchen, seeking her custodian. The person materialised as a tall woman, wearing baggy trousers, and an even more shapeless jumper. She smiled on seeing Harra, and before Harra could open her mouth, handed her yet another note, written in the same curling script.

'I am deaf.' The note read, and all of Harra's fury evaporated.

She nodded, taking the pen as handed to her by the woman.

'I'm Harra,' she wrote. 'Thank you for your medicine and food.'

The woman smiled, an odd arrangement on her face. The light of joy seemed to reach her eyes, but not the rest of her face. Harra watched her keenly, waiting to see if she would offer more. Only the custodian turned back to her meal, content she'd done all that needed to be done.

Harra turned to Jessy and offered her a shrug of confusion.

While the woman worked to prepare food for them, Harra reached for the piece of paper she'd written on, and thought about what else she wanted to ask.

'Why was I sick?' was her most pressing concern, but leaving a space for an answer, she also wrote. 'What are the animals following me outside, and howling?'

Then she waited, not wishing to startle the woman in her endeavours.

As a plate piled high with potatoes and chunks of meat was placed before her, another on the floor for Jessy, Harra handed over the piece of paper.

The custodian took this, and claimed a seat beside Harra, with her own plate of food before her.

She read the questions, but then placed the paper on the table, upside down, and began to eat with an appetite even more ferocious than Harra's. Harra curbed her frustration and tried the potatoes. They were good, a little salty, just the way she liked them. The meat was soft as well, requiring almost no chewing. She ate with appreciation. The custodian was a talented cook, even if the ingredients available were far from exciting.

Only when the woman had finished eating, did she return to the two questions. Pausing, with the pen in her hand, she began to write, her hand steady over the smooth paper.

Harra watched as she ate, unable to make out the words as the piece of paper was to the right of the woman, whereas Harra sat to the left. Impatiently she watched the paper fill with words in the same distinctive handwriting as the bath salts that had been left for her.

Harra examined the woman. She was impossible to age. She could have been young, or old. Harra thought she was probably a similar age to her mother. Perhaps.

At her feet, Jessy flopped to the ground, her plate licked clean, as Harra rubbed the contended dog's stomach, pleased she hadn't had the same upset belly inflicted on her.

At the thought, Harra's gut rolled unhappily, and she grimaced. Surely not again? Only it settled as quickly as it had complained, and now the woman handed the paper back to Harra.

She smiled her thanks, and then read carefully.

In response to

'Why she was sick?'

the woman had written.

'The toxins from the smog have worked their way into your body. It normally happens to everyone. It's to be expected. It'll not trouble you again as you journey north.'

That at least was reassuring. The answer to the question about the animals was lengthy and far from encouraging.

> 'Wild cats and dogs and other creatures live in the wilderness. They are not necessarily dangerous, but persistent. They are always hungry and, because they were once domesticated, they sense they should be with a person, not on their own. They have been known to attack, but normally just follow travellers, until they lose interest. I didn't know they howled at night. No one has ever told me that before.'

Harra nodded her thanks again, as she looked at the custodian, who was peering intently at her.

She grabbed back the paper.

> 'You are feeling better?'

Harra read the note and nodded. The custodian held up her thumb in reply, in what Harra took to mean 'good'.

The silence in the room seemed to overwhelm Harra. Bad enough to have to speak to someone she didn't know, even stranger to have to sit in silence with someone she didn't know. Once or twice she opened her mouth to speak but closed it again. Small talk would not be possible if everything had to be written down.

The woman nodded with understanding, and stood to clear away the dishes and tidy the kitchen area.

Harra settled to watch her, considering her options for the forthcoming night.

She had no weapon and nothing to beat off any animal trying to attack her, and yet the custodian didn't think it likely the animal would strike. But, and this worried Harra, none of the custodians knew much about life away from their own particular 'area' they controlled. That might mean there had been more attacks than the woman believed.

Unhappy with her thoughts, Harra stood and went to where she'd slept. The area was a mess, as was the bathroom, so she distracted herself with tidying everything away, and cleaning as she went, somehow hoping a way forward might just present itself to her. Jessy lay and watched her, vigilant but relaxed. Every so often, a scratching or a howl could be heard from outside. Whatever was out there, wanted to come in.

With her tasks done, and the words of the next stage memorised, Harra moodily took her backpack to the kitchen. On the table, a great wrapped package awaited her where she'd been sitting to eat her meal. Harra smiled a thank you again, before moving to refill her bottle and flask with water.

As she did so, the loudest howl of all sprang up.

She jumped, and then reached for the white paper.

'It sounds like there are hundreds of animals out there,'

she complained in writing, but the woman read it and simply shrugged her shoulders. This, after all, wasn't her problem to solve, and perhaps accounted for why she'd been given command of this particular place. If she couldn't hear the wild animals, she wouldn't worry about them.

Angry, Harra stomped to the cupboard in the kitchen,

opening and closing them as she searched for something she could defend herself with, if the need arose.

A tap on her back, had Harra turning, angry words on her lips. But the custodian held out a long metal bar toward her, inviting her to take it.

Harra stood and reached for it, gripping it firmly in two hands. It was a good weight, or so she thought, having no experience with weapons of any kind. The woman mimed swinging it from behind her shoulders and forward, and Harra tried. With her hands extended along the object, she felt more in control, but also knew it was just too heavy for her. It was just possible she'd lose her grip on it in a clash. But she held her tongue. It was better than nothing.

Jessy watched her with curious eyes, as Harra tested the improvised weapon.

The custodian stayed far away from her, while Harra practised in the empty space between the kitchen and the bathroom. Harra allowed time to run away, until sweat beaded her flesh, and she was out of breath and coughing.

Only then did she rest, grinning at the custodian.

The look she received back was perplexed, but Harra ignored it. Clearly, the woman rarely left the shelter of the building and had little idea of what lurked beyond the air-controlled doorways.

The strange silence stretched on, the custodian showing no hurry to leave, now she'd shown her face. Harra paced as her watch slowly clawed its way to 19:00, the time she was to leave.

As terrified as she was of the howling and scratching outside, she still thought it preferable to the silence of inside.

Almost with a skip in her step, Harra shrugged into her coat, placed her backpack in place, and reached for her and Jessy's breathing masks as the custodian waited for her at the first door.

Harra held out her hand to shake it, but a sudden look of fright crossed the woman's face, and she quickly retracted it. What did she know that Harra didn't? Why was the woman too scared to even touch her?

With half a smile, Harra tried to banish her sudden worry, as they stepped into the airlock. The rush of air had Harra bending to place Jessy's mask around her nose, before doing the same for herself. The custodian had taken a free hanging mask from inside the room and held it in place with her hand and nothing else.

Harra then gripped the metal bar in her hand, as the next door open.

She'd been expecting to see flashing amber eyes, but when she peered out the door, hovering despite the woman's eagerness for her to be gone, there was nothing there. Calling Jessy to her they both stepped outside, peering into the olive gloom, before turning to say goodbye to the woman. The sound of the door resolutely slamming behind her assured Harra thanks weren't needed.

'Goodbye to you as well,' Harra muttered, aggrieved.

Unusually, Jessy lingered by her side, and Harra redoubled her grip on her improvised weapon, swallowing heavily.

'Come on, girl,' she eventually said, beginning the walk back to the main road. 'If there's something there, we'll know soon enough.' Even she heard the wavering in her voice.

The only thing she had to be happy about was the lack of wind blowing into her face as she walked. Indeed, it seemed almost warm. Harra tried to decide if it was time for a new season to begin, or if it was merely a mild night after the deluge of rain.

Not that it took her long to change her mind. Sweat quickly sheeted her face, pooling in the breathing mask so it slipped down her face every time she took a step. It also fogged up as her hot breath hit the plastic making it difficult to see.

'Damn,' she complained, holding her breath so she could remove her mask and dry it on her sleeve. With it back on, she took the opportunity to remove her coat, and tie it around her waist. She'd have liked a swig of water as well but decided she'd not yet travelled far enough to justify it. If she drank now, she feared running out of water long before that night's eight miles were completed.

She reached for Jessy, just wanting to check the dog was okay, only to startle. The snout in her hand was soft and didn't wear an oxygen mask.

Looking down in terror, Harra met the whirling amber eyes of another creature, one she feared had been following her since yesterday. Jessy cried, at her other side, as Harra held her hand still, unsure what to do.

Would the animal bite her? Shining her torch over the animal, her weapon abandoned on the floor from where she'd been sorting out her coat, Harra gasped at the creature's length, and also at the marks, evidently from fighting, that marring the matted brown coat.

Swallowing for courage, she moved her hand away from the animal's snout. It whined. A soft sound reminiscent of Jessy.

'Hello,' Harra said, deciding to opt for the same greeting she'd given the abandoned dog.

'What do you want?' yet she thought she knew. Without taking her eyes from the animal, she shucked her backpack loose once more and reached inside grabbing the package the custodian had given her.

Harra ripped at the crinkly paper, while the animal sniffed delicately with appreciation.

Food, the way to any beast's heart, or so she was coming to realise.

Harra quickly peeled away one of the thick sandwiches and offered it to the animal. Eyes whirling with curiosity, it carefully sniffed at her hand, as Harra held her breath, fearing the creature would bite her hand.

A soft tongue crept between the teeth, tasting, and then the animal took a tiny bite, as though to sample what was being offered.

Whatever it had feared, it quickly took a bigger bite, and then a bigger bite as Harra dared to touch the animal's head.

A soft purr burst from the animal, as it took command of the entire sandwich and began to push the bread aside, searching for the meat inside. Jessy came out from behind Harra's legs to watch the animal, and when the cat, as Harra now realized it was, discarded the rest of the sandwich apart from the meat, Jessy stepped forward to snap it up.

The cat showed a moment of alarm, but its attention was focused on Harra's other hand, still holding the remaining sandwiches.

'Huh, hungry are you?' she offered, trying to extract the meaty filling from another sandwich, grateful the deaf woman had made her so many, even if she'd practically kicked her out of the shelter, and had refused to touch her.

The cat again sniffed Harra's hand as she offered the meat, a quick lick of the tongue to assure itself all was as it seemed and then it delicately stole the length of meat from Harra. It turned to settle on its back legs, the meat held in place between the front paws.

Harra chuckled. Such a tidy way of eating.

Jessy sat on Harra's foot closest to the cat, perhaps unsure, or possibly on guard, Harra couldn't determine. While the cat was distracted, Harra rewrapped her remaining sandwiches and returned them to her backpack. She couldn't share any more, not now. At the same time, she grabbed her water and drank deeply, offering some to Jessy, who lapped the water from Harra's hand, her breathing mask removed.

Another tongue quickly joined Jessy's, and Harra

hiccupped a laugh as the cat came for its fair share of water as well. Jessy growled just the once, before moving over, just the slightest amount, to make room for the other animal.

Harra looked from one to the other, considering whether she looked as ragged as the pair in the pale glow of the torch, clutched between her thighs as she knelt down. Jessy, despite being bathed the night before looked as feral as the cat, if without as many scars.

'What are we going to do with you?' she asked the cat, reaching out, now that the water was gone, to run her hand over the cat's head. It licked her hand as it did so, and then turned and stalked off, out of the torchlight.

Harra watched the animal go with a strange feeling, unsure whether she was pleased or not, at being so quickly used and discarded.

Harra watched the cat's graceful tail sashaying from side to side, until it disappeared from view, slipping back into the olive ooze without hesitation.

'Well, that was that then,' Harra mumbled, more of a complaint really. 'Steal my food and water and then sod off!' For some reason, a tear fell from her eyes, and she sniffed. She returned Jessy's breathing mask to her face and then standing abruptly, she returned her backpack to its place and set out walking again, resolutely in the opposite direction to that taken by the cat.

Sod the thing. She would have fed the cat somemore. But it apparently wasn't necessary.

The heat of the night quickly drained Harra of her anger and energy, as, with slowed footsteps, she made her way up yet another steep incline. Her breath wheezed harshly in her mouth and throat, as at the top of the hill she had to pause, and recover her poise. In some ways, not being able to see what lay ahead was a good thing. It meant, at the bottom of every single hill she'd climbed, she had no idea how much further there was to travel.

Now she coughed, clearing her throat, and then removing her mask to spit out whatever muck was irritating her mouth and tubes. Even in the light, Harra could tell it was thickly black, but it didn't taste of blood, so she resumed her walking, mask back in place. Clearly, whatever she inhaled had to come out.

Whatever leached into the atmosphere here, it was pretty damn destructive for the average human being. No wonder no one chose to live so far north.

Every so often, a faint tap-tapping reached her ears, but Harra chose to ignore it, refusing to hope the friendly cat followed her, instead renewing the tight grip on the retrieved metal bar time and time again.

As she walked, she talked to Jessy, or really just herself, desperate to hear a noise in the preternaturally quiet environment. How could the land be so still? Or was it merely that the people here slept at night, unaware of the steady leach of escapees along the broken road?

Every so often Harra pulled her mask clear from her mouth and coughed, clearing the gunk from her mouth, and for moments afterwards, she could breathe more freely. Until she resumed walking.

As her watch display glowed in the gloom, the time slowly draining away, she began to worry, as Jessy's lead stretched ever longer in front of her. Perhaps the black muck from inside her body shouldn't be so casually dismissed? Maybe it was causing severe damage with each and every breath?

When Jessy ground to a halt in front of her, retching into the breathing mask, which Harra quickly removed, Harra knew whatever the toxins were, they weren't good for either of them. Jessy's vomit, more spit, also glowed dully black in the light of the torch.

'Damn it,' Harra muttered, trying not to gag along with Jessy. With the mask back on, Jessy turned rheumy eyes her way, while Harra glared at her watch. It showed 03:14. They'd been walking for hours, surely long enough to have covered the distance they needed to reach the next staging post. But there was no sign of any shelter for the night.

'Damn it,' Harra complained again, but there was no one to hear apart from Jessy, and possibly the cat. If it followed them.

Casting her torch into the distance, Harra offered a swift wish for a place to stop for the night. But there was nothing.

Or rather, there was something, reflecting back the beam of the torch in fragmented shades that were no longer olive, but rather mustard-yellow coloured.

'What?' she said, coughing without realising, so her mask filled with her own spit and the black inky substance that seemed to pour from her.

'Urgh,' she exclaimed, breathing as deeply as she dared for the smell was hideous, before yanking the mask from her mouth. She scrubbed at the inside of the mask, with her hand, and then with her coat when her fingers left nothing but smudged trails in the muck.

'Damn it,' she said when her mask was back in place, visibility substantially reduced because of the mess she'd made trying to clear away the phlegm from her cough.

Torn between carrying on, and cleaning her mask thoroughly, Harra opted to move on. The mustard swirling fog enticed her.

Ten steps later, Harra emerged into an entirely new world, one lit by lamps, and somehow, devoid of all the olive and mustard fog.

'What the?' she asked, being able to see further than she had for a week.

Before her, a plethora of buildings had appeared, all lit with stringent white light cast high in the air.

'You can take the mask off now,' a voice called, and Harra turned, mouth dropping open, to stare at the young woman before her.

'I know. It's weird. But it's safe from here on. The foul stench of the middle lands doesn't reach this far.'

Pulling her mask from her face, Harra coughed again, huge dollops of black muck landing at her feet. Hastily the woman knelt to remove Jessy's mask, Harra being incapacitated, and almost on her hands and knees.

'Get it all out. The sooner, the better. It's not good to let it settle inside.'

If the words were meant to offer comfort, Harra failed to feel better, instead struggling to suck in air as liquid black pooled from her mouth. Jessy was faring no better.

'What is it?' she managed to gasp.

'Filth and shit,' was the far from reassuring answer. 'Just let it all out. Honestly, it's for the best, even if it doesn't feel like it.'

Long minutes passed, and finally, Harra felt able to stand, and then to rub her hand over Jessy's fur. The dog had recovered more quickly than she had. Now she moved forward, nose to the floor.

'Hi, I'm Racha,' the young woman said, holding out her hand to Harra. 'Welcome to Stage Seven, is it? I think so, but maybe I'm wrong.' Her forehead wrinkled as she spoke. Harra shook the offered hand, feeling the strength in the grip.

'Welcome to Darlington,' she gushed, 'to give its proper name.'

'Where's the smog gone?' Harra asked, turning to peer at the mustard cloud behind her morphing into the olive haze she'd spent seven days walking through. It stretched out behind her, but cut off, as though something physically restrained it. On the far side, the smog seemed to be alive, undulating and pulsing, but not here.

'Banished. Some clever air filtration system, a bit like your breathing mask, only on a much bigger scale.'

'Does that mean there won't be any more smog on the journey?'

'Nope, it's eliminated, past this point. Can't stand the damn stuff. When you get inside, you'll have to bathe, and we'll wash all your clothes again. Otherwise, it'll eat away at the fabric, and in no time, you'll have more holes than clothes.'

Racha laughed as she talked, indicating they should go forward.

'Come on, we'll get you sorted,' she cajoled, noticing Harra lingered.

'Can anything come through that?' Harra asked, thinking of her cat.

'Yes, there's no impediment, but not all can survive. Those who've lived all their lives in the smog, the animals mostly, can't cope with the purer air. They tend to survive a day or two, nothing more. It's sad.' Not that Racha sounded sorrowful, but Harra almost appreciated the sentiment, as she slowly looked away, hoping her feline friend didn't follow her for the promise of more food.

Abruptly Harra stopped walking. She was where she needed to be. Racha would have food for her. There was no need for the sandwiches wilting in her backpack.

'Just a minute,' Harra said, stopping, and throwing her bag on the floor to retrieve the wrapping.

'I left something behind. I'll just be quick.'

'Well don't breath in,' Racha cautioned, her lips pursed. 'Not now you've cleared it all out of your system,' but Harra was gone.

With a deep breath, Harra ploughed back into the smog, sandwiches in her hand. Going no more than ten paces, she placed the food on the concrete floor, an offering for her friend, or for any other animal that might come this way. Then she stood and dashed back through the olive cloud to the bright lights beyond.

Only then did she expel her clean air, and suck more into her lungs.

'Sorted,' she called brightly, indicating Racha should lead on, which she did.

There were many buildings here, some large, some small, some seeming to hover over the road. In the distance. In the distance. Harra laughed at the thought. But in the distance, she could see where the road ran straight through the settlement, until the bright lights faded and there was only the black of night of what must be 'normal' night.

Strange assortments of metal pulsed in the glow, some seeming to have a purpose, others perhaps long abandoned as mud coated wheels, and rust slowly grew along the metal work.

'What is this place?' Harra asked, but Racha shook her head.

'Can't tell you that, I'm afraid,' despite her cheerful tone.

'Oh, okay,' Harra hadn't expected the response but tried not to dwell on it. After all, she didn't need to know, she supposed.

'Here we are,' Racha came to a stop outside a building with the same metal doors Harra had become used to. 'No need to go through any air filtration systems, but as I said, we'll have to get you cleaned up. The dog as well. Then we can sort out food and stuff.'

'Okay, my thanks,' Harra said, mystified by the space she walked into.

She'd expected something similar to the previous nights, but this building was different. There was a glass roof extending far overhead, lit by the lights from outside, and instead of one open space, it was split into lots of smaller spaces, all of them with doors and numbers on them.

'The bathroom is to the left,' Racha said, pointing to the one door that was open. 'Dump all your clothes outside the door before you bathe, including any in your bag, and we'll get them washed as soon as possible. When you're finished, come to the door at the far end of the corridor,' again she pointed. 'That's where there'll be food. Oh, and don't forget to clean the dog as well.'

With that, Racha slammed the metal door shut behind the three of them, and practically skipped her way to the far door she'd indicated.

Harra shook her head. She'd never seen someone so jolly and energetic.

Quickly, she stumbled to the bathroom, a squeal of surprise at its palatial size. The bath was easily big enough for two, and already hot water steamed in the air, scented with a fresh fragrance Harra didn't recognise.

Hastily, she dug all her clothes from her bag, and then stripped, before placing everything on the other side of the door. She wrinkled her nose at her smell, not a little disgusted with herself.

Looking from Jessy to herself, Harra decided to take a bath first. She wasn't sure she fancied bathing in dog fur, even though it would mean she'd end up dirty again when she did put Jessy in the bath. Better to be clean herself.

On a tray across the bath, a number of bottles, and cloths had been left for her to use. Harra, letting the hot water ease aching muscles, reached for one of the bottles, an oily substance inside it, and sniffed. And sneezed, immediately.

The scent was exotic, strange, and yet, also enticing. Reaching for a cloth, she dolloped a huge blob onto it and then began to work it into her skin. Immediately on contact with the water, her arms, covered in the strange mixture, started to froth, and she giggled at the sensation on her skin.

Whatever it was doing, it was pleasant enough.

She worked to cover all of her body in the stuff, feeling the oily substance working lose muck she'd not realised was ingrained on her body.

When she ducked her head under the water, rubbing the stuff through her hair, thin tendrils of her hair came loose, and she surfaced, clutching handfuls of her long hair, tears of confusion stinging her eyes.

'Damn it,' she muttered. Perhaps it wasn't for the hair. Yet, the bottle had no label on it. Putting it back on the tray, with shaking hands, Harra again dunked her head under the water, trying to wash as much clear as possible. This time much less hair came away, and she considered that the hair she'd lost had been falling out anyway. Was it perhaps just another side effect of the olive smog? After all, she and Jessy had both lost hair and fur the night before, and the night before that.

Her enjoyment in the bath gone, she quickly finished up, and stepped from the bath, grabbing a towel for her hair and one for her body. Drying herself roughly, she pulled the towel away from her hair, almost fearing to look in the slightly foggy mirror. What she saw worried her as much as it soothed.

Much of her hair was gone, but a fuzz remained, covering all of her head, and riding low at the back. It was a shade lighter than she'd ever known it to be before, as she patted it, and tried not to consider the colour hair she'd previously shared with her mother.

'Damn it,' she exclaimed, although with a hint of pleasure in her voice.

Turning, she eyed Jessy, with a rueful smile. The dog, as though knowing the procedure by now, had her front paws up on the bath, just waiting to be given permission to jump in.

'Go on then,' Harra laughed, aware she had no clothes to put on.

Despite her worry, Harra used the same bottle to clean Jessy, less fearful when fur clumped in her hands, and Jessy emerged from the bath almost half the dog she had been.

Using the towel she'd dried her hair with, Harra rubbed Jessy clean, earning a lick from her in the process.

'There you go. You look far more presentable.' Harra laughed.

A knock on the door had Harra turning in surprise.

'I'll leave some clothes out here for you,' Racha trilled through the closed doorway.

'Thanks,' Harra had been worried she'd be left with only a towel.

She hastened to the door, opened it quickly and picked up what had been left for her.

They weren't her clothes, but at least she'd be dressed, or so she told herself, but first, she returned to the bath, now drained of water and cleaned away the swill. It was pretty damn disgusting, but rather she dealt with it than someone else.

Then she dressed quickly, in underwear that wasn't her own but which fitted well enough. She covered it with a bright yellow t-shirt and then plunged her legs into the body suit she'd been given. The knees were a bit baggy, and the legs too long, but once she'd hauled the sleeves over her arms, Harra fiddled with the trouser legs, rolling them three times before her toes even appeared, let alone her foot.

Jessy sniffed her speculatively and gave a small whine.

'It's okay, girl. It'll just be for a few hours.'

As tired as she'd been when exiting the olive smog, Harra was feeling invigorated after her bath and hair experience. With a swift glance for reassurance that the bathroom was presentable, she yanked the door open, the towels bundled in her arms. They needed a long soak in very hot water to get clean once more.

As instructed, she walked to the far door and entered a kitchen unlike anything she'd seen before. It was vast, and completely white, even the chairs and carpet.

Racha turned and smiled at her.

'I know, they've never been a good fit for anyone,' she commented, eyeing the bodysuit with a wry smile. 'I can only assume whoever made them had no idea how long legs truly were, or, perhaps they come from somewhere where legs genuinely make up seventy per cent of someone's height. Oh, just dump those in the machine, over there.' Racha pointed to a swathe of washing machines, only one of them currently busy and filled with Harra's stuff. It had a timer on it, but whether it counted up or down, Harra wasn't sure.

'Here, food for you. You might not have had it before, but we thrive on it here. Cod, a type of fish.'

'Fish?' Harra questioned. 'But I thought the seas were all poisoned.'

'Really?' Racha asked, shocked. 'Not around here. We have people who fish every day. It's an important part of our diet.'

'Okay,' Harra said, still unsure, but prepared to try the food anyway. It did look delicious.

'I take it you've had potatoes before?' Racha asked, almost a joke.

'Of course I have,' Harra retorted, a little stung. Racha was more outspoken than Harra was used to. While she appreciated the upbeat tone of her voice, she was also starting to tire a little of her implied 'we're better than you' attitude.

'Here you go doggy,' Racha bent and dropped a plate of food on the floor for Jessy. As unsure as Harra herself, Jessy sniffed the dish carefully, before trying a small morsel. Then she snapped the rest up, and Harra chose to do the same.

'After you've slept, I'll show you around a little bit. There's lots I can't tell you, but also some stuff I can share with you.'

'Okay,' Harra said, trying to smile around her mouthful of dinner. It really was delicious.

'You're to sleep in room three tonight. There's a number on the doors, so you know which one is yours. Now, I have to be off and leave you here. There's just you tonight so don't worry about bumping into anyone you don't know. I'll be back to give you breakfast, when I have my dinner.' Racha laughed at the funny, reversed situation.

'Sleep well,' she called, twirling buttons on the machine with Harra's towels in so the machine leapt to life with a low grumble. The one with all of Harra's clothes in had come to a swirling stop, and Racha moved the clothes from the machine with the dial now reading 0, and into another one, twirling a button so the clothes started to swirl around.

'Tumble dryer,' she explained closing the door behind her. Harra allowed herself a deep breath, pleased to be alone, even though she'd found the tediousness of having only herself and Jessy to talk to, tiring.

Even Jessy gave a sharp bark, as though in agreement, and then settled on Harra's feet.

Harra quickly cleared her plate, and then drank the glass of water left for her, before refilling the glass, and also pouring some onto Jessy's plate. She couldn't deny the water tasted delicious, but she was also too tired to fully enjoy it.

'Come on, girl,' she said, pushing back her white chair, in the blank room, and heading for the door.

'Room Number 3 it is,' she said aloud, following the numbers down the corridor, slightly amused to find that they didn't run in numerical order at all. Whatever reasoning there had been behind the odd arrangement of numbers, Harra failed to grasp it as she yawned, suddenly desperate to be asleep.

In the end Number 3 was the fifth door down from the kitchen. Pushing the door open Harra was greeted with a room as sterile as the kitchen. Everything was white, almost painful on the eye in the bright glare of artificial light coming through the glass roof, but the bed looked mighty comfortable.

With only her body suit to wear, she pulled back the sheets and collapsed on the bed, the mattress enveloping her, Jessy lying on the floor beneath her. Harra thought it would be impossible to sleep, with the reflection of the outside lights on the open glass above her head, but no sooner had she pulled up the clean smelling sheets to her chin, than the lights seemed to dim, and Harra closed her eyes and slept without dreaming.

When she woke, many hours later, Jessy was gone from her side, but her clothes had been restored to her and piled on the sideboard in the room.

For long moments, Harra just lay there, enjoying the silence, and the view out of the glass windows above her head.

The bluest sky she'd ever seen was out there, just waiting to be discovered, gentle clouds bobbing across her view. She felt tears gather in her eyes. Such a beautiful sight. Such a simple sight, and yet never seen before other than in old books her mother and father had cherished.

As she dressed and made herself presentable in the bathroom, Harra couldn't keep her eyes off the sky, but questions were forming in her mind. Ones she wanted answering.

In the kitchen, Racha was just spooning food onto a plate for her.

'A proper breakfast,' Racha crowed, pointing to the sausage, bacon, eggs and mushrooms, as well as a pile of toast, just waiting to be spread with butter. Again, something Harra had only ever seen in books.

'Where does all this come from?' Harra gasped, temporarily distracted from her other questions.

'Ah, you know. The farms close to here.' Racha shrugged as she spoke. Harra tried to be charitable about her nonchalance. It was evident Racha had never known what it was like to have so little. This abundance of food was just 'normal' for her, although it was a feast for Harra, and Racha knew it.

Hungrily, Harra dug into the meal, delighting in the tastes and textures of the food, slurping noisily of the warm beverage before her.

'Hot chocolate,' Racha explained to Harra. 'I know it's delicious.'

Whether Racha had learnt to be less exuberant in the intervening hours they'd spent apart, or whether she was just subdued at the end of a long day, Harra wasn't sure, but the woman seemed more convivial as she tidied up the mess she'd made in the kitchen.

'I made you sandwiches for tonight,' she offered, holding up a huge packet. 'Cheese, ham, coleslaw, a few chicken ones. I wasn't sure what you'd like but wanted to get them done.' She stifled a yawn as she spoke.

'My thanks,' Harra spoke around her mug of hot chocolate, her eyes almost goggling with the largess on display.

Only when Harra had finished eating, did Racha sit beside her at the table.

'It'll be easier going today,' Racha said. 'Much of it will be just straight up the road from here. Tonight's accommodation will be like this. I would arrange for you to have a lift with the Northern convoy, but it's not due to leave until tomorrow. You won't want to wait,' Racha said, somewhat dramatically, her hands raised in horror at the mere thought of suggesting it. 'No one ever wants to wait. But you could journey with it the next day, if you wanted to.'

'Convoy of what?' Harra was intrigued. 'And what is a convoy?'

'Um, you know vehicles, on the road, moving stuff.'

'What sort of vehicles?' Harra was thinking of the ones she'd seen in her stop at Stage 2.

'Electric. Slow but steady. Slow but safe.' Racha laughed, as though reciting something she'd heard many times in her life, her eyes rolling in her bright face. Harra couldn't determine how old Racha was, but she seemed young, perhaps little older than Harra. Her skin was clear and bright, her hair, long and lustrous, and there was no hint of deprivation on her tall frame. Harra could only think wistfully of the differences in their childhoods.

'With batteries?'

'No charged, for use.'

'But how can you afford the electricity to charge a vehicle?'

'Well, you know, we have lots of electricity here.' Racha offered, surprise in her voice for Harra's insistent questioning.

Harra's forehead furrowed. More questions.

'How?' she asked, hoping to trick Racha into answering. But there was no need.

'Come on, I'll show you. I'm allowed to show you that, just not, you know, the mines.' Abruptly she clapped a hand over her mouth and turned her back on Harra, but Harra had heard the word 'mine'. She held her tongue all the same. She didn't want Racha to change her mind about showing her outside. The blue sky and fluffy clouds were calling to Harra, and she was just about desperate to feel the heat of the sun on her upturned face.

Back through the metal door, they went, to the outside world.

Out there, the blue of the sky seemed even brighter, the clouds even fluffier, but Harra had to keep her eyes on the ground for fear of tripping over the uneven surface she followed Racha over.

Between the two buildings, it was impossible to do almost anything but look up. Only as they walked into an open space did Harra truly comprehend what she was seeing.

'Windmills?' Harra gasped, a group of them spotted on open ground seeming to run for miles and miles, slowly gaining height as it went further north on gentle slopes.

'Yep, you're lucky, it's quite a calm day, but it can be bloody windy for almost three hundred days of the year, and so we have windmills. When I was a kid, I used to think they were there to blow all the pollution away.' Racha laughed at her childish whimsy. 'I didn't really understand what they were for.'

Harra laughed along with Racha, but she was incredulous.

Windmills, here, so why did the rest of the country rely on smoky power stations, in need of repair and fuelled by choking coal that only added to the clinging smog?

Turning slowly around, Harra sought sight of the olive gloom behind her, feeling nauseous when she spied its inky swirling. It seemed filthy, grotesque, when all was so beautiful before her.

'I know, it does spoil a good view,' Racha smirked, following Harra's gaze.

'But how?' Harra asked, frantic to know the answer.

'You know, when England was walled off from the rest of the world, decisions had to be made about the future. Here, they opted to make use of what they had. Old industries, but good industries that didn't require the internet or being online or stuff like that. Proper industries that had to be taught to younger generations as the older declined. Stuff that people in 'London' and 'Parliament' were keen to stamp out.'

'But where does whatever you make go?' Harra probed because she knew it didn't end up in the areas covered in the smog.

'I can't really tell you that. But I could tell you the stuff from the mines goes south, the coal.'

'So you mine coal, but use wind power?' Harra asked, her forehead furrowed. Jessy beneath her fingers, the only anchor to all she'd ever known and understood about heat, energy and electricity.

'Yup, to start with there was more reliance on coal, but quickly they just built more windmills. It was for the best, and indeed it was. But, they needed the money made from the coal to do it.'

Harra was shaking her head in disbelief. It seemed to her

the area made money from the deprived south but shunned the goods it produced itself. She couldn't help thinking the situation was unfair.

'I know what you're thinking, but it was their damn decision.'

'You seem to know a lot about the past.'

'Well yes, they teach me that sort of stuff, for my role, as an ambassador for this place.'

'You're an ambassador? Where do you do your 'ambassadoring' work?'

Harra just couldn't imagine someone as outspoken and bubbly as Racha being used to speak to the dour people of the south.

'Well, I can't rightly discuss that with you,' Racha suddenly looked wary, as though she'd said too much. 'But part of my role is to greet the travellers heading north. To encourage them to continue. Quite a few just want to stay here, you know, they think to have a claim to what's been accomplished, but there's no claim at all. They can't just decide to be involved here when they've made no sacrifices to make the community work and thrive.' Racha's voice was tight with fury.

'Ah,' Harra was beginning to understand how this place was run, after only a few conversations with Racha. There was an entitlement here, one Harra had previously understood wasn't to be tolerated within England, where everyone was supposed to be equally miserable.

'You know, we're not the only part of England to resort to old industries,' Racha said, defensively, not enjoying the knowing look on Harra's face.

'In Cornwall, the old tin mines are open, and Kent still trades with Calais, although it's not supposed to do so. Calais is in Europe, in case you didn't know.'

'And how do you all get away with it?' Harra demanded to know, her own rage building. The bloody cheek of it. Her home town followed the rules and did what they were supposed to do. Why didn't these other places Racha spoke of do the same?

'You know, you just have to speak to the right people, pay off the right people, keep everyone happy. It's worth it, for a better quality of life.'

Harra growled angrily.

'But everyone should be the same. Everyone destined for a life cut short by ill health and lack of decent food, lack of electricity and other amenities.'

'Yes, perhaps, but some people made the decision to stay behind when The Wall went up, and The Dyke was widened, not because they had to, but because they could scent a good business opportunity.'

'You sound proud of that fact?'

'And why shouldn't I be? Here, we make our money from the south, and we use that to trade far and wide. The north, finally, has it much better than the bloody south. Damn fools. Anyway, my family set much of this in motion. They had the foresight to plan, unlike others.'

There was a slight there, but Harra ignored it, her anger growing fiercer.

'So you could have left, but you didn't?'

'Oh yes, all my family were entitled to leave when the ruling came in. Only, by then it was pretty obvious what was going to happen, and my grandparents opted to remain behind. Exploit the daft bastards from the south with their 'Out means Out' slogans with regard to Europe.'

'You don't invite people here, from the south?'

'Why would we? If the south came here, how would we make our money? The need for coal is going nowhere. I doubt it ever will.'

'I think I'll go back inside,' Harra said, no longer feeling any enjoyment in being in the gentle breeze.

'If you want,' Racha said, a look of confusion on her face, as she led the way back through the closely built buildings.

Harra left her as soon as she could, returning to Room Number 3 and all of her possessions, as paltry as they were. Her head pounded with the injustice of what she'd seen.

Everything she'd ever known had told her equality ran throughout her country, everyone united in their misery, but at least alone from interference from foreign powers. England shunned by all, just as it wanted to be. That, now, didn't seem to be the case.

Harra paced her room, her thoughts running wild.

Why couldn't they let other people come to this veritable paradise? Why was it always all about money? She thought back on what she'd read in her father's journal. She'd thought his complaints about self-interest and pig-headedness the rantings of someone who understood too little of what it had been hoped would be accomplished. Now she wasn't convinced at all. Had he, after all, understood what was only just becoming clear to her?

England, a once great nation, was nothing but a sick pseudo-democracy. Elections happened every four years, but all that was ever spoken about was maintaining the status quo by politicians who'd been in power for so many decades no one could even remember a time when they'd not been there.

No one contested elections. There was no point. Everyone, at least in principle, wanted the same thing. Yet, it appeared to be a fiction, all of it.

Some suffered, while others prospered, much as she remembered being taught about the great British Empire, which had stretched around the globe, growing fat and rich from the exploitation and torture of others. It seemed that superiorism was far from dead, only now being inflicted on the English people by other English people.

She felt sickened.

But who was to blame?

She'd always condemned her grandparents for what had happened to her, but was she right to do so? Had they simply believed the lies and then been brave enough to live with the consequences, as they saw them. Was that why her grandmother had arranged for her to leave, as her cousin had? Was it genuinely some form of punishment for prior, foolish behaviour?

Harra stumbled to a chair, tears blurring her eyes.

This had seemed a haven to her when she'd come to it earlier. Now it felt like a lie, built upon other lies, and perpetuated as a truth.

If she felt like this here, how would she feel if she made it through The Wall, into a place she didn't know or understand?

She already knew the final stage of her journey was fraught with danger, the people on the other side of The Wall doing all they could to prevent unlawful entry. But what happened when she bypassed their failsafes? If she did?

'It's nearly time to go,' Racha eventually called through the door, not knocking, but rather poking her head around it.

'Come on. You'll get the best views if you head off now.' Racha spoke to entice, but Harra's legs felt heavy and her will far from strong. Longingly she gazed at the bed, where Jessy watched her. Couldn't she just curl up for the night, perhaps get this convoy tomorrow, as Racha had suggested?

'Most people are quite jubilant,' Racha said sourly, but Harra ignored her, dragging herself to her feet, and then to her backpack. Hastily, she searched through her bag for her water bottle and flask, and then stuffed her clean clothes inside, being careful not to disturb her father's journal or her bag with its gloopy contents.

Racha took the bottle and flask from their place on the floor.

'I'll fill these for you. Meet me in the kitchen.' Racha

marched from the room, as Harra gave it one final once over to make sure she hadn't forgotten anything.

Far from content, she walked to the kitchen and wordlessly packed her water, flask and food parcel, Jessy silent at her side, Racha watching her with confused eyes.

'My thanks for your care of me,' Harra burbled, not one to stint when praise was due, even if it sat uneasily with her.

'A pleasure, as always,' Racha smiled brightly, her full-fronted approach of yesterday back.

'Now come on. You get to leave while the sun set's tonight. The colours will be amazing, and then, of course, the streetlights will come on. You probably won't even need your torch. At all. But, you'll possibly encounter more people out and about. Not many use the road after dark, but with the convoy due tomorrow, there might be some work going on.' Racha shrugged again, as though the news meant little, but it infuriated Harra.

She was used to walking alone, and in the dark. The thought of encountering more 'jolly' people such as Racha wasn't one to hold anything but apprehension for her.

Outside, Harra spared a glance toward the swirling oily olive mass, held back by something she couldn't see, and she shuddered. To think, a life outside the murk was possible, and within England as well.

'Go that way,' Racha advised, pointing northwards. While the last vestiges of daylight illuminated a road that was well repaired, running ever northwards, Harra could see far in the distance. It was, she noticed sourly, perfectly flat, the vegetation held in check at the side by barriers and careful management so those who passed by wouldn't need to skip over twisted roots, or poking up tarmac.

'Good luck,' Racha called, perhaps hoping it would send Harra on her way, yet still she paused. A moment of real indecision. She wanted nothing more than to go back through the oily haze, to tell her mother of this bright future here, to inform every one of just what could be achieved, and yet she had to go on. This was no place for her or her family. Or so she tried to convince herself.

Hesitantly, as though unsure, Harra took a step and then another, trying to plaster a smile of thanks onto her face, but in the end, she kept her eyes firmly forward, not allowing herself to consider what lay behind. Who lay behind.

Of all the steps she'd taken on her bizarre journey, whether through rain, winds, or a thick soupy air that infected her, nothing had been this hard.

Crying softly, she set her shoulders, called Jessy to her side in a shaking voice, and walked away from all she'd known, and all she'd understood to be the true nature of her home.

Tears dripped down her cheeks, snot from her nose, and the sky could have been on fire, but Harra wouldn't have noticed, too caught up in her misery.

CHAPTER 9
STAGE 7

'RETURN TO THE NORTHERN
ROAD AND WALK NORTH FOR
FIFTEEN MILES.'

THE DARK CAME QUICKLY and with it the comforting anonymity that had accompanied her for so much of her journey.

She welcomed it, like a thick cloak around cold shoulders, hunching into it, revelling in it, allowing it to black out much of her surroundings.

Racha had been right. Lights illuminated the road, but they faded away with distance from the huddle of buildings. After that, only occasionally did a small crowd of them arise again, always to show a parting of the road or a collection of other small buildings.

Harra even tried to block the noise of the swirling windmills, or the whisper of the wind, as it swung around her, a little more strongly as the night advanced.

Such wealth here, yet others starved or died from the resultant smog caused by the constant choking smoke of coal powered power stations and the fires in peoples' homes.

The surface of the road, so smooth, was easy to walk over, and yet her feet quickly ached. At one point, she slumped to the ground, again feeling she couldn't go on. She couldn't abandon her family.

How, she thought angrily, had her cousin managed to make his escape and not come back for her, and the rest of the family? Had he known, when he left, Harra would follow on soon? But what of everyone else?

Riddled with self-loathing, as she stood and marched ever northwards, Harra was blind to much she walked over. She had her torch and the occasional clusters of street lights, but she saw nothing, concentrating only on moving one foot in front of the other, her vision fading to the blackness of the road and nothing else. Jessy was silent at her side, staying close to her, unhappy to stray more than ten steps either forward or backwards of Harra's plodding steps.

She would do as demanded of her, but then, well then she'd do something about this enclave of peace and tranquility, set in motion only to prosper from the misery of others.

Those thoughts gave her the strength needed to keep walking, always walking. Higher and higher she went.

Jessy matched Harra's speed, occasionally whining in sympathy, as though that might help. Harra tried to banish her anger, but no matter how fast her legs pumped beneath her, it followed her. It was as though she was stalked by the remnants of her old life, clinging to her with oily hands reaching out from the artificial barrier holding the smog at bay.

Breathing heavily, she again crashed to the ground, her hands failing to grip the tarmac below her so her chin hit the ground, her teeth snapping shut as she bit her tongue.

Tears of anger melded with tears of pain, as she lay there, sobs of despair wracking her body. Jessy nudged her, but she ignored the inquisitive nose, and eventually, Jessy merely sat beside her.

Harra's breath ran ragged, and gasping, her sobs quietened to small puffs of air. Her torch, abandoned on the ground, shone brightly back the way she'd come, as she rolled, her face still low to the ground to search for it. Like a beacon of light, it cut through what darkness there was, while Harra sniffed.

The torch illuminated the oily, olive smog of her home in the far distance, as she inhaled and exhaled the clean air she now breathed. Harra sighed. Going back would mean her death, too young, from something that would first rob her of what little dignity was left to her.

No one lived long any more. The older generation, with their better upbringing and prior access to free healthcare, were the last of their kind to expect to live into their seventies. No, going back home was the sure means of cutting her life too short. But could she, could she genuinely allow herself the luxury of a longer life, with the knowledge she now carried?

'Ah,' an old voice whispered. 'It happens to almost everyone,' it continued, conversationally. 'Come on dearie. Nearly there. A good day's sleep and nothing will truly seem as bad as you believe it to be.'

'Who are you?' Harra gulped, still unable to move.

'The custodian for the night. I take it you met the bubbly, self-serving Racha? Come, learn the truth or the truth as it should have been told.'

'What?' this caught Harra's attention. She lifted her head and turned it to seek out the person the voice belonged to. To start with she saw only black boots, the rubber soles thick and rubbery. Looking up, she encountered baggy trousers, a shirt that might once have been white, and a head covered with a beard, moustache and shoulder-length hair. But the most interesting feature was the piercing blue eyes that shining from a face coated in wrinkled skin.

Harra didn't think she'd ever met anyone so old, and slowly she sat upright, Jessy abandoning her in favour of the gnarled hands rubbing her fur.

'Hey girlie,' the voice said. 'You look hungry and thirsty, and sunrise isn't far off.'

Harra realised the custodian spoke to her and the dog.

Harra sat upright.

'Did she lie to me?' Harra wished she could banish the wistfulness from her voice.

'She told you the version the young 'uns get told. It's one version of events. I can tell you another. It usually helps.'

Harra stood quickly, scrubbing at her face, feeling as though her tears had been a waste, subsiding in the face of his implacable calm.

'That's it. Now, off we go. It's not far.' He pointed with his hand, along an arc of light illuminated with his own powerful torch. Harra bent and picked up her possessions, including her flashlight, and with a final look back at the oily olive gloom, resolutely turned to follow the older man.

He walked with rolling footsteps, his legs a little bowed, and his back hunched. Harra held her tongue from asking any more questions. The small piece of hope she carried within her was too new to be extinguished just yet, should his words prove to be less than she needed to hear.

The road she'd followed, as was so often the case, had split, and now she followed a secondary road toward a massive array of lights. So bright were they it appeared to be daytime, even though the sun was yet to rise. Indeed, the glow was so intense even after walking through areas illuminated with street lights, she had to shield her eyes from the glare.

'Best to walk with your head down,' the man cautioned her, when she fell behind his rolling gait. 'Don't focus on them. It's easier that way.'

She did as advised, and quickly made up the space between her and the custodian.

'Here we are,' he said, reaching out to swing open a small gate made of silver threaded wire in diamond shapes.

On the other side, the tarmac was pitch black, perhaps newly laid because it showed no cracks or holes. Harra assumed it would lead, as always, to a building into which she'd pass the day before the next stage of her journey.

Yet the custodian walked on, past the building, and into the area that was so brightly lit. Harra's jaw dropped open when she realised what it was.

As far as the eye could see, heavy machinery crawled its way around a never ending black field, similar to the tarmac she'd walked over.

The machinery, alike that she'd seen during her stopover for Stage 2, was yellow and shiny, busy like ants about their business, or so she'd seen once in a book.

'What is this?' she asked.

'The mine,' the custodian said. 'For the coal, that's sold to the south and also overseas.'

'All this?' she asked, shaking her head in surprise. She couldn't imagine such a vast expanse in her wildest dreams. The mine filled her horizon, miles upon miles of busy machinery trundling about their business, some looking so small they could have nestled in her hand.

'Yes, and when it's gone, it'll be gone, and that'll be that. There are no other deposits to be found in the north, not any more. But we've done well out of it.'

'So you sell it while you have it?'

'Yes. It's been many years now, but it won't last forever. That's why we've already converted to windmills for our electricity supply. The south, they don't believe what they're told. They've taken no action to ensure the future, to open up their own old mines. They have no idea of what's coming, and sooner than they think.'

She nodded with understanding. But this was similar to Racha's statements.

'They could do the same, easily,' he continued, 'but they

choose not to do so. They've always thought the north backwards. They blamed our ancestry, and they said it made us different to them. And maybe it did. But maybe that's why we survive and thrive. They thought to exploit us, but we made better decisions in the end.' He spoke eloquently.

'Come, see what we do.'

Quickly he walked onto the black field, gesturing for Harra to follow him. She did so but hesitantly, not used to seeing machinery moving and unsure whether it was safe or not. Jessy walked so close to her it was as though she was an appendage of her left leg.

'This is where we mine it from,' he said, running his hand over the interior wall. Harra was amazed by the size of it. The walls of the mine towered higher and higher, and Harra shuddered at her own insignificance, down at the very bottom.

'These areas were mined long ago. It's all exhausted now, and the machines have to travel further and further each day. One day it simply won't be cost effective. But for now, the machines travel the ten or fifteen miles each day, deep inland, that they need to, and come back at the end of each shift, with the precious coal. Soon, we'll have to charge the south more, to cover our increased expenses. They might pay it. Depends how desperate they are. And we are.' He shrugged as though of no concern to him. 'I imagine they'll pay whatever levy we put on it.'

The thought of the cost of electricity increasing chilled Harra, even as she looked at what had been done to the landscape in the name of heat, light and warmth.

'Aye, it's not pretty,' the custodian agreed. 'But it makes money and powers the future.' His tone was rueful. Here then was someone who understood the irony of the situation.

Harra yawned, despite her interest.

'Ah, come on. Apologies. I should have fed you and let you rest. There'll be time later for more conversation.'

Harra trailed him back to the building they'd passed. Inside only a few stray lamps illuminated a vast space because few more were needed. Like the night before, the roof was made of glass, and the light from the mine spilt inside.

The smell of a cooked meal greeted Harra's nostrils, and she thought of the sandwiches she'd not eaten. A waste, but her travels had been too difficult for her to think about food.

As in other nights, she bathed, ate and then went to her bed. The custodian spoke to her but only in passing, and she was grateful for his taciturn, bluff mannerisms.

Yet, as she lay in bed, she was tormented still and finally reached for her backpack and the journal inside. She'd not read it for some time. Now she hoped to find something in the words to help her.

Hastily she flicked through the pages she'd already read, stopping on a headline that caught her eye, and the scrawled words of her father.

'The world has gone mad,' her agitated father began.

> 'All I hear is news of natural disasters, shootings, stabbings, children starving to death, the possibility of war with Russia, of spies in England, of our own spies elsewhere. All is madness, and what do people concern themselves with? This bloody Brexit business. The United Kingdom, like the USA, is a laughing stock, the rest of the world watching with wry amusement as the 'special relationship' countries both tear themselves apart. I tried to speak with Rebecca about it all, but she laughed at my concerns and worries. 'It'll never happen,' she said when she asked me what was wrong. 'No one wants it.' 'It doesn't matter,' I said to her. 'Democratically it must be done by this government.' 'Someone will oust the mad bastard, and soon. My father says so.' 'Who?' I asked her. 'The democratic will of the people must be done.' 'But you said it wasn't a legally binding referendum.' 'Yes, but just like in America, no one will move against the voters. They're all too scared to question democracy even when it's all gone to shit.' She just shook her head and kissed me, laughter in her voice. She believes that it will never happen. I don't see how it can't. Not now.'

Harra felt tears in the corner of her eyes. Her mother, always so firm in the past, had apparently been a gentler soul as a child, or perhaps, like so many others, she just hadn't understood, any of it.

The next page in her father's journal.

> 'It's been agreed that they lied when they campaigned to Leave the European Union. They committed election fraud. The results should be invalid, and yet no one in Parliament questions it.'

His writing was scratchy, the fluid curves gone, his fury evident to hear even over the passage of so many years.

Harra's eyes closed on the words. Sleep finally coming, but her sleep was far from restful, and when she snapped awake, the bright blue told her it was far too early to be awake. Trying to convince sleep to claim her, she closed her eyes, but they refused to oblige, popping opening time and time again.

Annoyed with herself, she stood and dressed, making her way to the kitchen where she'd eaten only hours before. It was deserted apart from two items. One was a covered bowl of food, and the other intrigued her so much she sat and was leafing through the large book, filled with colours, before she even lifted the cover from the bowl to see what lay inside.

A bowl of porridge greeted her when she remembered, still warm somehow, as she flicked through the pages of the book, eating distractedly as she went.

Whatever title had once been on the book had been rubbed off, but its intent was clear.

There were black and white photographs at the beginning, evidently of the surrounding area, or so Harra surmised. More urgently she flicked through, the pictures finally turning to colour, hazy shades, and then brighter ones and ever clearer and more vivid.

She grinned time and time again at the faces of people caught in the photographs, enjoying themselves when the images were in colour, but dourer when they were in black and white, or sepia. All of them were moments caught in time, forever, so she could see them now. A reminder not everything had always been bleak.

'They teach you so little, in the south,' the voice was understanding as the custodian stood in front of her, gesturing to ask if he could join her.

Harra nodded.

'Tell me, when does your history begin?' he asked. Harra

thought he knew the answer already but answered all the same.

'In 2016. They don't call it history. They call it current affairs.'

'And teach you nothing of the past?'

'No, nothing. It's as though the world began in 2016 and there hasn't been anything before.'

'I've never been a fan of learning, but even I know that to learn how to be better, we must first learn how not to be. History is the great leveller. This area, so reviled by all those in the south, has a rich heritage for always being a little bit different, a little bit 'separate' to the rest of England. As I say, they blame our heritage, a wonderful combination of the ancient tribes of England, the Saxons who invaded during the 'Dark Ages,'" he laughed as he said that, pointing back the way she'd come.

'And those who came to challenge the Saxons, the Viking raiders, and many, many more since then. We didn't much like the Normans, the next round of invaders and they didn't much like us either. They committed great atrocities against the people of the north, and the same still goes on. Those in the south, with their equally mixed blood, look upon us as somehow strange, our language too difficult for them to understand, our accents thick and heavy.'

He laughed once more, a harsh sound, and Harra shivered at the threat in his voice.

'So, you are a people with many ancestors?' she asked. 'Not native to England.'

He shook his head, a hard edge to his eyes.

'England is an island. Few could be classed as 'native' in the way you mean it. Some would argue the ancient Iron-age tribes are the most 'native', but they live in Wales and Scotland, not England. England is a mixture of French, German, Scandinavian, and Italian and just about everything under the sun, from as far around the World as it's possible to be. Britain was once an Empire, after all. The north is the same.'

Harra felt her eyes cross with confusion, and he held his hand up.

'They tell you lies, all of it lies. Lies they cultivate to make them true. They said them, and then they believed them, and somehow, they decided it made them true. It's not the case.'

'But Wales is part of England?'

'No, Wales is part of what used to be the United Kingdom. It's free now, The Dyke dividing Wales and England, just as England and Scotland are divided by The Wall. Cornwall would do the same if it could.'

'Your England is a foolish fiction, and rather than admit the truth, your politicians just became more and more engrossed in their own lies. You have no democracy, for there's no choice any more. You're worse than many other societies forced to their knees by overlords who think they know what's best, but have no true idea.'

'So why did you stay?'

Harra could feel her anger growing, at the continued criticism, at all she'd ever known. Fair enough for her to cast doubt on it all, but to hear this old man, who must surely have cast his vote all those years ago, criticise in the same vein was almost too much for her to bear.

'I stayed because I had to do so.' A simple reply.

'And you, did your family stay because they had to do so?'

Harra nodded. 'As I understand it, yes.'

'So they never told you, either?'

'Told me what?' Now her mind flicked to yet another page in her father's journal. Words repeated over and over again. 'Leavers to Remain. Remainers to Leave.'

'Tell me?' she demanded.

'Everyone had a choice, as I'm sure Racha told you. Some

chose to remain who initially voted to leave. And vice versa. None were forced to it.'

'So my family could have left. It wasn't down to the initial decision in 2016?' This perplexed Harra, as she shook her head softly from side to side as though to deny his words.

'They could have gone. But again, I suspect many lies were told. So many of you believe it's the fault of your own family but I'm led to believe this is a fiction told to all. Another lie. Always lies. All built on a lie and a promise that, even though it was shown to be incorrect, was allowed to dictate policy. All because the politicians wouldn't ever admit to the truth!'

He sounded disgusted, and Harra shook her head, trying to deny what he said.

How was it even possible?

Yet there was something in her that couldn't deny his logic.

All this time, it had felt so wrong, so contrived, so bloody stupid!

'And the lies, they're still accepted?' she spoke with a whisper, already knowing the answer.

'No one will highlight the lies. The English are too damn proud to accept they're at fault. Not that they're truly English. They simply have this island, for now. One day they'll all die out, and then the Scots and Welsh will reclaim the extent of England. An irony of history, a reversal of all that's ever gone on before, from the Romans to this day.'

Harra didn't know who the Romans were, and she wasn't sure she wanted to know who they were, and yet she asked all the same.

'These Romans? Who were they?'

Now he chuckled again, enjoying their conversation.

'The Romans were the first fools to think this island could be divided. They too were conquerors, from Italy, two millennia ago. They came with their weapons and their straight roads, and their building techniques and aqueducts, and they fought the ancient tribes, the so-called 'native' English, or Britons, as they're known to history.'

'The tribes became their subordinates, or were just beaten in battle, and then the Romans came to Scotland. Then it was known as the land of the Picts, and the Picts were canny warriors. Still, the Romans built a wall in Scotland, staking their claim to the land. But then they suffered defeats, and so abandoned The Wall and built another one, just to the north of here. A different border, for a different time. To keep the Picts out, or so they say. I think it was to keep the Britons in myself.'

Harra was leaning forward, her head resting on her hands, as her elbows balanced on the table, just below the book. She could scarcely breathe for all she was being told.

'How could they keep them in?' she exhaled.

'They had military camps, all along The Wall. And it was built so high none could climb it, not without risk of being seen from the regular watchtowers, visible from one to the next. The Romans, for all they left these shores so many years ago, their Empire in ruin for trying to achieve too much, were good at taxing their subjugated provinces. They ruled all of Europe, well, much of it, and then the bickering of politicians forced it to crumble, as with so many other nations. Better that the politicians had been ousted rather than the United Kingdom crumble. But politicians don't study the past, only the polls.'

'The polls?' Another word she didn't understand.

'Yes, politicians used to live and die by the polls, a survey of whether people supported policies and people or not. They don't happen any more. Not for a long time. Not when there's no opposition.'

'One day,' and he pierced her with his eyes. 'Your politicians will all have died. There'll be no one left to perpetuate the lies, and then there might be hope once more if the rest of the world hasn't long ago abandoned England.'

'So there's the possibility of reversion?' she asked, caught up in the excitement of all he told her.

'It's never too late to make good old mistakes. All it takes is admitting the mistake and being prepared to remedy it. That, sadly, isn't going to happen anytime soon, not in my lifetime, of that I'm sure.'

'You speak very eloquently,' Harra suddenly said. 'You could go into the smog. You could tell people the truth.'

'It's not my truth that's needed,' he said, sadly, shaking his head. 'They need to question, to ask for clarification, to understand. As should you. You should not just go from believing one interpretation to believing another just because it's more to your liking. You must learn to question, to find the truth for yourself.'

His voice had turned hard, harsh even, and yet his eyes were kind with understanding.

'I've had many years to work out my own version of events. Perhaps I, like Racha, tell you only what I think you should know. Perhaps I have my own political agenda.' He spoke with bright eyes, his mouth curled up to show he teased her, just a little, but Harra felt tears forming in her eyes. She was genuinely desperate for everything to be as he'd told her.

'How,' her voice wobbled. 'How would I find out the truth, for myself?'

'You can begin when you escape,' he assured her. 'I don't know what will happen beyond The Wall, but I hope they'll educate you and then you can question the sources of that knowledge. You'll become like an investigator or a historian. You must question everything, and only then decide.'

'And then what?'

'You'll not be alone, beyond The Wall, I'm sure of it. Many, many others have gone before you. What you must do is find them, and work with them. And then, well then I have no idea what more you can do, but the right path will make itself known to you.'

'Is this what you say to everyone?' she asked, a weak attempt at a joke as she still cried.

'What? Do I try to build a resistance from outside England? I think I should lose my role as a custodian if that were what I did. No, I speak only to those who have the capacity to hear. Most are more indoctrinated than you. Most are not yet able to hear the wavering line through which you must cross to find your own 'truths'. I hope I've not taken liberties?'

'No, no, not at all. Here, wait. I would show you something.'

Hastily she returned to her room and found her father's journal.

When she returned to the kitchen, the custodian had already stood, perhaps preparing to depart, a denial already on his lips.

'My father, he died, but he kept a journal, see. He. I don't know. It started as something for fun, but in it, he wrote his thoughts, and they're angry. Look.'

Harra passed the journal over the table, and the custodian, clearly not expecting such an item, returned to the table and ran his hands over the front cover.

'A truly priceless artefact,' he smiled, and then sat to leaf through the pages, as Harra had done with the photographs.

'Is this your mother?' he asked, pausing on the front page, but Harra could only nod her agreement.

'You're very similar to her,' he said, just in passing, and then his already creased forehead, creased even more, as he looked and read, sometimes stopping to read entire pages, and occasionally just shaking his head in dismay.

Harra turned away from him, her own eyes on the photographs in the book. Still, she flicked through, and then she came to a section that arrested her eyes. An image of what she must imagine was the ancient Wall he spoke about.

Fingers tracing the image, she said.

'Is this a photograph? Of The Wall?'

He looked up, distractedly, to see where she looked. A tired smile creased his face.

'No, a drawing, a reconstruction of how they believe the old Roman wall looked when it was complete and not in ruins. There were no cameras to take photographs. Not during the Roman period.'

'Oh,' she said, determined not to feel foolish. It wasn't her fault she'd never been taught such things.

Eyes glued to the image, Harra was wholly engrossed by what she saw. Even the digits advancing on her watch didn't distract her, as the light began to drain from the sky, turning it first to a muddy blue, and then deepening dusk.

She could immediately see what the custodian meant, or she sort of could. To her, it looked as though it was impossible to get over The Wall from the north, but she supposed ot also made it impossible to get over from the south, apart from through the gates. And tiny looking warriors, with what seemed to be long knives in their hands, guarded them all. She couldn't tell for sure.

On the next page there was a more complete image, showing how the Roman wall had once run from coast to coast. This too absorbed her attention.

'How narrow the neck seems,' she mused, but her ally in knowledge either didn't hear her or chose not to reply.

Harra noticed something else as well. The image, while showing where the Roman wall had been also showed her more, much more. Indeed all of England, Wales and Scotland were shown on the map.

Eagerly she sought York, keen to see where she'd lived her life, but the words seemed strange, the letters all jumbled up.

'What does this say?' she asked the custodian, pointing to a jumble of letters.

'Ah, that book shows the Roman names of everything. Why, what do you wish to see?'

'York, where I come from.'

'Ah, then that is easy. Here, this is York, or Eboracum, as they used to name it.' He pointed to a particular spot on the page, after carefully examining it. Harra traced her fingers from York to the Roman wall.

'Then I don't have far to go?' she asked, surprised.

'Ah, that boundary is different to the one that stands today. Today you must go to here, to reach The Wall.'

His finger again traced the page and settled much further north, where the neck of England continued to narrow.

'Oh,' Harra couldn't hide her disappointment.

'But tonight you can travel with the convoy north. It'll mean a night off your feet. Oh, hello,' he looked up from the page, as Jessy's nose settled on the table next to Harra's hand.

'Hello girl,' Harra greeted, the dog whining slightly, perhaps concerned at waking and finding herself all alone.

'You must be hungry,' the custodian said, standing abruptly, although his hand lingered over her father's journal. 'I can cook and read,' he mused, and busily set about his task. In all honesty, Harra wasn't hungry, not after her porridge, but Jessy made her own demands clear.

'I'm sorry,' she tried to apologise.

'There's no need. I was caught in the journal. It's a fascinating insight into what happened in York, you say? It's so close to here, no more than fifty or sixty miles, and yet the lies prevailed, and the truth didn't. Not like here. I find it strange, and upsetting.'

'How does the filtration system work, here,' she asked reminded of the olive haze once more.

'It's simple really. We don't use fossil fuels – coal – we rely on energy from the wind and from the sea.'

'Is that all it takes?'

'Well yes, but also investment so the windmills could be built, and likewise with the wave energy. It all had to be paid for, and now it has to be maintained. Again, through money and having the right skills. There are many skilled mechanics within this area. Parents teach their children, as they should. Education is important. We use men and women for more than just collecting taxes, to squander on buying more coal. It's a vicious cycle.'

'Now, you tell me. What happened to your father?'

'He died. My family couldn't afford the treatment costs when he was told he had cancer, and so he died.'

'So medicine isn't free then, or health care? I'd heard rumours but didn't believe them.'

'No, everything has a cost attached to it, some of them very high.'

'And what did you do, before you left?'

'I worked in an office, filling in tax forms for people who couldn't do it themselves. They had to pay for that as well.' She laughed, bitterly. 'They had to pay me to work out how much they had to pay. It was stupid, all of it stupid, and people never had enough to pay their taxes and have a good lifestyle.'

'What do people do for fun?'

'Oh, there's no fun. Just work, and sleep, and then more work. I don't know for sure, but I think the population declines, quite alarmingly. I believe that's why the taxes get higher and higher.'

'Well, it makes sense to me. If there are fewer people to tax, then they must be taxed more, if the Governments only concern is to maintain the status quo.' His tone was hard again, his back to her, rigid, and she nodded. Speaking to him made so much more sense than any other conversation she'd ever had in her entire life.

'Here, eat up young lady,' he bent and placed something on the floor for Jessy. The dog scampered to his side, and after a quick sniff, ate quickly and neatly.

'Yours will be ready soon, and then we'll need to get you ready to move on.'

At those words, her hands grabbed instinctively for the book. She couldn't imagine leaving it behind.

'You can take it on the convoy. Just hand it to one of the attendants before you leave. I only have the one copy.' He spoke as an apology, and she grinned.

'Not to worry. I'll read all I can, while I can.'

'You have a keen mind,' he offered, perhaps surprised to realise the truth in the words. 'Like your father. He was intelligent as well; it's clear to see from his writings. He begins as a lovesick teenager but is quickly acutely aware of what's happening and the true implications. Tell me, what did he do for a living?'

Harra's forehead creased.

'I don't think I know. He was just my Dad.'

'Ah well, not to worry. Being a Dad is enough of a job.'

'Do you have children?' she thought to ask, and now he sucked in his cheeks, as though considering a reply.

'Not my own, no. I couldn't have my own children, but I looked after all the waifs and strays here. That's why I ended up as the custodian. I was offered the job because I was used to talking to the young 'uns, like you.' He laughed then. 'I feel as though I've had hundreds of children in my time, and I hope they all made it to their new life, and remember me fondly.'

Harra swallowed against the lump in her throat his words elicited.

'Then you have my sincere thanks,' she offered, reaching out to touch the back of his wrinkled hand.

'Aye,' he sniffed quickly. 'Aye. It's always been a pleasure. Now, here you go. Eat and drink. I'm just going to double-check what time the convoy is due. Did Racha not say you could wait for it? That girl!'

'No, no, she did, but, well…'

'You didn't want to spend another day with her. That's fine. As long as you knew.'

He left then, his slow gait rolling from the door, and Jessy went with him. Harra watched her go with a lopsided grin. The dog wasn't a great fan of anyone other than her.

She turned her gaze to her steaming food, but as she did so, the page he'd been reading in her father's journal caught her eye, and she pulled it toward her.

'2nd February 2029,' the newspaper clipping read. 'THE WALL WILL BE BUILT, THE DYKE TO BE ENLARGED,' the words screamed at her from across the years. But it was the second newspaper article that surprised her. 'European Court to rule on Human Rights issues surrounding The Wall and The Dyke.' She didn't read the article but again turned the page.

There, in stark black and white, was a picture of The Wall she was heading towards. She gulped in shock at the size of it. A few people stood beside The Wall, and it towered over their heads, at least ten times as high, built of stone that seemed smooth, white and utterly impenetrable.

On the opposite page was another article. This heading she was more familiar with.

'Leavers to Remain. Remainers to Leave.'

The words had always confused her.

'European Court of Human Rights says Remainers may Leave.' The smaller heading below reading, 'All Remainers have permission to begin life in the European Union again. English government must provide compensation.'

There was another black and white photograph, this time of

people queuing at The Wall, in cars and vans stuffed to overflowing with possessions.

'The photographs are amazing,' the custodian said softly, returning to her side, Jessy with him. 'I remember it all, perhaps too well. Come on, eat up,' he chivvied. 'The convoy is leaving in forty minutes. They're just filling up, but they're going to wait for you and Jessy.'

Harra understood a 'hurry-up' when she heard one, and ate quickly, clearing her plate, while he whistled tunelessly and made her a stack of sandwiches. As he sat at the table again, she turned the journal toward him.

'Sorry, I turned a page or two. You carry on, while I check I've got everything.'

As she turned to leave, an image in her own book once more caught her attention, but she banished her curiosity. Now wasn't the time. Not when she could read while she travelled. Hopefully, that would mean a night off her feet.

CHAPTER 10
STAGE 8

'RETURN TO THE NORTHERN ROAD AND WALK NORTH FOR TWENTY MILES.'

WHEN SHE FOLLOWED the custodian outside a bit later, hundreds and hundreds of lamps lighted the sky, even more than when she'd arrived the day before. She looked around, wondering where the convoy was, and what it would look like.

At her side, Jessy and the custodian walked a little in front, because they knew where they were going. When the road she'd walked the day before came into view she gasped in shock. There was a line of perhaps thirty vehicles stretching both in front and behind her, all separate and yet clearly following one another. They were a uniform grey, apart from at the front, where the trucks seemed similar to the ones she'd seen on her second night. That, she assumed, was where the driver sat.

'What do they transport?' she turned to ask, but her custodian was gone, already talking with a group of people, while she hovered behind. No curious eyes watched her, and yet she could detect their interest in her all the same, perhaps in their studious avoidance of her eyes.

They were all dressed in a similar way to the old man. All

had over-alls on, slashed with material that seemed to reflect back the light, and with thick soled boots on their feet. She felt jealous. The boots looked waterproof. Much better than the tatty boots she wore.

'This is Harra,' the custodian said. 'Forgive us if we don't share our names. It's just easier that way,' he further explained for her sake. 'And this is Jessy. She's a good dog. But she doesn't like many people.' It was a caution and a welcome all in one sentence. Harra smiled tightly.

'You can jump up in there,' a finger pointed, and Harra gulped. She'd never been in an actual moving vehicle before. What would it feel like? 'Take the dog as well, and our custodian, here. There's more than enough room for us all.'

Jessy jumped up the three steps and quickly settled herself on the floor of the vehicle. Harra was less keen to follow her, but, if her dog could do it, then so could she, or so she told herself.

Her own ascent was slower, the steps steep even for her legs, and she turned to help the custodian in. He gripped her offered arm a muttered thank you on his lips, as his older legs also struggled with the steps.

'Damn things,' he muttered, settling in one of the chairs.

There were four of them, in a tight group, with a fifth separate, no doubt for the operator of the vehicle. Jessy looked from one to the other, and then settled herself, head on her paws, contentment flowing from her.

The custodian fiddled with something besides him, and a table popped out from the arm of his chair. 'There's one for you if you want it,' he confirmed, placing the journal on his own table. Harra nodded but laid her own book on the chair beside her. She wanted to watch what happened when the convoy started, she wanted to see all that she could.

'So what's in this vehicle?' she asked.

'It's not coal, if that's what you're thinking. They don't

need our coal. We trade other goods, and sometimes the vehicles are empty, sent only to bring foodstuffs back.'

Harra understood his answer to be purposefully evasive, but she left him to his secrets, for the person who was to occupy the fifth seat was making their way inside.

He turned, a wry smirk on his young face in greeting, and settled himself behind the controls. Harra thought there should be a steering wheel, but there was merely a series of levers to be manipulated.

'Forwards and backwards,' he answered, without being questioned. 'And for the hills, a bit more boost on the way up, and a bit less on the way down. No steering wheel. The lead vehicle controls all the others.'

'And it's all electric?'

'Aye, all of it. No dirty petrol or diesel here. Too bloody expensive, anyway.'

Harra was aware of doors slamming up and down the convoy.

'Do you take many passengers?'

'Sometimes, that's why there's room for so many.'

She lapsed into silence, a faint tremor running through her seat as the operator twiddled with some of the levers. He wore the same uniform the others did, although around his neck there was an extra bit of material, stripped with red, yellow, blue and green, and tied just below his chin. She didn't know what it was and was too embarrassed to ask the question.

'Here we go,' the operator called, a chuckle in his warm voice, as Harra gripped the seat tightly, more worried than she wanted to admit.

'You'll get used to it,' he offered sympathetically, noticing her actions. 'I felt the same way the first time I rode a horse.'

'A horse? What's a horse?'

'An animal, four legs, you can race them or use them to move stuff.'

'Oh, I never knew you could do that,' she muttered, feeling foolish all over again.

'It's how people used to get around before there were cars,' the custodian reached for her book and flicked through. 'There you go,' returning it to her, Harra saw a black and white, or rather, brownish photograph of a four-legged animal standing beside a man wearing an over-all similar to the custodian's.

'They used to till the soil, that's some contraption for turning the soil before they planted seeds.'

Abruptly the vehicle was plunged into darkness.

'Sorry,' the operator said. 'I'll turn the internal lights on. I don't always when I'm on my own.'

Before the light came on Harra caught a glimpse of the road to either side of the vehicle, flashing passed with regularity.

There seemed to be a high wall flanking them on both sides, and small lights were spaced at regular intervals into the walls. They seemed more to guide than to actually illuminate the way.

Then the lights came back on, and Harra could see little but her own reflection in the windows. She settled to her book, finding her place again, moving on from the Roman wall, for all it fascinated her.

'How fast are we travelling?' she suddenly asked, thinking of her instructions for this stage.

'Hardly at all. Just a couple of miles an hour. It's slow going, but it's better than walking,' the operator said, his hands holding one of the levers forward. 'Here, we'll go up a steep hill in a minute or two. Enjoy not feeling it in your calf muscles.'

Harra watched his hands, fascinated as the vehicle started to slow as it began to climb, only for him to move a second lever, to make the vehicle run at the same speed as before.

'See, it's quite simple really.'

'How do you get to do this?' she suddenly asked. 'You know, be chosen to have such an important job?'

Now he laughed, turning to face her, blue eyes bright.

'It's not an important job. I just had to have some basic training. It's the engineers that we all rely on. They can fix the vehicles. I just drive, and help load and unload.'

'Oh,' Harra felt her mouth drop open in surprise. To her, this seemed like a far more responsible job than the one she'd ever had.

'And where do you live?' she asked. 'Close to the custodian, or at the end of this road?'

'Close to the custodian, but I travel up and down the convoy twice a week, going all the way to the borderlands, and back again. I meet a lot of people. Some of them can be quite unruly.'

'Shush,' the custodian hissed, and Harra turned in surprise.

'You can only be told what you need to know about this stage. Don't listen to him. The unruly lot won't concern you because you won't see them.'

The operator, rebuked, turned away, with a shrug of his shoulders, as though used to being berated in such a way by the older man. When he was sure the custodian wasn't looking, he turned and winked at her.

'So, it's not like this all the way to the border then?'

'No, just around here. Once you cross the river, it'll get a bit rough again. Not that rough, but the area north of here is more disjointed. They like to do it their own way. I'm sure you can understand that.'

'And what do you trade with them?'

'Food, they're farmers. Good at it as well, for all its bloody cold and windy all the time. You think I look funny,' the custodian chuckled, 'wait and see what the old girls and boys look like up there.'

Again she turned to her book. Almost at the back now, she

didn't relish running out of photographs to pass the time. She thought it would be enjoyable in the vehicle, but it just seemed a bit tedious with nothing to do but chat and look out of the window, and in the black of night, there really wasn't a great deal to see.'

'What do they grow?' she asked.

'Root vegetables, grains, animals, all sorts of things I imagine you can't get away with in the south under the gloomy skies. They fish as well, as do we. It's a different life up there, both harder and easier. It's simple really. They didn't want to give up on their livelihoods. Land isn't easy to get hold off elsewhere, so I hear, you know, in Europe. Especially when people didn't want to buy it, because they couldn't sell what they were leaving behind. Nothing like a mass exodus of people to have land prices bottom-out.'

Jessy stirred at the conversation, standing and stretching, before resting her chin on Harra's knee. She thought the dog was probably bored as well but didn't want to be seen complaining when they thought they were helping her out with a rest. It seemed, however, that her body was now used to walking at night, even better now the air she breathed was so much cleaner.

'Come on girl,' she cajoled, trying to entice her to sit or sleep once more. But Jessy simply whined a little.

'Let her up on the chair,' the operator called. 'It's not a problem.'

Almost as though understanding the words, Jessy leapt up, and settled herself to look out of the window, as Harra was. She chuckled.

'Nosy beast,' she cautioned but was content to sit back with Jessy and watch the small lights on the wall flashing past. It would have been nice to see more of the landscape, but that would have taken daylight, or the bright outdoor lights she'd encountered earlier on her journey. They seemed in short supply now.

'It won't be much longer,' the operator said, as though sensing her itchy feet. 'The custodian will probably take you in for the night, but he,' and here the operator nodded in the direction of last night's custodian, 'might let you see a bit of what's going on, if you keep close to him.'

'Aye. I don't mind. It's a bit early yet for you to be getting here.'

'Who will I see?' she asked, but the operator tapped his nose, in the uniform sign for a secret, and Harra held her tongue.

'Here you go,' her custodian said. 'This is fascinating, and you should try and keep hold of it, if you can, when you cross The Wall. There'll be people there who could help you with it. You know, with the actual truth.'

'My thanks,' Harra said, returning it to her backpack. The thought of not taking the book with her was troubling, but equally, so was the thought of taking it. Her mother had cautioned her, but so much of what her mother had known had been wrong. Harra tried to smile.

'And my thanks to you. For this,' Harra handed his book back, equally as reluctant to part with it.

'There'll be plenty more,' he offered with a soft smile. 'The schools there, even the Universities, will be stuffed with items such as these.'

A thought struck Harra.

'What happened to all the books in the south?'

'Daft bastards sold off all the items of value, to rapacious collectors around the world. The irony, hey! Didn't want anything to do with them, but happy to take their money when times were hard.'

'Ah,' the operator said, turning quickly. 'You been filling the girl's head with your nonsense again?'

Her custodian, far from looking outraged, actually looked pleased with the harsh statement.

'Just because you've heard it a million times doesn't make it nonsense. Anyway, you know everything I've told her, and you've made your own decisions. A well-rounded education was never denied you.'

'No, no,' the operator said, holding his hand up as though to ward off a blow. 'Please, please, don't tell me all this again. I know, I know.'

But Harra was intrigued.

'What do you disagree with?' she asked.

The operator fixed her with a serious look.

'In all honesty, very little. He doesn't embellish what he knows. He's a good teacher, always has been. Should have become more than a custodian, but hey, someone needs to help you kids, and I'd rather it was him than anyone else.'

Harra beamed at the words, pleased to hear an endorsement from someone else.

'Now look, see our 'Angel,' the operator said, pointing out of the front window.

Harra was confused by the words, her eyes lingering on the operator, while the custodian chuckled at her confusion.

'Just look,' the custodian enticed, and so Harra did.

Her mouth dropped open at the vision coming into view before her. She'd never seen a monument such as this.

Lit by a gentle glow of yellow light, a massive metal structure was coming ever closer to the convoy, sheened in the rust of age. It was a larger than life figure, proudly guarding its hilly vantage point. It had the shape of a body with huge wings sticking out to either side.

'What is it?' she breathed, while both men shared a low chuckle at her expense.

'The Angel of the North. Our monument,' the custodian said, pride in his voice.

'Through the darkest of nights and the most terrible of times, the Angel has stood as a bastion of all that is wonderful about 'The North."'

'He's beautiful,' Harra gasped, straining to look upwards as the convoy came ever closer, hoping to see more and more of the monument.

'She is,' he chuckled. 'I always think she's a she,' he offered by way of an explanation.

'How did she get there?' Harra asked.

'She was made for The North, by a world famous artist. I forget his name. Ever since then she's stood, on watch, a welcoming sight for all travellers returning to the north.'

Harra lapsed into silence, absorbing the sculpture as it loomed too large in the front window, and she turned her head to watch it pass.

Silence filled the cab for long moments, as they all considered The Angel, and then abruptly, the booth filled with harsh light, almost blinding.

'Here we go then. It was a pleasure to meet you, now stay close to him, and you might learn a few things before the next custodian hooks you. As I'm sure you might have realised by now, not everyone's as good at their job as your custodian here!'

With that, the operator opened his door, having twiddled and reset many of the levers, so the vehicle quietened from the faint hum, the only evidence it had been moving.

'I'll leave this here,' the custodian said, patting the book onto the chair beside him. His table was already stored away again, and he stood to open the door cautiously.

'Come on,' he said, a conspiratorial grin on his face. 'There's no sign of your new custodian. Let's see what we can see. But you go first, and help me down.'

Harra did as instructed, her backpack in place, Jessy already scampering down the steps.

The air outside felt dry and free of all wind. That surprised her, until she looked up, and realised they were inside a massive building. The lights were blinding when she tried to peer upwards. Quickly, she reached for the hand of her custodian, and he ambled down the steep steps as well.

'This way,' he pointed, heading toward what Harra took to be the rear of the convoy. There were few people around, but they were making their way toward a well of conversation, and Harra called Jessy to her side. She didn't want to lose sight of her dog when there were so many new and exciting smells for her to examine.

Ducking down behind one of the vehicles, Jessy was faced with what she could only describe as a vast market. The convoy was to the far side of the building, on a strip of road she assumed must have been purpose-built for this reason. The rest of the building was filled with market stalls, and also small machines, driven by people, unloading the convoy and delivering goods.

Harra felt her mouth drop open in shock. She'd never seen so many people in one place before, or so much business being transacted.

'It's a hub,' the custodian informed her, as he worked his way closer and closer to the market stalls. 'Goods from the north meet goods from the south, and there are a few other things in-between which it would be good if you pretended you'd never seen.'

'Here,' and he stopped abruptly. 'This row contains all the produce that has to be sold quickly, or it goes rotten. Look, carrots and onions, potatoes, foodstuffs like that. Fish and meat as well. This row,' Harra tried to look, along the long line of stalls, but he was urging her on from his place between two stalls on the next row across. 'This row has food items that last longer. Grains, flours, stuff like that.' Again she paused, but he gestured her ever onwards, an impatient look on his lined face.

Avoiding one of the small machines, and grabbing Jessy before she too walked out in front of it, Harra rushed to catch up. She was beginning to suspect he had something specific he wanted to show her.

'Clothes and cloth,' he announced, pointing down the next aisle.

'Mechanical and electrical goods,' the next aisle.

Only then did he stop, and beam, Harra almost out of breath from apologising to everyone she'd crashed into trying to keep pace with him.

'Knowledge,' he pointed, and now Harra understood the rush. Down this aisle were as many stalls as all the others, and not one of them that Harra could see, didn't have books and old items on it, the patina of age adding a particular shine to mirrors, wooden cabinets and all wonder of strange objects. Smiling, she strode before the first stall, hands behind her back to stop her from touching. How perfect it would be to one day have access to such books.

She read the spines on them all, they included words like 'maps,' 'encyclopaedia,' 'dictionary,' 'thesaurus', 'coding,' 'cookery.' She laughed with delight.

'Is this where you come for all your books?' she asked, but he was shaking his head.

'No, no, knowledge such as this comes at a price I can't afford to pay, not alone.'

'Then who buys it?' she asked, far from missing the fact the knowledge he told her about was rationed to the poor, just as medicine was. Perhaps not everything was quite as civilised in the north as he'd implied.

'Schools, corporations, cities and towns. Anyone who can afford it. Just not custodians.'

'Do custodians not earn much money?' Harra asked, shocked, but the stallholder shook his head.

'Not at all. But that never stops my friend here from coming to visit. He knows more about my stall than I do.' The stallholder had a pleasant voice, an enjoyment in his interactions with her and the custodian Harra was unused to feeling. Did everyone like the man who'd guided her here? It was a strange concept for her.

'Damn, she's on to you,' the stallholder warned, with a sharp whisper.

'That was quick. But never mind. You got to see what needed to be seen. And now Harra, I'll bid you goodbye and safe journeying. Remember what I've shown you here. And more importantly, be careful when you leave the enclave. There are some nasty people out there, as well as the nice, they shouldn't concern you, but be on your guard all the same.'

With that, the custodian slipped from sight, leaving Harra to face a woman with a red face, hurrying towards her. She was perhaps the fattest woman Harra had ever seen, parts of her body seeming to move of their own free will, and Harra felt her jaw drop open.

'Aye, she likes her food, this one,' the stallholder confirmed in an aside, turning away so he wasn't caught up in the following exchange.

'The bloody fool,' was all the greeting Harra received. 'Come with me and be quick about it. No one should see you. He thinks it's a game. I'll have to inform 'them' again of what he's done.'

Harra hastened to obey, a smile of thanks for the stallholder, as she was propelled through the rest of the market. Her eyes tried to take everything in, but the woman, despite her size, moved with great speed, and everyone jumped out of the way when they saw her barrelling toward them.

Harra grew tired of apologising and knew a moment of fear when Jessy disappeared from view. Luckily, the dog caught up fast, a piece of some purloined meat in her mouth.

Only when they were through the market stalls, and behind a metal door, did the woman pause to catch her breath.

'My apologies,' she said. 'He's not very professional, but you're here now, and that's all that matters. Now, come on. Food and a bed for the night, and then you'll need to prepare for tomorrow. I imagine the last few days have been a relief for you, but come tomorrow, you'll leave the enclave, and there are things you need to know. Information that can't be written down for fear of upsetting those making their escape. It's best that way.'

The woman spoke as though expecting questions but never gave Harra the chance to actually talk. Recognising she should just hold her tongue, Harra followed her as they opened and closed a few doors, before coming to a set-up Harra had become used to.

Again, the roof was glass, the lights of outside illuminating the neat and tidy row of doors hiding beds, the bathroom and kitchen as well. Jessy immediately sniffed her way to the kitchen, Harra holding back a bark of laughter, and then she was being sat at a familiar white table, with white chairs, and white kitchen appliances.

A plate was brought to her, and Harra dug in hungrily. She might not have walked that night, but she thought with a wry smile, she'd exercised her mind instead.

'Now, sleep, and then meet me here at 16:00 to go through the information you need for the next stage. Then you can be ready to leave at 18:00 when the bridge is down.'

Harra nodded, not truly understanding the words.

'My thanks,' she offered, standing. Her watch read 04:19.

'Your custodian from last night. He means well. But don't let him distract you from what's really important.'

With that, the woman turned her back to Harra, busy tidying away items in the kitchen. Harra stood to leave, unsure where to go.

'Room 3,' the woman said. 'And the bathroom's the last door on the right.'

Not for the first time, Harra considered what lay behind all the other doors lining the corridor, but she didn't want to arouse any more annoyance in the woman. So, although her hand hovered over the handles of more than one door, she made quick use of the bathroom and then returned to her bed.

Her watch flashed in the bright room, 04:45. If she wanted, she could have nearly twelve hours of sleep, but of all the nights, Harra thought this the one where she needed the least amount of sleep. For all that, she settled in bed, and while her mind sought her father's journal and the treasures it contained, her body slept, and Harra didn't even dream.

CHAPTER 11
STAGE 9

'LEAVE AT 18:00 HOURS, WHEN
THE BRIDGE IS DOWN.'

SHE WOKE GROGGY, and grouchy, annoyed at the banging on the door, and then when she saw her watch read 16:01, annoyed with herself for sleeping so long.

'Hurry,' the stringent tone of her custodian demanded, as Harra peered around bleary-eyed. Only a pressing need for the bathroom made her leave the bed, and even then, she'd have happily returned to it, if the custodian hadn't shot out of the kitchen again looking for her.

'Hurry,' she said again, as though the only word she could say.

'I'll just get dressed,' Harra yawned.

The kitchen appeared much as the day before, a plate of food piled high for Harra, and a bowl with something similar in for Jessy. Harra patted her stomach, convinced despite all the exercise she was doing, the good food was adding to her slight frame.

'No doubt you were skin and bones,' the woman said, eyeing Harra's movements. 'It's better to show no bones through your skin, you know.' She spoke without warmth, and Harra quickly sat and began to eat, horrified by her appetite.

'Now, we must talk about your next stage. As I said, at 18:00, you'll cross the bridge. It only gets used twice a day, at 06:00 and 18:00 hours. The Far Northerners can be a feisty lot, but they had the foresight to build the bridge so when the tunnel collapsed, it was still possible to trade.'

Harra nodded, as though understanding what she was being told, even though the words meant nothing to her. What tunnel?

'From the bridge, you need to find the old road, for they don't necessarily maintain it as we do, that's why the convoy only goes this far. They prefer their horses and other modes of transport. Now, and remember this, should you ever lose sight of the road, and be unable to find it, there's a railway line, to the east. It goes all the way north, but it's little used. It will help you orientate yourself.'

'Railway line?' Harra wasn't sure what one was.

'Yes, for trains. Ah, I forget, they teach you nothing. It's a narrow width of metal track, with other pieces of metal running across it.' As she spoke, the woman's large hands wobbled as though trying to enact the railway line for Harra. 'It's small, no more than a few feet across, but it's survived this age almost intact. Easier to maintain than the bloody roads, which I understand were always in a terrible state of repair, even before this damn Wall was built.'

'Now, the Far Northerners have no centralised living space, as we do here. You'll walk through many deserted villages and every so often, meet people. Your custodians will be harsh and rough with you because they think they should be. But they're good, honest people, who have your best interests at heart. I like the Far Northerners. They say what's on their mind. There are certainly no filthy, lying politicians there.' She spoke with approval rich in her voice. Harra was surprised but held her tongue.

The vast number of different personalities she'd encountered on her journey amazed her. All so different and yet all working as one, for her, a total stranger.

'I have a small item to give to you. Be careful with it.'

The woman handed over a metal object, heavy and with a sharp blade.

'I've not heard of any attacks in years, but all the same. There are desperate people between the settlements. They might attack, or they might just steal from you and leave you with nothing but your life. Either way, be wary and alert. The lack of smog means people will be out and about at night. Until now the darkness has been your ally, but in the land of the Far Northerners that's not the case.'

'But,' and the woman babbled. 'Don't fear too much. If anything should happen, your custodians will look for you. Not like further south, where they let young men and women choke on their noxious gases from the coal fires.'

Harra nodded, but with uncertainty. She'd sort of hoped the remainder of the journey would be as gentle as the last few days, perhaps even with the chance of riding in another convoy. It seemed not.

'From here you've more than enough days to reach The Wall. You shouldn't need them all, but it's more than enough time. You may arrive early. If you do, try not to go to the final place until you're supposed to do so. Hide somewhere else. Anywhere. The less time you're there, before The Wall, the less chance you have of being found and returned home.'

Harra nodded. She'd just been told a great deal of information in a short space of time, and now she needed to think about it. Indeed, the custodian had told her more than any of the other people she'd met so far. Only the custodian hadn't finished.

'The Wall, and the chance to escape, no longer concerns many people. They've grown used to how life is. As your own family must have, wherever you came from. There are few, in the Far North, apart from the custodians, who would help you if you got into any difficulties. They'd be more likely to just keep you, or even inform the authorities. Some believe they'll be paid for catching potential escapees. It isn't true, but the thought of easy money will make people act in strange ways. Be warned, and be careful.'

'If it all goes wrong, can I come back here, if it's my only choice?' Harra thought to ask.

'Yes, you can. But you'll struggle to get across the bridge. You know, no one has ever asked that before. But yes, say you're with the convoy and got lost. That should get you back across, and from there you can decide what to do. But I hope it doesn't come to that.' As the custodian lapsed into silence, her chin wobbled, an approximation of a smile on her face.

'Now, let's get you ready. Give me your water bottle and flask. I doubt you used them yesterday, but it's best to always have fresh.'

Harra returned to her white room and retrieved the bottle and flask from her bag, as she did, running her hand over the gloopy bag.

When she returned to the kitchen, her expression was pensive, and the custodian noted it immediately.

'As I said, don't let his words confuse you, or cause conflict. Proceed as you've been instructed. That way lies success, and after that, when you're free, you can consider whether it was all necessary. Don't take chances now.'

Harra was surprised by the woman's insights but silently agreed all the same. She didn't fail to understand the circularity of her thoughts. Only a scrappy piece of paper had told her to allow the strange procedure in the first place. And with that piece of paper, she'd done as instructed. It was just one person's word, against another's. Is that really all it had ever been? All this mess, with The Wall and leaving Europe?

Ready at last, Harra checked her watch one last time, as her custodian handed her a large packet of food. It showed 17:51.

'I know, it's probably too much, but eat it or leave it. I won't be offended.' Harra, as so many nights before, pocketed all the food offered to her. She didn't know when she might need it. However, she removed the previous night's sandwiches, half eaten and then discarded. Perhaps that had been why she'd been so hungry when the woman had given her food early that morning.

'Now, stay close to me, and when I say go, you must go. Remember, you need to find the old road over the bridge as soon as you can. It's not far, but it'll be dark. They have the bridge, but they choose not to light it well. I think they thrive on the secrecy of the whole thing.'

Shrugging into her coat, Harra slipped her backpack in place, her torch in one hand, the knife she'd been given, buried in the top layer of her clothes in the backpack until she might have need of it. Jessy was keen to be gone as well, her black and white tail slapping against the side of her leg.

'Stay close.' As earlier, the large woman walked in front of Harra, once they were outside, as people dashed out of the way, keen not to get in the way of the custodian. Harra murmured soft apologies, but no one seemed to hear or to be particularly offended.

This time, they walked around the massive building the convoy had stopped within. Harra tried to assess its vastness but gave up. She was small and insignificant compared to its height and length. She amused herself trying to decide if it was big enough to house all of York she'd known as a child? The answer was far from comforting.

If possible, the path they followed grew ever brighter with harsh lights, buzzing softly, the lack of wind a pleasant surprise once more. Yet, for all that, it was cold, and Harra was pleased she had her coat on, as they neared the area of most confusion.

Squinting into the too-bright glow, Harra tried to see what was happening. The custodian was right though. She could hear the rush of flowing water far below her, as the old road she'd walked along for so much of her journey came to an abrupt end just in front of her.

Below, unseen because the lights didn't go that far, Harra imagined she could see the river flowing unchecked, too deep to cross without swimming, and maybe too dangerous even then. The need for a bridge made Harra assume it was all but impassable without it. After all, the custodian had also mentioned a tunnel. How wide did the river stretch? Could it, perhaps, have been used as a divide between the Far Northerners and those here? Was that indeed the use it was put to? Division seemed to run very deep within the areas she'd visited, and indeed, the derogatory comments she'd heard about the south only reinforced the notion.

Not that she could see. The lights were too intense to allow her to focus on anything but floating shapes far to the east and west, the course the river followed, or so she took them to be. It was impossible to focus clearly with the bright lights.

'Stand clear,' a loud voice ordered, and then an ear-piercing siren sounded, adding to Harra's general sense of confusion, as she grabbed for Jessy, while the custodian grasped for her.

'It's just a warning. You're well clear of it.' The voice was almost kindly, but Harra fought for freedom. She didn't want to be enveloped by the custodian's ample frame. She'd come this far alone. She wasn't scared of a bloody siren! Or at least, she didn't think she was.

Harra expected the bridge to be lowered from above and kept looking upwards for it to appear, but instead, it rose up from below, settling in place with a gentle clang, and then a much louder clunk that sent a ricochet of movement through the tarmac she stood on. She fought for balance, others being better prepared with their legs further apart. She wished the custodian had warned her.

The bridge, Harra noticed when she was fully upright once more, sloped gently down, and no one stood on it, waiting, as they did on this side of it. Rather, a barrier prevented anyone from the northern side from standing on it, until the siren stopped, and then the barrier dropped with a loud metallic clang and people surged forward.

'Go as soon as you think there are enough people to mask your movements,' the custodian instructed. 'Take the less popular route.'

'My thanks for your help,' Harra muttered, and a small smile touched the wobbling cheeks of the larger woman.

'It's a pleasure, and I wish you safe travels.'

Harra turned back, to measure how much longer she needed to wait, only for the woman to have disappeared into the crowd when she swung her head around. Harra shrugged. These custodians were a strange lot, all of them.

She peered at the people walking toward her. Some pushed barrows, others carried backpacks, there was even a small procession escorting a coffin, yet none of them looked any different to her. Their clothes were just as well-worn, their faces pinched by the wind. Harra suppressed a wry smirk. Why would she expect them to? Probably because the custodian had told her they were a wild lot!

She needed to learn to make her own assumptions and not rely on what others told her, just as she'd been cautioned by the custodian of two nights ago.

Once the mass of people met in the centre, those from the far north, and those from what was now, to all intents and purposes, the south, Harra made her way quickly across the bridge, feeling strange as her feet passed from the side she knew, to the unknown, the bridge seeming to sway slightly in the wind. Not that there was any real difference in the surface of the road.

The lower she walked along the ramped bridge, the more she noticed the scent of the river, not necessarily a pleasant smell. Her nose wrinkled, and she peered to either side, hoping for a glance of the water, but there were still too many lights, blinding her. A vast abyss could have been below her feet, and she'd never know. Jessy was staying close to her side, as people swirled around them, coming and going, exchanging gruff welcomes and goodbyes, trading where they stood, and Harra reached for Jessy in reassurance time and time again.

She wasn't used to vast groups of people, and it unnerved her. She felt as though all watched her movements, when in fact, no one did.

What surprised Harra, when she reached the bottom of the sloping bridge, was the lack of any oversight as to who went which way. No officials stood with clipboards demanding to know name and business, or address, or anything like that. She couldn't imagine such an exchange of people and goods taking place near her home without such officious administrators getting involved, and demanding payment for their services and the right to travel and trade.

At the bottom of the ramp, there were two options to choose from. The wider road led straight into a building similar to the one she'd seen the market in, last night. Most people with barrows, or balancing precarious loads, went that way, but Harra followed the other path. It was smaller, less well lit, but the custodian had told her to follow the less well-travelled path.

Only a few people walked the pavement in front of her, and they were engrossed in conversation and paid no attention to her, or to Jessy. None at all.

Abruptly, piercing lights lighted up an area of the path, and Harra lifted her hand to shield her eyes from the glare.

In front of her, all of the other people had disappeared, and for a moment she panicked, fearing she'd done something wrong.

'Well are you crossing or not?' a grumpy voice asked, and Harra jumped at the sound.

'Um, crossing?' she said, an answer but also a question.

'Yes, you know, to the road below. Where everyone else has gone. Come on girlie, I haven't got all night. I've got a warm bed and supper to get home to.'

Harra had the words of an apology on her lips, but she still couldn't see who spoke. Walking quickly, toward the light, it abruptly dimmed as soon as she'd walked past a particular spot, and she was plunged into almost darkness, her eyes fuzzy from the too bright lights. She stopped, unable to see anything with the sudden darkness, and then someone walked into her, and they both tumbled to the ground.

'What did you stop for,' the same grumpy voice complained.

'I couldn't see anything when the lights went out,' she tried to explain, in a tangle of arms and legs as Jessy complicated matters by sticking her nose close to Harra's face, to reassure herself all was well.

'Well, I'm sorry,' the voice complained, close to Harra's ears, but still not in focus. All she could see was a hazy shadow.

'I thought you were through, and I know the path so well, I don't even need a torch.'

At those words, Harra reached out to grab her own torch, from her pocket, and clicked the switch to highlight the person speaking.

Surprised, she stared, and then stared again, for the voice, while sounding old, seemed to belong to a young man, perhaps her own age.

'Ah, that's better,' he whined once more, untangling

himself, and then offering a hand to Harra. They both stood, and dusted themselves down, although there was really no need.

'Apologies again,' he offered, and then walked off without a backwards glance, down a short flight of steps to where the surface of the road began again. Harra followed, more slowly, casting her torch from one side to another. It was a unique layout, almost as though the road had once run through here, but had been cut in half, either on purpose or by the river, which she was now far too close to. The smell was overwhelming, a mixture of almost sewage with the hint of something a lot more pleasant.

Perhaps the smell of sea tangled with the rank aroma of river-dwelling.

She wasn't sure why there needed to be a crossing for the pedestrians, which she believed this to be, when she couldn't see how any vehicles made use of the road, stopping as it did only a few feet to her right, but she hastened across the expanse all the same.

Behind, she heard a strange metallic scraping sound, and when she turned back a huge piece of machinery stood on the edge of the road, doing something to the river water she couldn't determine. Or at least, she assumed that was the cause of the gurgling sound.

For a long moment she stood still, trying to decide the purpose of the machine, but perplexed, she quickly turned her thoughts to the instructions she'd been given about getting on the road north.

This seemed to be where she needed to be, but she was unsure. Was she just supposed to walk along the road? Her instructions hadn't been clear.

Harra walked a little further along the path the others had long since disappeared down, hoping another road would appear, but stopped after no more than fifty paces. It was just a path. It didn't lead to a road, but into a residential space. Perhaps this was where the bridge operator lived.

Hastily, she retraced her steps back to the road and the strange machine, making gurgling noises as it went about its work. Well, it seemed there was little for it.

Quickly, she stepped onto the tarmac and began moving forward, Jessy following her. There was a loud clang, as though something settled, and Harra turned in surprise. Above her head, unseen until now, she could see the bridge, and it was coming down, as though it would land in the river.

She watched, confusion knitting her prow, as the bridge descended, stopping just short of the water. At the same time, the massive machine began to click and purr and then moved forward once more. Alarmed, Harra rushed on. She didn't need to know what the bridge and machine were doing. Even she knew her footsteps were too fast and that she almost ran away from the strange object.

The road here, then, was well maintained, and Harra wondered how much of what the custodian had told her was right when she came across a long trail of vehicles, similar to the convoy she'd travelled on the night before. That it seemed empty made Harra feel better, as she strode past all of them, without seeing another soul.

The astringent lights of the river crossing were quickly fading behind her, although a haze of blinding white stained the blackened sky behind her. In front, she could see where all street lighting trailed away. Running her torch along the surface of the road, she thought it might be a long walk, if a relatively hidden one.

Her feet slapped on the surface, and as she passed a shadowy hulk of a sign on her left, she stopped and ran her torch over it. 'The North' it proclaimed at the top, and then beneath it, a list of names, Ponteland, Morpeth, Ashington, Alnwick, and Berwick. All the names were bright, as though only just painted on, although the bottom name had been obscured, the paint peeled away from the letters.

Still, it didn't take any sort of genius to decipher 'Edinburgh' as the missing name, the empty shadows on the old sign as visible as if the white paint had still been there. The name meant something to her but she couldn't place it in her memory.

Jessy ran in front, and Harra let her go. There was nothing to fear, not here. Indeed, she could feel the emptiness of the place as she crossed from a wide road, to one that was narrower. No doubt, it would soon become even narrower, reflecting the past, when people travelled the roads in increasingly smaller numbers the further they'd gone from the centre of the settlement housing the bridge.

Still, whatever had or hadn't happened in the past, this road was in a good state of repair and could easily allow a convoy to pass over it. Perhaps, she suddenly thought, it was simply not necessary to do so very often. Maybe that was why it stood abandoned on the road, and yet still within easy reach of the bridge?

Under the flicker of her torch, Harra peered at the surrounding landscape. Under the olive gloom of the smog, she'd been scared to veer from her set path. Here, there was just darkness, and even that didn't appear to be complete. Every so often, she could make out the shadows of buildings, perhaps even homes, all empty now. In her mind, she could hear the sounds that might once have rung through the air, if they could be heard above the roar of the cars and lorries.

As her watch display glowed in the gloom, the time moving on at a decent enough speed, Harra amused herself with thinking about life during her father's childhood. How different it must have been. Better, of course, but also very different.

Her father had once delighted her with a story of him

getting sick from eating too many sweets. She'd laughed and laughed as he'd described the sugary mass of chocolate he'd consumed, from a box containing many, many different varieties of sweets, all in separate wrappers. His description had been so good, she could almost have tasted them.

Chocolate and sweets, just a part of his childhood that had never been a part of her own.

As the road further narrowed, a breeze sprang up, becoming progressively fiercer as she continued walking. To the side of the tarmac and old barriers, she could hear the rustle of the wind through trees and other vegetation, but the breeze felt far from cold, and the noise far from worrying. A plant wouldn't hurt her. Not unless a branch fell from a tree.

Quickly, she recognised a part of the road where other roads veered off to go who knew where. She'd have liked to follow just one of those divergent roads, but knew better. Indeed, only here did she see any signs of decay, for some of the smaller roads, twisted high into the air or rather once had. They'd since crumbled to the ground beneath them. No one had bothered to repair them, or even felt the urge to do so. Were the places that had been on that collapsed road as abandoned as the buildings she'd imagined walking past?

Was the Far North as desolate as everywhere else she'd seen on her travels? Had so many people truly abandoned England vast swathes of it had been left uninhabited?

It seemed it was the case.

On she walked, her feet never seeming to tire, although the watch glowed 01:23 which meant she'd been walking for hours now. Her instructions for the day had been to walk twelve miles. Harra had worried the distance was too great, but now it seemed too easy. She wasn't convinced she even wanted to stop for the night. Not yet.

Ahead, a haze of lights came into view, and Harra knew she'd come to the end of the night's travel. Yet, as she walked toward the source of the light, no one came to greet her, and her curiosity grew for she could hear a strange sound, a sort of metallic whining. Cursing her inquisitiveness, Harra continued on from where she thought her custodian should have greeted her. She walked down a shorter road, riddled with overgrown grasses and potholes, sloped, strangely toward one side.

Down both sides of the road, there were houses, sleeping quietly, and Harra was convinced they were all occupied, the sound of soft breathing seeming to seep out of barred windows and doors.

On she walked, the source of the noise, and the lights, slowly came into focus.

A group of people, no more than twenty, stood encircling a huge machine that made Harra gasp in surprise. It seemed to have but one or two windows, from which interior lights spilt forth, and it was exceptionally long, appearing to trail off into the distance, snake-like. But also straight.

Train lines.

Harra realised what it was as soon as she saw it. This then was what the custodian had spoken to her about. If she got lost, she was to follow the train line. The custodian hadn't mentioned there might be an actual train on the train line!

Not wishing to be seen, Harra found an abandoned piece of machinery to crouch behind, just to the side of the train line, where she could see all that was happening, but far enough away none should see her.

Her torch was angled toward the floor, Jessy hopefully sniffing her backpack, and Harra quickly relented and pulled out one of the sandwiches for the dog to eat. She also splashed water onto her hand for Jessy to lick, and the dog settled then, head on her paws, utterly uninterested in what so transfixed Harra.

While the lights here were bright, their purpose was to guide the work being undertaken, and not to warn off any who might consider stealing what wasn't there's. It enabled Harra to see much of what was being done.

The twenty or so people stood around in a variety of poses, some bored, others keen while yet others worked together. Harra quickly decided the machine must be broken, unexpectedly, and those who waited were the ones who wanted to make use of the train but couldn't. Not until it was repaired.

Harra wondered what they were transporting. The custodian had told her the Far North grew crops, all sorts of crops, yet, she couldn't see any food waiting to be loaded onto the train. Instead, she thought the barrows were filled with mechanical parts. Were they making goods that needed to be sent along the train line?

Harra squinted. The train was heading north. So it was going toward The Wall, or perhaps toward one of the smaller settlements there. But, the custodian had made it clear none of the settlements worked together. She'd said they were fractured and unlikely to help another.

Harra wasn't quite so convinced, even from what little she could see. Unless, and she did consider the possibility, this was just another case of those who had something, taking advantage of those who didn't, and charging them for the privilege. However, on this occasion, it didn't seem to be working.

For the length of time that Harra crouched, watching what was happening, she didn't see the train move. Indeed, the people waiting gradually melted away until only three remained, arguing back and forth in the good-natured way of someone trying to solve a problem.

Only when her left leg began to spasm did Harra look up, realising the skyline was flush with the coming pink of day. Reluctantly, she turned and made her way back up the small road she'd walked down. Now her feet were aching, and her belly rumbling, but there was no one waiting for her.

The time on her watch was flicking round to 05:34 and

Harra began to feel nervous. She didn't want to be caught here, alone, that much was sure.

Frustrated, Harra walked to the rear of a building where she thought she was to meet her custodian. It was ramshackle and falling to pieces, or at least the façade was. Finding a door, she knocked and then pushed it open, her nose wrinkling at the astringent smell.

'Hello,' she called, her voice small and barely reaching her own ears. Jessy whined softly.

'Hello,' she called again. But the reply came from behind her, and not in front.

'Ah, there you are. I've been looking for hours. It's a long walk, I know,' the custodian answered his own question. 'But come on, sunrise is but minutes away.'

Following in the man's footsteps, away from the decaying building, Harra reached another building, nothing like as huge as ones she'd seen in the past, but ostentatiously for the same purpose.

'Here you go. Whoops,' the voice suddenly high as he beckoned Harra through the door. 'I better just check the food. You're in room number 3. Dump your things and come to the kitchen.'

Quickly, he sealed the open door behind her, and sprinted into the kitchen.

Harra still hadn't had a good look at the man, other than a shock of blond hair, and long legs, but she did as instructed all the same. She was too used to the same routine night after night, not to follow it.

When she entered the kitchen, the faint smell of something burning permeated the air, and the custodian, an older man than the hair suggested, was frantically trying to clear the air with a cloth in his hand.

'Help me or the bloody smoke alarms will go off.' His face was twisted in annoyance, and Harra grabbed another cloth and coaxed the faint trace of smoke toward a loud fan. It seemed to suck the smoke from the room.

'My thanks,' the custodian said, finally ceasing his frantic efforts. 'I'm always doing that.' He spoke ruefully. 'Sometimes it triggers the overhead sprinkler system, and everyone gets wet. I wish I could disable the damn thing.'

As he spoke, food appeared on a plate before her, with a flourish, just a few brown spots showing where it had caught when cooking. She wrinkled her nose at the strange smell, and he laughed.

'No, that's what I thought. Never had cheese and pasta. It's nice, but it catches easily under the grill.'

Harra was not used to considerable variety in her diet – root vegetables and potatoes, some meat as well if she was lucky. This though was something entirely new.

With a long fork, she poked amongst the food, and then finally tried it, a smile stretching across her face.

'This is good,' she smirked, and the custodian laughed.

'And for you, little lady,' he placed a bowl on the floor for Jessy. 'Some finest bacon and general meat and vegetables. My own dog used to love it.'

Jessy had no such reservation to try the food and dug in hungrily.

'It was a long walk?' the custodian asked again, and Harra shrugged and then nodded.

'Well yes, but I was over there. Looking at the train line.' She pointed where she thought the train had been.

'You must have walked quickly,' he complimented, not at all concerned by her admission.

'It was easy going. The road is in good repair.'

'The main one, yes, to here at least.' He offered nothing else, seemingly more interested in Jessy than in her.

'From here on up, it's not as easy going. We rely more on the train than the road.' It was as though he didn't want to offer the information, but felt obligated to do so. 'I could arrange for you to travel on the train so you get a day ahead of yourself, or thereabouts. Let me know so I can organise it, if I need to do so. The custodian for tomorrow night won't mind either way, and neither will the night after. But beyond that, you'll be back on the road. The train only goes to the Far North every so often, and it's just come back from there.'

Harra nodded, the idea an attractive one. Watching the world fly by from the train would be interesting. Well, she was assuming it went more quickly than the convoy.

'Will it be fixed?' she asked, suddenly remembering.

'Oh yes. It does that sometimes. The engine prefers short journey's, that's why it doesn't go to the Far North all that often.'

'Ah, okay. Then yes. I'll take the train, if I may.'

'Of course,' now he smiled, as though relieved. Harra almost dreaded to ask what worried him so much about her walking along the road, but held her tongue. The woman of the night before had made it clear it would be difficult. Perhaps she hadn't known about the train.

'Do many people use the train?'

'Yes, well, from between here and a place called Alnmouth, yes. It's a bit of a pain that the train doesn't just go to Alnwick, but they've been building an extension to the track for years now. I doubt it'll ever be completed. There's just not enough willpower for the project to succeed. Don't worry though,' he hastily continued. 'I'll make sure you get to Alnwick with the custodian. I'll write you some new instructions. It's only a few miles. Nothing for you with the speed you'll be travelling, and it'll mean you're back on the road for the next stage of the journey.'

'My thanks,' Harra offered, surprised by the suddenly talkative nature of her host. He'd seemed entirely monosyllabic when they'd first met. Perhaps it was talking about the trains that excited him so much.

'Do you go on the train often?' And indeed his face lit up.

'Oh yes, all the time. Ever since I was about this high,' he mimed the height of the table and Harra grinned.

'Just a little lad then?'

'Yes, my grandfather taught me. Said I should have a trade with all the shit storm going on. Said being an engineer would never not be fashionable. He was right.'

'But you're a custodian as well?'

'Well, being a custodian is only an 'every so often' thing. My Dad used to do that. I got both their jobs when they died.' His excellent cheer evaporated as he spoke.

'I'm sorry,' Harra said softly, the edges of his grief clear to see.

'Ah, it's not as if it wasn't expected. Old gits, both of them. Lived good lives, despite everything. Healthy to the last and both dropped dead doing what they loved. I won't grumble about that.'

'Now, if you've finished, I'll get tidying away and then you can sleep. I'll sort out your train ride for tomorrow. It normally goes a bit earlier than you might have been hoping to leave. So, say no later than 16:00 to be back here, ready to go.'

Harra nodded, and yawned, suddenly exhausted.

'I'll bathe. Is that okay?'

'Oh yes, of course. Whatever you want. Make use of the facilities as you would anywhere else. And so I bid you good night,' with that he looked at her hopefully, and Harra realised his pleasant small talk was over.

'Good night,' she called over her shoulder, hastening to her room to settle Jessy before taking herself off for a bath. Only then did she realise that for the first time in three nights, she had a roof over her head that wasn't permanently illuminated. She might sleep better. She just might.

CHAPTER 12
STAGE 10

'RETURN TO THE NORTHERN ROAD AND WALK NORTH FOR 10 MILES.'

SHE WOKE AT 15:01, with a bang on the door.

'The train leaves at 16:09,' the custodian called through the door.

'Okay, I'll be ready,' she tried to shout, although her voice was thick with sleep.

'Food will be ready at 15:30,' he further added, and Harra groaned as her stomach rumbled loudly. Jessy whined at her side, as Harra closed her eyes, considering just continuing the journey on foot if it meant she could sleep longer.

'No,' she berated herself. 'Get your lazy ass out of bed.'

Flinging back the covers, cold air assaulted her body, and she shivered. Either the weather had changed outside, or the custodian was less than generous at keeping the stopover warm enough to be pleasant.

Grumbling, she sat and said good morning to Jessy, before reaching for her clothes.

She was starting to run short of clean clothes once more. She should have considered that last night. Hopefully, she'd have time to wash them that night, when her train journey was made.

Unlike the ride in the convoy, as slow and ponderous as it had been, Harra was excited by the thought of being on a train. She was sure it would travel faster than the convoy, and she also hoped it might allow her to see more than she had from her place beside the older custodian. After all, the train track could surely not be lit the entire way to the place she was heading. She wracked her brain, trying to remember what it was called, but gave up.

When she was dressed, she made her way to the kitchen.

A huge plate of food waited for her, this something she could recognise. A meaty stew with potatoes, almost a staple diet for her, although the meat was often not what it appeared. She didn't think to complain this was an evening meal when she'd only just woken up.

'My thanks,' she said, but the custodian kept his back to her, and she considered he might not have heard her, or didn't want to speak with her. She fed Jessy titbits from her plate when it seemed there was no food laid aside specifically for her.

Hungrily she dug into the food, thinking of what she needed to do.

'Water bottle and flask?' the custodian asked, when he finally turned to her, to find her plate empty. As always happened, he handed her a packet of food, no doubt sandwiches, and she exchanged her bottles for it. This time, she'd kept her backpack with her, checking the room before she'd left that nothing had been left behind.

'Okay, good,' he announced, satisfied. 'I'll walk you to the track. It's still light out, and my presence will stop people from questioning who you are. Everyone around here knows everyone else.' He continued, by way of an explanation.

'My thanks for your help,' she offered, standing.

'Oh, the custodian will meet you off the train. She might be late, so please don't go wandering off at the end of the journey.' He spoke with a smile to his lips to take the edge from his criticism of her earlier behaviour, and her eyes strayed to her fingers in faint embarrassment. All these strangers, offering a judgement on her when they hardly knew her. It was becoming trying.

'Oh, put your coat on,' he ordered. 'It's raining outside.'

After doing as he'd suggested, she followed him to the door, Jessy weaving in and out of her legs, and then they were outside.

The day was heavy and overcast, rain hitting the ground with a resounding thwack, so large was it. Yet, as she peered around, it cast a delightful menace over the area, the promise of better to come evident in the hints of blue blurring with the grey at the edges of her vision.

The walk back to the train line was done quickly, although she felt eyes watching her and her dog from the houses that had been so sleepy when she'd made the journey before. She felt jaded in her travel weary clothes and didn't enjoy the scrutiny. At her side, the custodian was silent, his stares at those who looked for too long at Harra, effective. Only when they came within sight of the engine and the long straight track, did he speak.

'It won't be long. Here, you and Jessy can sit in here,' he manipulated a complicated looking door handle, and stepped inside, up the three steep steps.

'There's only you in here, so enjoy it, but remember, don't wander off at the other end.'

'How will I know when to get off?' she asked, worried she'd be alone.

'Ah, the train won't go any further. If you can't get the door to open, the window slides down, and you can open it from the outside. I suggest you sit facing that way?' He pointed the way they'd just walked onto the train and her brow furrowed.

'That way is forwards, the other backwards. Not many like to travel backwards. Now, safe travels,' he offered, turning to leave without glancing back.

'My thanks,' Harra half-whispered, suddenly feeling alone and not a little afraid. At least she knew what to expect with a road. She had no idea with a train. Would it be like the convoy?'

Outside, there were voices raised in conversation and laughter. She peered out of the window, to see the three men from yesterday speaking to another.

'She's fine. A bit of muck in some of the pipes. You know what it's like. She does like to run clean.'

'You sure. I don't want her conking out on me before bloody Alnmouth.'

'I'll eat my hat if she does that,' the one said, with a wink, only for the other to scowl.

'You don't wear a bloody hat,' he stomped off, perhaps to get into the train. Only Harra couldn't determine which because the train was too straight for her to see anything other than what happened outside her own window.

To either side, she could see houses, clearly lived in, with clothes blowing on washing lines, despite the rain, and neat and tidy gardens, with green plants growing everywhere.

This little place then, despite appearing to be much, much smaller than York, was prosperous and happy. Despite everything. She imagined much of that came from the close proximity to the coal-producing region to the south, and then also the train. Anyone with a train at their command was inevitably going to have a better quality of life than those who didn't even know such things still existed.

With a screech of metal, Harra was flung back into her seat, Jessy losing her grip on the floor so she slid slowly toward Harra, a confused expression on her doggy face.

'Come here girl,' Harra said when she'd recovered her wits. 'Let's look out of the windows.'

Jessy was only too keen to join her, jumping onto her lap, and together they fogged up the glass as the train moved along the railway tracks, bouncing along with a strange regularity that had been missing on the convoy. It was a bizarre experience, and as Harra watched grass verges, fields, and abandoned buildings flash past, she knew they were travelling much faster than the convoy had.

She tried to enjoy the experience, always so keen to see the areas she travelled through, but just as the custodian had warned might happen, she slowly began to feel nauseous and closed her eyes to banish the sensation. Jessy remained on her lap, her tongue hanging from her mouth. The dog wasn't at all bothered by the journey.

They stopped a few times as they travelled north, but never anywhere that looked particularly inhabited. The number of abandoned buildings far exceeded any signs of life, such as lights in a house, and the darkness soon closed in, making it difficult for Harra to see anything.

Slowly, Harra began to feel better, allowing herself to drift, half asleep, until the train came to yet another stop, this one brightly lit, and Harra knew she'd reached the end of the line. She checked her watch. It read 19:54. She'd come a long way in only a very short space of time. Four hours of walking would have meant eight or ten miles to her. She had no idea how far she'd come on the train in that time.

Standing, she grabbed her backpack and made her way to the door, only for it to fling open before her.

'Evening,' a jolly voice called. 'Enjoy the train? Good, good,' again, no time for an answer allowed. 'Just a short walk from here, well, maybe an hour,' was then added. 'And then you can rest and anything else you need to do.' The woman held Harra's hand as she jumped to the ground, swaying a little with the unexpected cessation of movement. Jessy made the move look easy.

'Can I wash my clothes?' Harra asked quickly.

'Yes, yes, of course. A thorough clean before the next, and almost final stage of your journey. It'll be nice to get there with something clean to wear,' the custodian joked. Harra nodded, trying to decide whether the custodian was young or old. She was wreathed, from head to toe in a thick coat, fur or something at the collar and cuffs, so Harra could see little but piercing green eyes in the lights surrounding the train.

'Just up here,' the woman explained, not pausing to allow Harra to catch a final glance of the train. It was so long it snaked into the darkness beyond the lights. Harra had no chance to find out whether it carried cargo or not, and certainly, no other person clambered down its sides to walk along the smooth tarmac beside the slotted grooves the train needed to travel over.

'It's always good when you can get the train instead of walking. The road isn't safe to the south. Or so they say.' The woman shrugged her shoulders, as though sharing her deepest thoughts. 'The people who walk it never really say anything, but I have my suspicions.'

Harra nodded as though she knew what the woman spoke about, but really her mind was on what the train was being used for. Was it just to take foodstuffs to the south, or was it something else? What did these people trade to ensure they could afford to provide electricity to run a train? At least, she thought it must run on electricity. She hadn't determined any other means of propulsion for it, and certainly, it didn't smell of coal and smoke.

'Now, we have to go down a steep hill, and then up another one, and so on, until we reach the stopover point.' Only Harra wasn't listening and had indeed come to a stop. She looked at the woman.

'Is that the sea?' she asked, peering to where she thought she'd heard the slosh of waves.

'Oh yes, the sea and the river. You can see it, in the glow of the moon. See.'

Harra looked where she'd pointed, and her eyes feasted on the image. Before her the ocean stretched black and endless, yet calm and reassuring, while a small settlement was backlit by the moon, standing proudly on a promontory close to the sea.

'Alnmouth,' the woman said. 'Where the sea and river meet. It's charming, on a warm sunny day,' she laughed. 'Not that the sea is ever warm.'

'Warm?'

'For splashing in. You know, without your shoes on, and wearing shorts.'

'But isn't the sea filled with toxins here?'

'No,' she laughed, 'not at all. Honestly, they do come out with some rubbish in the south.' She sounded amused, not angry, as Harra turned back to watch what she could see of the sea in the gleam of the moon.

Out here, away from the train, there were few, if any lights, and although Harra had seen the blue sky a few times now, this, she felt, was the first time she'd truly seen the night sky. Above her head, a pale moon shone, and tiny pinpricks of light filled what felt like an enormous space above her head. Stars. She'd never seen one before.

'I think I'd like to splash my feet in the sea,' Harra said, wistfully, finally turning to stare once more at the sea. The crash of distant waves on distant shores excited her. How much her mother would have loved this!

'And one day you will, but come on, we should get back as

soon as possible. No point saving a day, if you're too tired to enjoy it.'

Leading on, a bright torch in one hand, the woman walked onwards, as she'd said, down a steep hill, houses to either side, clearly inhabited, and then along a flat stretch of land, and across a faint trickle of a river.

'A bridge, but just a small one,' the custodian commented.

Harra flashed her own torch from side to side, taking in the sights she could see through the narrow beam of light, content to walk in silence until the sound of the sea had ebbed from her hearing.

'Is this a road?' Harra asked, surprised by how narrow it was in places, the overhanging trees entwining their branches.

'Yes, but only a minor one. Still, it gets used a fair bit, even now.'

To either side of the road, fields and fields lay drowsing under the faint glow of the moon. Harra could smell the ripeness of manure and a more pleasant one of greenery. It was peaceful, even with the calls of hooting birds, and the occasional scamper of some animal in the undergrowth.

To the far right, Harra could make out a too bright glow of lights.

'One of the farmers. Tending his crop at night. It's quite common,' the woman conversationally informed her. 'Out here there's no one to tell you no.'

Quickly, the constant going up and going down forced Harra to break out in a sweat, and she paused to suck on her water bottle.

'Not that much further,' the woman smiled, unconcerned by Harra stopping. 'Not long, and you'll see where you need to walk tomorrow. I take it you've been warned about the road around here?'

'Well, I was warned about the one to the south of here,'

Harra said, alarmed at what she might yet face when it had all begun to feel quite secure.

'They say that to scare all the travellers into taking the bloody train, so they can brag about it. Damn fools,' the woman complained. 'The true danger is to the north of here. Wild country, for maybe thirty miles, until you reach the next settlement. Oh, there are outcroppings of houses, and of course, the land is all farmed, but still, there are some people who might have slightly strange ways of doing things.'

The woman's tone was ominous, and Harra shivered, as they stopped on another bridge running over a road illuminated in the beam from the torach and Harra stared ever northwards.

She searched for lights, or some sort of sign the woman spoke the truth, and didn't just try and scare her, but only the area her torch illuminated could be seen, and it showed nothing but the usual surface, occasionally overgrown with greenery, although not too badly.

'It's a double road here?' she asked, pointing down, trying to make sense of what she saw.

'Yes, but it stops in a few miles. Then it's just two lanes, one heading south, and the other north.'

'Ah, okay,' Harra nodded. 'And the railway line. Is that close to the road?'

'Not really, or so I understand it. The railway line is close to the coastline, not the road.'

The custodian didn't query her questioning, and Harra was pleased because she didn't know why she'd asked either.

'Ah, at last,' as they walked up another steep hill, the custodian pointed Harra toward a turning. 'It's just along here. Down and closer to the road. It's funny the road doesn't go this way, but there you go.'

Harra wasn't sure what the custodian meant, but fatigue

was muddling her thoughts, so she merely smiled, and followed on, once more going downhill.

In front, a small glow of lights came into view, and Harra welcomed the thought of food and sleep.

'There'll be a meal waiting for you,' the custodian reassured you. 'And then you can sleep, room number 3, as always. Wake when you want tomorrow. I'll check in on you every so often to make sure you're okay, and then you can decide when you want to eat, and when you're going to leave. If you plan on staying an extra night, which is fine, let me know, and I can ensure I'm available to keep you company. Not much to do around here in the middle of the night.'

Her tone was again warm and inviting, and yet Harra also detected a faint reserve. Maybe the custodian didn't want her to overstay her welcome, or demand too much of her time.

'My thanks,' was Harra's only response. She wasn't yet sure what she wanted to do come the next day.

'And here you are,' the custodian opened a metallic door, and Harra stepped into yet another building following the same pattern as all the other ones she'd slept within, even down to the placement of the doors and the bathroom.

'I'm sure you know your way around,' the custodian said. 'I'll meet you in the kitchen.'

Harra nodded, keen to bathe before she ate. She felt sweaty and grimy, even though she'd walked a fraction of the route her instruction sheet demanded.

But Jessy whined at her feet, so Harra took her through to the kitchen first.

'Sorry, she's hungry,' Harra offered apologetically, but the custodian was already placing a plate on the floor, which Jessy quickly appraised with one sniff, and then began to devour.

'I'm going to bathe,' Harra said, unsure whether she told Jessy or the custodian. Neither responded, all the same.

Quickly, she made her way to the bathroom, turning the

taps to fill the large bath, smelling all of the label-less bottles before she chose which one to add to the water. It smelled of heat and light, and Harra liberally doused the water so bubbles frothed up quickly.

She giggled as the bubbles touched her skin on entering the hot water, and quickly relaxed.

A day of doing nothing beckoned, but she banished the thought from her mind, the better to savour what had been accomplished that day.

CHAPTER 13
REST DAY & STAGE 11

'LEAVE AT PRECISELY 20:00 HOURS. RETURN TO THE NORTHERN ROAD AND WALK NORTH FOR 10 MILES.'

HER WATCH DISPLAY glowed 14:56, but she didn't move, savouring the warmth of the bed and the delight of waking naturally from what had been a long sleep.

Her limbs were free of all aches, but neither did they want to move. She could tell from the odd twitched she tried. Beside her, Jessy slept on, her hot dog-breath a comfortable waft across her face.

Harra sighed, looking upwards, but seeing nothing. There was no glass ceiling here. Nothing to hint at the events going on in the world outside her sanctuary.

A faint tap on the door and she turned toward it, her eyebrows knitting together in confusion.

'Hello?' she called, softly.

'Ah, you're awake then,' her custodian bustled into the room, smiling when she saw Jessy still asleep.

'I'm going up toward the old town, if you want to come along?' the woman offered, 'you know, see some of the place while you can. I'm going in about thirty minutes, if that's enough time for you to get ready.'

Harra was already nodding, as she gently moved Jessy over so she could exit the bed.

'Yes, yes, I'll come. My thanks for offering.'

The custodian smiled and turned to leave, and then stopped, placing Harra's clean pile of clothes down on the side table, rolling her eyes at her inattention. Harra chuckled and leapt free from the bed as soon as the door closed.

She stretched muscles slack from too much rest and turned to face Jessy's eyes, which watched her sleepily.

'We're going for a walk,' she offered, brightly, 'but not a long one,' she hastily added, when Jessy looked far from impressed, as if she understood the meaning behind the words.

'I'm getting dressed. You can suit yourself.'

Half an hour later Harra and Jessy made their way to the kitchen. The custodian eyed them with amusement.

'Good sleep, the pair of you?' She didn't wait for a reply. 'Here, a hot drink before we go, and then I made you these to eat on the way.' She handed Harra a pack of the ubiquitous sandwiches, but filled with something different, for the smell that wafted to Harra, as she placed them in her backpack, was delicious.

'My thanks,' she gulped, swallowing her drink quickly. Harra was keen to see what she could before night fell once more.

'If anyone asks who you are, just leave the talking to me,' the custodian cautioned before they walked through the metallic door to the outside world. 'It won't be a problem, but just to be on the safe side.'

Harra nodded and knew a moment of worry. She'd almost forgotten her journey was being accomplished under the utmost secrecy.

'Of course. I'll just stay dumb, unless they ask me about the weather or something like that.'

Yet the custodian shook her head again. 'It's best you say nothing. Your southern accent might give you away. Okay?' she added that, no doubt to take the sting from her words and Harra smiled, to show she wasn't offended. All the same, she thought about the way she spoke. Did she have an accent? She honestly didn't know.

She was greeted with a clear blue sky when she stepped outside. All the same, she shivered.

'A cold day,' her custodian confirmed. 'But a good day for a quick walk. If you're lucky, we might be able to catch sight of the sea. You were quite transfixed by it last night.'

'Are we far from the sea?'

'A few miles. No more. It'll depend on how clear the coast is as to whether you can see it. Sometimes it'll be glorious sunshine here, but there'll be a fret along the coast.'

'A fret?'

'Yes, cloudy, I suppose,' the custodian confirmed, leading the way for Harra to walk. 'Where the water is colder than the clouds. It blows in from the sea and settles over the coast like a vengeful beast. Still, there's a certain charm to a sea fret.'

As Harra walked, puffing a little because her legs didn't want to tackle the slight hill they climbed, her head regularly turned from one side to another. This then was what a place that had been somewhat abandoned looked like.

In York, the olive gloom had prevented her from truly appreciating the scale of decay. Here, she could see it clearly, as they walked past a cemetery, locked, dark gates forbidding entry, and then buildings which might have once been residential or businesses.

The road was reasonably well maintained beneath her feet, but to either side, the vegetation had reclaimed the raised parts, reaching claws seeming to toy with the notion of taking the road as well.

'No one lives in this part of the town any more,' the custodian confirmed. 'They've moved back into the areas close to the market and also the castle.' She spoke with a little derision, and Harra wondered why, until she continued talking.

'The castle is old, and long abandoned by its owners, the Duke and Duchess. For all their wealth and investment in this place, and indeed the whole area, they scuttled off soon as you like when they realised what was going to happen. Good riddance to them is all I say. I imagine the rest of the landed nobility of England have done the same.'

'A few fools live in the castle still, amongst the ruin of the wealth, thinking as it was once a bastion against marauding Scots, it can be again. Damn fools. The Scots have their Border Drones and The Wall. Why would they bother with a castle?'

The notion fascinated Harra. No one wanted England, so it seemed, not even the people within it.

'Ah, here we are,' the woman announced, pointing to a squat building before them raised a little from the side of the road. 'I thought you'd like to see this. I've got the key.'

Harra's forehead furrowed in confusion, as she had no idea what the building was.

Stepping inside she smelt a strange smell, as the custodian turned and manipulated something that cast the building into dim light.

'Ah, the aroma of rotting knowledge, with the occasional whiff of wood smoke.'

Harra looked around, unsure what she was seeing, as lights flickering on overhead.

'This used to be the old railway station,' the custodian announced. 'Long since turned into a bookstore, and long since abandoned, but I thought you'd like to see it all the same. This is about all this place has going for it now.'

Harra finally focused on a sagging bookcases, stuffed with books, the spines showing in a profusion of shapes, sizes and colours.

Her jaw dropped open.

'I know. So much crap, all in one place,' the custodian confirmed, but even she was running her hands lovingly along a shelf of books. 'Come and see it all,' she continued. 'I've tried to ensure the building stays as airtight as possible, to preserve the books, but it's a losing battle. It's as drafty as when the top-hat station master used to patrol up and down the line, just waiting for royalty, so he could escort them from the platform.' She smiled sadly at the words. 'This place used to draw people from miles and miles around. Now its long forsaken, just as it was before it became a bookshop.'

Harra was nodding, although the words made little sense to her. So many books. In one place. She could scarcely believe it.

'When I was a girl, we used to have a library too. Filled with books, we could borrow for free. All that's gone though. But I have this because no one else wanted it.' Again, the custodian laughed morosely. Harra could imagine her spending a great deal of time in the building, reading by the light of a single solitary lamp. She almost wished to do the same.

But she followed the custodian deeper into the great vault, bristling with books and other treasures, some of them seemingly behind glass cases, others just open and on display.

'I change them every so often,' the custodian said, noting Harra's interest. 'Just because I can. These books were made to be read, not forgotten about.'

'I met a man who would have loved this place,' Harra whispered, aware of a sharp gaze from the custodian. She knew not to mention the people she'd encountered but did so all the same. A faint smile touched the custodian's lips.

'I'm not the only one who pines for lost knowledge then?'

'Nope,' Harra confirmed, pleased to see the outline of a

genuine smile on the woman's face. A moment of joy to be savoured.

'This here is my favourite,' the custodian smirked, leading Harra toward one of the glass display cases. 'The colours in the pictures get me every time.'

Harra looked where she was instructed, and giggled. Before her was a picture book, perhaps meant for children, she didn't know, but depicted on it were small children, playing around a giant tree, decked out with what seemed to be glowing lights.

Harra laughed as well.

'It's so pretty,' she agreed, desperate to pick up more of the books and see what they said.

The custodian noticed her gaze.

'I think they all used to be sorted in certain categories, but now they're all mixed up. Some of them have pictures of food in them, others have page after page of black and white letters, and others only have a few words. For children. But look. See if you can find any answers to your questions. I'm just going to lock the front door, and check the doors out the back. But no one will bother you so enjoy yourself.'

Harra needed no further urging. Already she was turning to decide what to look at, while Jessy sniffed her way around the bottom of the shelves, clearly perplexed by the odd mix of aromas.

Titles flashed before Harra's eyes, some tired and barely visible, others bright, as though the books had never even been opened. The words said 'diet', 'cookery', 'geographic', 'build', 'doctor', 'biography', 'war.' All enticed her.

Her hand hovered over the titles, almost fearing to pull one of the books off the shelf and open up the knowledge it contained. And then the one that finally won over, 'A Short History of England.' History, a topic denied her, or so the ancient custodian had told her.

She held the book in her hand, just a small thing, and

flicked through the pages. It seemed so little and yet contained so much within the small volume.

Flicking to the back, she held her breath, hoping for some insight into the England that had existed before she'd been born. But deflated, she realised the book ended too soon. Was there perhaps another book, with the information she needed or had it yet to be written? She was beginning to understand why the old custodian had been so enamoured of her father's journal. Perhaps her father had written what needed to be shared. Perhaps. The thought excited her.

Turning to the beginning of the book, she found herself reading a list of 'Contents', starting with something called the 'Saxon Dawn' and ending with 'Epilogue.'

She paused, considering where to start, only to feel someone at her side.

'Take it,' the custodian said. 'Take it back to your room, and you can read it tonight. I'll bring it back here, next time I come up.'

Harra nodded.

'We should go.' The custodian warned. 'I don't want people to see the lights on in here and come investigating.'

Harra felt the groan of anguish pour forth before she could stop herself.

'I know,' the woman sympathised. 'But one day maybe you'll have time to read all you need to. I wish I did!' There was a note of whimsy in her voice Harra could well understand.

'But before we go back, I'll show you a bit more of the town, maybe even the castle, if we have time.'

Harra turned to place the book in her backpack, again looking around the vast room, filled with books.

'Come and see this first though,' the custodian called, and Harra followed the woman into a smaller room, ransacked and stuffed with boxes clearly containing even more moldering books.

'Look,' the torch flashed to reveal a picture on the wall, the lights not reaching far enough into the room.

'The 'top-hat station master," the woman said with a wry tone to her voice. 'Doesn't he look smart?'

'My, he does,' even Harra was impressed by the height of the black hat upon the older man's head. This then must be the 'top-hat' she'd mentioned to her. He also wore smart black trousers, and a jacket that looked too tight to be comfortable, a small tie around his neck.

'The shit people used to be concerned with,' the custodian muttered, but Harra could tell she'd rather be bothered with a top hat than this current excuse of a nation. In silence, they walked back to the front door of the building.

Outside, night had fallen in the time they'd been inside. Harra flicked her torch on and peered around her. In the near distance she had an idea of hulking buildings, but then her torch flashed over something white.

'What's that?' she asked. The custodian looked where her torch was.

'Oh, some old monument to the Duke and Duchess. It's broken now. It was one of the first things to go when they left. People were pleased to see the back of them. Always meddling, so some said, and building things that no one bloody wanted. Come on, I'll show you the castle, and then another famous ruin as well.'

Harra followed the custodian along a short road, flanked with buildings, again some clearly occupied, others not. They went through a small arch, and Harra saw a few exterior lights revealing what she knew to be shop fronts.

'Not a lot here,' the custodian said. 'But, if you look back over the years, there never really was.'

'What's the arch for?'

'Stop traffic or some such. It should have been moved years ago. But now it will stand forever, no doubt.'

The shops were all closed, their doors barred, heavy shutters covering what Harra knew to be windows. She had only the names of shops to point her in the right direction as to what goods could be bought and sold in Alnwick, as she'd been told this place was called. And as the custodian said, there was little, but the basics, mainly food shops, all offering little in the way of variety, or so Harra presumed.

Walking down another path, again buildings on either side, Harra was struck by how quiet the place was. For all there was no choking olive smog, no one was out and about. Was the place really so lawless? It looked harmless enough.

'Ah, the castle,' the custodian said, pointing. Highlighted against the rising moon, Harra could make out towering walls, and an impressive looking wooden gate bared tight against the night. No lights showed through the walls, or indeed any sign of a fire burning inside.

'They have their own windmills,' the custodian offered, anticipating the question. 'On the other side, and on the hills, over there.' She pointed in the general direction of north. 'Snooty lot,' she sighed, before turning away.

'Not very bloody impressive, is it?' Yet Harra just grunted. She thought it looked awe-inspiring.

'Here,' the custodian said, a few minutes later, stopping before a twisting, black metal gate. 'Sneak in here. See the greatest of folly's.'

Harra didn't know what a folly was, but she followed, all the same, avoiding the reaching green growths, seemingly desperate to escape through the gate.

'Flash your torch over there,' Harra did as instructed, and so too did the custodian.

In the glare of the twin torches, Harra could see what

looked like a series of giant steps, surrounding an odd round shape.

'What it is?' she asked, walking forward, only for the custodian to haul her back.

'It was a fountain once, when I was a girl. People came to see it from far and wide, but they turned off the water when they left. It's been silent ever since. They also grew poisonous plants, and the damn fools left them behind when they left. Now the gardens are safe for no one.'

'So that's why I shouldn't go any closer?' Harra asked.

'Exactly, nor Jessy.' As they talked, Jessy was sniffing excitingly, but Harra called her back.

'Heel,' she commanded the dog, and Jessy obeyed, perhaps scenting danger. Harra wasn't sure.

'You'd like to see all of this restored to your childhood memories?' Harra quizzed.

'I should like the whole world to be the way I remember it,' the custodian smiled sadly. 'But it will never be the same. Some steps are irreversible. This is one of them.'

As they spoke, the custodian was leading them back toward the road that led to the sanctuary.

'Anyway, I suppose some things are better,' the custodian laughed. 'No bloody visitors any more.' However, her laughter rang hollow.

They'd seen no one on their journey. Only now did she think to question why it hadn't been possible to press on a day earlier, because of the train.

'I have no means of contacting the custodians to the north,' the woman explained when Harra asked. 'It's all supposed to be a secret operation, obviously, but with the train running sometimes, we've set up a method of alerting a few of us, if there's a deviation from the normal routine.'

'But you don't know who any of the other people are?' Harra asked, just to be sure.

'No, the only people who know who everyone is are those making the journey, such as yourself.'

'And obviously, whoever sets each journey in motion.'

'I suppose so,' the custodian agreed, her face pensive. 'Not many know what you're doing is even possible. But sometimes the authorities get wind of certain strange events, and there have been problems in the past. They never last long though. There are always new people willing to take chances.'

Harra fell to silence, content to eat the meal that had been prepared for her. The history book weighed on her mind, and she was keen to reach for it but didn't want to appear too rude, not while the woman was so chatty.

Only hours later was Harra free to do as she wanted. She settled, a drink in easy reach, and opened the book before her.

As before, she scanned the contents, wondering where to start discovering knowledge previously withheld from her. Biting her lips, she considered, turning first to one chapter, and then to another, mirroring numbers next to each section heading.

The distant past, with each chapter containing the years covered, was evidently not as relevant to her as what had happened just before her father's own lifetime, and yet she wavered, unsure.

'Get your things together,' the custodian was suddenly before her, holding the door closed behind her, fury on her face.

'You'll have to leave. I'm sorry. Take the book with you.'

'What?' Harra stumbled, already standing.

'People are coming, who can't see you. It's my fault. I shouldn't have taken you to the old station. There's always some nosy bugger sticking their nose in.'

The woman had stepped away from the closed door now and was busy banging and crashing through cupboards.

'Get your things, from your room. I'll prepare food for you, and then you must go.'

'But the next custodian isn't expecting me yet?' Harra tried to argue, only to feel firm hands on her back.

'If you don't leave now, you might never. Mark my words; you don't want to meet these particular people. Nasty bastards, if ever I saw them. Better to risk it out on the road. Quickly.' Urgent panic made the words fall hastily one after another, almost without a break in-between.

It was infectious, and Harra dashed to her room, stuffing clean clothes into her backpack, and hastily ensuring she had everything she needed. Even running to the bathroom to reclaim a few stray pieces of clothing.

All the time Jessy watched her, confusion in her eyes at what was happening.

Returning to the kitchen, Harra was handed a packet of sandwiches, again, and stuffed them into her backpack as well, forgetting she already had some from earlier. Well, she surmised, it might be a while before she had a good meal again. She shouldn't leave anything behind.

'Right, when I open the exterior door, you need to walk down to the road. It's easy enough to see, and then head north, which is that way,' the woman indicated by holding her hand out. 'You'll know you've done it right because the wide stretch of road will only last a mile or two more. If you go the wrong way, it'll last for about seven or eight miles. If you hear sounds of pursuit, head off the road, and aim for the train line, which is that way.' Again, the custodian pointed with her hand. Harra nodded, swallowing her fear as she sealed her backpack, her torch in hand.

'Keep your dog with you. If they see a stray dog, they might think it a bit strange. I'm not saying they will,' she cautioned. 'Lots of farm dogs around here. But they might. That's all. Now, are you ready?'

Harra nodded, and hastily they made their way to the exterior door. Harra had been looking forward to a full day of rest, and now her feet were complaining inside her boots, already starting to ache against the miles they needed to cover.

'Wait a minute,' the custodian cautioned, only then opening the door, and looking around her before beckoning Harra outside.

'It's clear, come on, go, go, go,' the urgency had Harra running before she was even outside, a whispered, 'My thanks,' floating behind her in the air.

In front, with the torch turned off for fear of being seen, Harra made out the smooth surface of the road, and then stopped, confused, as the road seemed to go three different ways at once.

'Damn,' she muttered, coming to an abrupt stop. But Jessy had no such compunction and raced on, Harra following her, hoping the dog knew better than she did.

Even when her feet hit the tarmac, going the right way, Harra didn't stop because behind her, a welter of lights had exploded on the skyline, a loud noise accompanying them, as though two huge metallic machines had crashed together, erupted, shaking the ground beneath Harra's feet and causing Jessy to whine.

'Run girl,' Harra cautioned the dog, the torchlight bouncing from one side to another, as she took her own advice.

'Run girl,' Harra said again, her feet being joined by her calf muscles in protest. Yet she pushed on, ever northwards, hoping the light would fade, and she'd hear no one else on the road behind her.

Only when the road narrowed, as the custodian had warned her, did Harra pause her running, and only then to try and listen, because her breath was chafing in her throat and she could hear nothing but herself.

In the distance, bright lights still flickered, casting a glow that almost reached her, and the bridge she sheltered beneath. With a start of recognition, Harra knew it to be the bridge she'd walked over the night before, on arriving.

She hesitated, suddenly torn. She could scamper up the side of the road, to that bridge, and head back toward the train line. She could take her chances there, far from the main course of her intended path. But, if she did that she chanced not finding the next custodian, and if she didn't find the custodian, there was a risk of being discovered.

Harra waited, straining to hear, but it was impossible. Tongue lolling from the side of her mouth, Jessy watched her carefully.

'Which way, girl?' Harra asked the dog, desperate not to make the wrong decision herself.

For a long moment, Harra watched as Jessy turned to face the way they'd come, and then the way forward. The dog sniffed the air, perhaps sensing something Harra couldn't and then she began to walk, along the road they were destined to take.

Harra fell in beside her, one minute of worry making her wish they'd chosen the other route, and then she banished it. The decision had been made. The way to The Wall was along this road. It always had been.

Walking into the dark, Harra felt uneasy. The night before, with the custodian, a night-time walk had felt pleasant, almost a treat, now she startled at every small sound, sure that at any moment, she'd be discovered, and then what would she do?

The night was wreathed in shadows. The moon, which before had cast a welcome light over the castle in Alnwick, was gone, hidden by fast-moving clouds scuttling their way inland.

The wind was cold as well, Harra trying to make her coat cover her more, until giving up, she found another jumper to fling over her head, beneath her coat. The pleasant conditions that had prevailed when she'd arrived on the train had fled as quickly as she had.

Harra paused only once, when the road narrowed, to look back the way she'd come. The bright lights seemed less intense from so far away. That didn't mean they'd dimmed, or gone away, and Harra knew it was too soon to be convinced there'd be no pursuit.

Looking into the fields that sprang up from the very side of the tarmac, Harra peered intently, looking for the eyes of watchers, or the lights of farm equipment. But she heard nothing. It was as though the entire world slept, apart from her.

Her watch read 23:13. Shaking her head, Harra thought of the instructions for the following night's journey.

They'd been simple enough. 'Walk ten miles north,' but now she didn't know what to do. The custodian was expecting her in more than twenty-four hours. They'd be no one waiting for her. Should she just press on? Or find somewhere safe for the night, and just wait?

It was impossible to know.

Shining her torch forward, Harra was surprised at how far her torch's beam penetrated, all of it reflecting back the inky surface of the tarmac. None of it distorted or overrun with vegetation.

Whoever lived close to here, and she was sure some people did, otherwise the fields wouldn't have been tended with neat shoots, all of the same height, poking through the muddy soil, they still used this road. That much was obvious.

What would they make of a young woman walking alone at night, with nothing but a dog for company, should she be discovered?

The worry nipped at her heels, hastening her speed so she almost ran once more, Jessy keeping up easily, her black and white tail bouncing up and down.

Harra continued to argue with herself.

What was different about this night, after all? All her excursions had taken place under cover of darkness, with only her, or with her and Jessy. No one had yet questioned her. No one.

In some places, the further south, closer to where she'd lived all her life, what she did was a complete secret. In the bright lights of the mine, it had been more of an open secret. Here, well, she was no longer sure who knew, and who didn't. Indeed, the people who plied the train line had seemed to recognise and accept what was happening.

Perhaps she should have gone that way after all?

She walked on, her footsteps sounding loud in the quiet of the night, now the wind had dropped.

Her watch read 03:32 and Harra considered how far they might have come in the time since she'd left. And then she heard it. The sound she'd been fearing. A clicking, whirling sound, that meant either pursuit or a low flying drone. Quickly, she flicked her torch to off, and called Jessy to heel, striding free from the easy-going tarmac, and into an open expanse of field to her left.

Jessy came to her quickly, keen to rest, and Harra cautioned her with a stern finger in front of her eyes, as she bent beside her. They needed to be quiet, and not to move. They couldn't be spotted. Not now.

Overhead, a small red light appeared, accompanying the click, click whirling noise and Harra almost forgot to breathe.

There were warnings about the Border Drones in her list of instructions. No suggestions on how to avoid them, just merely an admonishment they must be avoided.

Harra squinted, concerned because the Border Drone's came from the south, and not the north, as she expected. She worried about the custodian of the night before. Had her part in Harra's escape been discovered? Was she in danger?

Harra held still as the light came ever closer, occasionally hovering over something that seemed to interest it, perhaps a wild animal or some such, or perhaps someone else trying to escape.

Closer and closer it came, the red light of its sensors pulsing with a life of their own. Harra closed her eyes, not wanting to see the moment she was captured. But a long minute passed, and Harra heard the click, click whirling grow louder and then suddenly, quieter. Still, she held her place, eyes screwed tightly shut.

She could afford to wait an entire twenty-four hours if she needed to do so.

At her side, Jessy shifted, a very low whine asking the question.

'No,' Harra shook her head, the words so low they escaped more as a vibration in the air than actual sound, but Jessy understood all the same.

They both stayed quiet, still, almost not breathing, and then she heard it again.

'Bastards,' she expelled, watching as yet another red light slowly made its way toward her. Click, click, whirling.

This time she watched as much as she could as the low flying object swung its piercing laser from one side of the road to the other. Was it hunting for her or was it just hunting? And who'd sent not one, but two Border Drones down this deserted stretch of road supposed to be free from such scrutiny? The people of England, whether they could or not being irrelevant, were free to roam, as they wanted to do so. If they wanted to do so. Most were too fearful. Strangers were not welcome, even if they were English.

Harra knew it could only be whoever had scared the custodian so much. But why would they have command of Border Drones?

She waited. She wasn't about to get anyone in trouble for helping her. Whether it was a crime to provide succour to travellers was a mute point. It was where she headed that would cause the problems.

As before, the Border Drone passed overhead, and Harra expelled air, but still hesitated. Then she screamed, turning abruptly, her heart beating too loud, her other leg working its way into a kicking motion, for something had hold of her right leg.

'Shush,' a voice cautioned. 'I mean no harm. Come, I can keep you hidden for the night.'

Fumbling for her torch in the mud, Harra miss-hit the 'on' button and had to try again, shaky hands forcing the light upwards, not into the face of whoever spoke.

'Give that here,' the voice complained, reaching out for the torch, and in the process releasing the leg. Harra shot backwards, on her butt, but ready to flee now she had both legs.

Only, the person who spoke had twisted the torch so that it his face.

'See, not a scary monster from the deep or a bloody enforcement officer. Now follow me. You need to be off the road for the rest of the night.'

Harra nodded, still unsure, but Jessy was already making friends with the newcomer, no worry in her demeanour, as she allowed the stranger to pet her.

Harra stood, brushing mud from her clothes.

'Go on then. I'll follow,' she said with a wobble to her voice. She wished the torch was in her hand. And then it was.

'Here, I don't need it. I know my way around here whether it's light or dark.' As he spoke, he turned to leave, but Harra paused. Should she risk taking help from this total stranger, when by rights she could just carry on walking the road? The Border Drones were gone, after all.

'There'll be more,' he advised, with some insistence now, his head turned to the south as though straining to hear.

'There's always more, when they do this. For twelve hours they'll send out the Border Drones at random times.'

'How do you know so much?' Harra asked, reluctantly deciding to follow.

'I listen,' was the less than helpful reply.

'Where are we going?' she further demanded, the mud of the field already sticking to her boots, forcing her to take exaggerated steps where her knees were raised higher than usual. He didn't seem to be having the same trouble, and already she was breathing hard.

'Just up here. To the farm. But I have to retrieve my tractor first. I left it around here, somewhere,' now he peered into the dark, as though unsure, before crying out with delight, and turning to walk at a tight angle to their path.

'Follow me, you can jump into the tractor, and then we'll get you back to the farm. Bloody Border Drones. Shouldn't be allowed. Not here.' He complained as he walked, and Harra almost smiled to hear the rich vein of exasperation in his voice. This then was not a new occurrence, but rather an old one, repeated continuously.

'Do you know who I am?' she thought to ask, fearful of the answer, but driven to ask all the same.

'I have my suspicions, but there's no need to confirm them. Just,' and here he stopped so Harra nearly walked into his back, as he reached upwards. 'Hop in here, with your fine doggy friend, and we'll spirit you away in no time at all.'

With the clang of a door opening on whatever was before them, Harra saw a pale light illuminating a wheel and a seat, a few steep steps as well.

'Is this a tractor?' she asked, the word unfamiliar to her.

'Yep, old beastie. Runs on all sorts of nasties that I'm not supposed to have access to, but the old ones are the best. The very best.' He spoke with pride as he hopped in, turning to help Harra. There was no room for her in the tight cab, and yet that didn't seem to bother him.

'Just wedge yourself in behind me. There. It's not comfortable, but you're in. The Border Drones will leave us alone. They know a tractor when they see one, even if they don't necessarily expect one to be out at this time of night.'

As he spoke, Harra hit her head on the back of the machine, where a window gave out onto the back of the machine, and yelped. But Jessy was comfortable on the floor and was unsympathetic enough to Harra's plight to bark, just once, as though telling her to get on with it.

'Thanks, friend,' Harra scowled, but the man was fiddling with some arrangement beneath a thin wheel, and suddenly a thrum of movement juddered the tractor, making conversation impossible, as a loud noise filled the small cabin. He spun the wheel, and the tractor began to slowly turn, as bright lights swept over nodding crops, disturbing them from their sleep.

'Bloody muddy,' was all Harra heard, trying to watch what was happening, in case she needed to make a quick escape in the event of this farm he spoke about being less than salubrious. But it was impossible to tell which way they went in the cramped confines of the small cab, where her head hit the roof with every bump and judder the machine gave.

Even its smell was worrying, a strange half-burning, half-screeching aroma jumping into her mouth so she could taste it as well as smell it. Neither did the old tractor seem that keen to move. As the man turned the wheel, he also stomped on something on the floor, and thrust a stick from side to side, as though it was imperative it move, despite the accompanying crunching and screeches.

When they eventually came to a stop, about fifteen minutes later, Harra could scarcely breathe and felt nauseous. He, however, jumped through the open door, with a cackle of delight for his 'beastie' and allowed Jessy to jump down, and then offered Harra a hand as well. She took it, worried without it she'd tumble down the steps.

'What you think?' he asked, waving at his tractor, which Harra could now tell was a muddy brown colour, whether from the fields or by choice she wasn't sure. They were in a building that smelt of 'fresh', and she could hear the shuffling of feet. Surprised, she turned, wondering what had so intrigued Jessy, and met the staring eyes of huge four-legged creatures, held back only by a small metal gate.

'Ah,' she cried, almost falling over in shock once more.

'What, you've never seen a cow before?' the man laughed, and then sobered. 'No really, you've never seen a bloody cow before?' he asked again, as Harra shook her head. Jessy was on her hind legs, the front two resting on the metal gate, as she sniffed the air. One of the creatures, or cows, as he'd said, turned to meet Jessy's inquisitive sniffing with soft brown eyes.

'Cows, fine beasties, but damn smelly,' he explained. Still chuckling softly. 'They won't hurt you,' he offered, as an afterthought, moving away from his tractor, and hauling on a huge wooden door to close it against the darkness beyond.

'I'm Ted,' he said, finished with his task and turning to greet her, his hand outstretched. She shook it, feeling callouses beneath her hand. He was evidently a hard working man.

'I'm,' she began, but he shook his head.

'Oh no, sorry, don't tell me your name. Best if I don't know, but I recognise the look alright, and when it all kicked off down there,' he pointed with his head, 'I thought I might find one of you on the road. Damn bastards,' he muttered, appraising Harra quickly.

'You look much better than most of the skin and bones I see on the road. Clearly, you're a healthier specimen, and so I'll keep you intact while the Border Drones ply their useless trade. Then I'll take you back to the road tomorrow. When it's safe again.'

'Now,' and he paused, a wry smirk on his lined face. Harra watched him. It wasn't that Ted was old. He just looked well worn, as though he'd made a great deal of use of himself. He was tall, but not so tall Harra had to tilt her head too high to meet his gaze, and his eyes flashed a unique grey she'd never seen before. His hair was brown and close-cropped, his face showing a series of scars, perhaps from trying to tame the bristle that grew thickly on his chin and cheeks.

'Would you like to meet a cow?' he asked, smirking with delight. Harra glared at him, but then reconsidered.

'Why not,' she breathed. 'Jessy seems to like them.'

'Aye,' Ted agreed, walking to where Jessy and the cow were still communicating, in some way, their eyes on each other.

'This here is Petal, and she's a big lady, but very friendly.' As he spoke, he rubbed his hands over the cow's nose and then patted her just above her eyes.

Harra reached out hesitantly, unsure whether she wanted to touch a cow or not, but not prepared to be laughed at any more.

'There you go. She's a dairy cow. All of them are. Keep them for their milk, which gets shipped down south, somewhere.'

'Milk?' Harra squawked, another laugh coming from Ted.

'Yep, you know, white stuff, put it in tea.' Harra nodded, a little numb. Milk was a delicacy where she came from. Extremely expensive and served only by those with too much money, which meant just about no one.

'You have had milk, in tea, right?' Ted asked, but Harra was shaking her head.

'Too expensive,' she offered, a tremor to her lips.

'Well, come on then. Let's get you a nice cup of tea, with

some milk, and then you can thank the old girl when you leave tomorrow.'

With that, Ted walked to a smaller gate in the wall to the one the tractor had driven through, and paused, perhaps to listen for another Border Drone.

'This way. The house is about fifty steps away. We'll be fine.'

Jessy was reluctant to leave, and Harra didn't want to leave her behind. When she refused to come as instructed, Harra grabbed her gently and directed her toward Ted. Jessy went, but was unhappy about it.

'Damn dog,' she muttered.

'Curious dog,' Ted amended, and then Harra was outside.

The wind was fierce, and as she paused to gaze at the sea, under the pale moon, lingering still, Harra realised how high up they were.

'It's always windy here,' he offered. 'Windy Farm, well, that's what I call it now. I think it had another name, once, but no need now. Windy is fine with me.'

He led her across a tarmacked area; clear of all mud, which surprised Harra before fiddling with a locking mechanism on a wooden door, and indicating she should step inside.

'Take your boots off, please,' he softened the command. 'And doggy, you need to wipe your paws as well. Here,' he flung a linen at Harra, and she grabbed Jessy's front paw and began to wipe the mud from it. Jessy thanked her with a soft lick on her arm, and Harra smiled.

Only when all four paws were clean did she stand and look around. Not that there was much to see.

It was a smallish room, lined with rows and rows of shelves, on which all sorts of strange and familiar items resided, from muddy boots to coveralls, to mechanical looking pieces, and a row of torches, all standing upright.

'Come through here, this is just the staging post,' Ted

advised, opening another door, a blast of warmth enveloping her.

She stepped inside, soft carpet underfoot beneath her socks. Harra didn't know where to look first. The interior of the house, lit by only a handful of low lamps, was the most impressive thing she'd ever seen.

A huge fireplace dominated the kitchen, gentle flames visible through the door of a stove, impressive wood beams visible overhead, and a huge wooden table dominating the centre of the kitchen.

It was spotlessly clean, and hunks of machines lined the wide work surface. Harra had heard of all of the items but had never seen them, not all in one place. A kettle was a necessity for every household of course, but Ted had many other things besides.

Ignoring her, he walked forward, pressing various buttons as he went, before he stopped and turned to look at her.

'What?' he asked, but she shook her head, more amused with him than her. It seemed he had more than just an ancient tractor to his name.

'I like to tinker,' he advised her. 'During the dark nights, when I don't need to be outside tending to the beasties or checking the crops. Here are all the kitchen appliances I've managed to maintain and keep going.'

'But where does all the power come from?' she asked, mystified.

'Oh, I have a few windmills as well, just behind the farm. They provide all I need.'

'Is there just you, then?' Harra asked, peering into the recesses of the house, dark behind a closed glass-fronted door.

'Yep, just me and a hundred beasties. It's a good enough life,' he offered, a grin splitting his face as he plonked a huge mug before her.

'Tea, with milk. There's sugar too, if you want,' and he pushed a pot toward her. 'I'd taste it first. But not yet,' he cautioned as she lifted it to her lips. 'It'll be bloody hot,' he cautioned, a roll of his eyes. She snatched her hand from the mug and took a seat instead, Jessy sniffing the kitchen to determine the best place to lie down.

'It can be a bit lonely,' he explained, stirring a simmering pot on top of his stove, 'but it's better this way. Not many like the isolated life of a Far Northerner farmer, and I'm not the most tolerant of men.' As he spoke, he was swiping at the work surface, as though it had offended him.

'I like to be clean,' he explained, with a shrug before sitting before her.

'Don't we all,' Harra replied, understanding all the same. Her time walking north had shown her she appreciated her own company more than others.

'So, you're headed north?' he questioned.

'Yep, away from the smoggy gloom of my birth town. A quest for fresh air,' she inhaled sharply to highlight what she meant.

'You're brave,' he offered, respect in his eyes. 'To leave what you know for what you can only imagine.'

'When what you know is shit, it's not that hard, believe me. If I lived somewhere like this, it might be very different.' He allowed that and sank into quiet contemplation.

Harra reached for her tea once more, cupping the mug in both hands, blowing softly over the surface. She was keen to try the drink, but, not wanting a nasty surprise, was prepared to wait, as directed.

'Wouldn't you think of leaving, if you could?'

'I could leave. I don't much want to. I imagine it's bloody busy out there. Not like there weren't enough people already, getting in the way and generally inflicting their lives on others.

No, I want to be left alone. This is probably the only place where I can guarantee that will happen.'

'Well, you seem friendly enough to me,' Harra muttered.

'Well, I know I can kick you out if I have enough of you. And anyway, you'll only be here for a finite amount of time. I can almost count the hours down in my mind as I speak to you, now.' His eyes bulged wide as he spoke, teasing her. She sipped her tea, minded to ignore him.

'This is good,' she acknowledged.

'Aye, a good old brew,' he agreed, drinking from his own mug, suppressing a yawn as he did so, checking his watch.

'Are you staying then?' he asked, rubbing his eyes as well now.

'If that's alright with you, yes. I'm a day ahead. I can wait, and head out tomorrow.'

'Good. In that case, bring your tea, and I'll show you where you and beastie can spend the night.' Jessy looked up then, a loud rumble running through the room.

'I, I have food, don't worry,' Harra quickly responded, but Ted smiled at the dog.

'Not to worry. I have something she'll like.'

Reaching for a bowl, he removed the lid from his pot on the stove, and placed a generous portion into the bowl.'

'Proper meat,' he said, leaving it to cool on the table. 'None of that substituted stuff you get told is meat.'

'What?' Harra asked. Ted nodded.

'Aye, I know. Another lie. They ship the good stuff off, you know, trade deals that are allegedly no longer legal. They do all that. But not round here. We have the proper stuff.'

Harra's gaze switched to the cooling food, licking her own lips at the juicy lumps and bumps it contained. But she held her tongue.

'It'll be better tomorrow,' Ted assured her. 'Leave it, if you can, and then tomorrow we can dine on this and the bread that'll be delivered, come the morning.'

With that, he yawned once more and lowered the bowl for Jessy. She, of course, spared not a thought for Harra and wolfed the lot, thrumming with delight.

'And now, let's go this way.' Ted opened the glass-fronted door, and Harra murmured in surprise as muted lights sprang up without him doing anything.

The kitchen was homely, and everything she'd always thought a kitchen should be. By contrast, the rest of the house was entirely functional. Hard wooden floorboards stretched across a vast space, leading to a corridor with three doors branching from it, while the central area was occupied by another wooden table, a few stand-alone chairs, padded for comfort, and little else. Not that she could see, anyway.

'Here,' he said, pointing to one of the doors. 'You can sleep in here. It has its own bathroom through that other door. It has a lock as well,' and he showed her how to work the lock, his hands twisting from side to side in a grinding motion. 'I'll be in my own room, at the far end of the hall. I'll lock my door as well, and then neither of us need worry about the other's intentions when we're fast asleep.' His tone was light, but Harra gasped at the implication in his words. He smiled, to remove the sting.

'There's no need for either of us to trust the other.'

With that, he opened the door wide and walked away. Harra listened to his departing footsteps, and then, when they faded away as he opened and locked his own door, hastily shut and fastened the door, as quietly as she could.

Only then did she truly take in the room offered for the night. It was, as the main room of the house, entirely functional. The bed, however, was wide and looked comfortable, the sheets, smart and fresh smelling. Behind her, a chair and desk waited, to take her backpack, and the door to the bathroom revealed a smart and tidy space with a bath, washbasin and toilet, all sparklingly clean.

'If he was so damn antisocial, why did he keep a guest room like this?' Harra thought. Fear she'd not yet encountered sneaking into her thoughts as she questioned her quick acceptance of him.

Damn him for saying that.

With thoroughness she'd never employed before when stopping for the day, she checked the room, making sure there were no hidden entrances or exits, but heavy shutters barred even the windows. As he'd said, it was secure.

Harra sat on the chair, Jessy coming to her with a low whine of contentment. Harra tried to relax, but it had been a strange day, and she felt wide-awake, even though her watch display read 04:37.

Reaching for her backpack, she pulled out not the history, as keen as she was to read it, but rather her father's journal.

Hastily she turned to the newspaper articles he'd curated, perhaps not from an actual newspaper as the paper was thicker than that, and had nothing on the rear of it, and gazed at it. This was her ultimate goal. This was where her future lay. All the same, a well of fear rushed through her.

The Wall had seemed like a target that was forever just out of reach, but she was now almost within sight of it. The appearance of the Border Drones was a sure sign of that. So many times she'd worried and argued with herself about what she was doing. Now it felt real, possible, and terrifying. Ted's words had resonated with her.

The chance for freedom hadn't been her decision to make. Her family had opted for it on her behalf. No matter the misinformation behind that decision, the systematic lies of the establishment, Harra still needed to assure herself this was the future she wanted for herself.

She'd met many different custodians on the way north, and

now Ted as well. They'd all told her something at variance with what she thought she knew. She was just beginning to determine where the truth must lie, or so it seemed to her. But, did she know enough to be assured her decision was the correct one? Couldn't she just stay? After all, or so she'd been told, the opportunity to leave could be taken whenever she wanted to take it.

Or could it?

This time she reached for her list of instructions.

The final stage was exceptionally detailed, almost minute-by-minute, the only time to avoid the Border Drones.

But, and Harra finally realised she'd not asked this question before, if she could genuinely leave whenever she wanted to, why were there Border Drones in the first place?

If no one knew they could leave, then why have them? If everyone was free to go whenever they wanted to, then why have them? The circular argument made her rub her forehead.

Harra picked at her lip, running her eyes over the grainy photograph of The Wall. Even with the poor copying of the image, it was an imposing structure, reaching as far as the eye could see from one side of the coast to the other, or so the map attached to the article implied.

Once more, she ran her fingers over the thick paper.

Why hadn't her father known he could leave? Why hadn't he taken the chance when his illness had proved to be terminal? He would have received treatment if he'd only left England?

Words caught her eye, ones she'd not seen before. They were tiny, shaky, as though written at a later time. Perhaps her father had self-edited it. Maybe, he'd meant for her to have this all along.

'Truth is more painful than the lies.'

She starred, just to make sure she'd read the words correctly.

Harra glared at the image of The Wall again, pondering the words.

What was it that her father had learnt before his death that had made him write such a thing?

What had he come to realise when it was all too late?

CHAPTER 14
STAGE 12

'LEAVE AT PRECISELY 20:00 HOURS.'

NOT THAT THE mystery kept her awake all night. Indeed, it was as though saying the words aloud lulled her to sleep, an unpleasant sleep of horror and dark foreboding.

She woke, sweat-drenched and almost crying from reliving the day of her father's death. No more than a child, she'd understood all the same, that she'd never see him again.

So final.

She glanced at her watch, glowing faintly.

13:04.

She could sleep for hours yet but didn't want to do so. Instead, she leapt from the bed, and headed for the bathroom, hoping for hot water.

Pleasantly surprised when the tap ran with steaming water almost immediately, she filled the bath and submerged herself into the hot steam, eyes closed, trying to ease a headache that pounded behind her eyes. It caused flashes of bright light to appear sporadically, as though she walked with her torch in front of her, the light coming and going with the gait of her steady steps.

Outside she could hear nothing but silence and a strange whistling sound. She strained to hear, for a moment concerned it sounded similar to the noise of the Border Drones. And then she realised what it was, as the light flickered, just a little, above her head. Ah, the windmills. It was they that whimpered, disturbing her bath.

She relaxed once more, fighting for an inner calm denied her when she slept. It hovered, just out of reach, until a new sound infiltrated her room, the sniffing of her dog.

Opening one eye only, Harra chuckled at Jessy, hanging over the bath.

'Morning,' she offered, reaching to rub a wet hand over Jessy's nose. 'You slept then?' she asked, but Jessy was looking urgently toward the exit.

'Oh, okay,' she complained, understanding the need. Quickly she leapt from the bath, dried and dressed. She hastened to the door, unlocking it, and marched into the hallway. Jessy led the way straight back to the glass doors to the kitchen.

All was quiet in there, and yet the stove was warm, and Harra saw a puff of steam from the kettle. It seemed Ted was awake, but elsewhere.

Jessy whined once more, as Harra rushed to help her friend.

The door they'd used to gain access to the house was closed but unlocked, and Harra, pausing to listen, just in case, opened the door and let Jessy slip outside as she hunted for her boots.

Before she found them, Jessy was back, Ted trailing in behind her.

'Afternoon,' he offered, inspecting her. 'You did not sleep well,' it was a statement, not a question, and he sounded dismayed as he closed the door behind him. 'My apologies, I didn't mean to worry you,' he offered. 'I was teasing. My sincere apologies.'

Harra shook her head, keen to assure him it wasn't his fault.

'Nightmares, nothing to do with your words.'

'Ah, then, I take back all my apologies, and invite you to eat.' He gestured back toward the kitchen, and Harra, Jessy in tow, trailed back through.

'Have you been awake long?' she asked him.

'I don't sleep well,' he explained. 'That's why I was up in the field last night. I've milked the cows and seen to some other mundane tasks.'

'The lights flickered?'

'Yes, they do, just every so often. There's a problem in the mechanism. I should fix it, but it's been happening for so long, I'll miss it if I do so.' He shrugged as he talked, boiling the kettle and fixing her another cup of tea, a bowl of water for Jessy on the floor.

'I'm not sure you'd appreciate milk. After all, you're not a cat!' He offered the dog, head canted to one side.

'Now, let's eat. It's a pleasant enough day out there, but I think it'll be cold tonight. I'd recommend you wrap up warm when you leave.'

Food appeared before Harra, a steaming bowl of meaty stew, and she inhaled deeply as she waited for Ted to join her.

'Don't wait on me,' he urged. 'Just eat up, while it's hot. I'm keen to see if you like it as much as your canine friend.' Now he placed another bowl on the floor for Jessy, this one though contained only some meat and not the root vegetables or potatoes.

'I portioned it out for her earlier. I didn't want her eating too much rich food. It might upset her digestive system.'

'This is good,' Harra complimented, savouring the juices

and texture of the meat. Ted was right. It was much better than anything she'd eaten before.

'I know,' he grinned, enjoying the compliment all the same. 'You're lucky. Sometimes I experiment, and it's not always a good experience. Yesterday I just opted for plain and simple. So you know, I've seen and heard no Border Drones this morning. But I did hear more last night. Damn things. Sticking their noses in where they aren't needed.'

'Not that they stay long. Just enough to remind everyone that they exist, for another few months.'

'My thanks for all your help,' Harra was scraping her bowl clean with her spoon as she spoke, while Ted carved her a thick slice of bread from a squat shaped loaf. He gestured for her to spread it with butter from a waiting plate on the table, wincing when she spread the barest amount. 'I hope you didn't take too much of a risk.'

'Not at all. And please, load your bread. Nothing here is in short supply,' Ted smirked as he spoke, her hand hesitating over the bread knife. 'They can't do anything, not without capturing you, anyway. So, provided you make your escape without detection, I'll be fine.' He spoke with relish, the possibility perhaps exciting him more than it should. Harra considered that he didn't truly like living alone after all.

'I promise that if they take me, I'll not mention your name,' she giggled, swept up in his fantasy.

'Then no harm has been done. None at all.' His arms flung wide, as though he were about to bow.

'Still, it was good of you. I take it you don't normally lurk in your tractor waiting to pounce on people?' She said it with a smile, but he paused, his spoon halfway to his mouth, his own bowl now before him. She gasped in shock, only for him to wink, laughter lines stretching along his cheeks.

She rolled her eyes at him.

'Fool,' she complained.

Hours later, when they finally parted company, Harra felt a twinge of sadness. It would have been good to meet Ted many years before, and to have more time to get to know him. But, such things were not to be.

He'd driven her to the road in his tractor once more, her head banging on the ceiling while Jessy tried to grip the floor. His face had been pensive, perhaps a trace of worry there.

'Good luck,' he said, reaching out to shake her hand. 'Remember, any problems, head for the railway line. It's further toward the coast but will get you north all the same.'

'My thanks,' she said, a tightness to her throat she'd not experienced before when bidding farewell to any of her custodians. But then, Ted wasn't a custodian. He'd helped her because he'd wanted to, not because of any other reason.

'Enjoy 'the other side," he stated with a quirk of a smile.

'I will,' she trilled, trying to mask her lingering moroseness with too much cheer so her voice squeaked a little.

With that, she turned away, stepping onto the tarmac of the road, and vowing not to look back. No matter what.

But, no more than fifty feet up the road, the roar of the tractor springing to life made her turn, whether she wanted to or not, she raised her arm in farewell, even though it was doubtful he'd see her in the darkness. The lights flickered on the tractor, just briefly, and Harra turned away wondering if it had been intentional or just the engine playing up.

Her steps were more onerous than in the past, for all the road was pleasantly flat and the wind little more than a gentle breeze playing around her face. Even the moon was cooperating, bright and high behind her as the watch proclaimed it was 20:01.

She had ten miles to walk that night. A relatively short distance, in the grand scheme of her journey. Ten miles today, and ten tomorrow, and then, and here she swallowed thickly; it would be time to make her way to The Wall. To finally see it for real as opposed to only in photographs.

Jessy scampered before her, refreshed from her excellent food and good night's sleep. Harra still chased the memories of her nightmares, although she tried not to think about them.

She listened carefully, because the wind was so gentle, for the sound of any Border Drones behind her. All was silent, the night a comfort as she strode through the dark. Only once did she look behind her, about an hour later, convinced the lights of Ted's tractor were still visible to her, even from such a distance, but she knew they weren't.

Harra was met by a worried looking man at 00:05.

'I've been looking out for you. I was concerned you might have been walking last night?' There was a demand for answers, but Harra refrained from speaking until they were inside the usual looking complex and the metal door was barred behind her.

'I was. I hid.' For some reason, she didn't want to mention Ted's name or that he'd helped her the night before.

'All night?' the man asked.

'Yes.'

Her custodian for the night was almost painfully thin and extremely tall. He had to duck his head as he moved around the building, walking in and out of doors, and Harra wondered how often he forgot and bashed his head. His movements were short and spikey, betraying his anxiety.

'With your dog?' the man was less impressed with her companion than any of the other custodians. She was convinced that, if he could, Jessy would have been forced to stay outside.

'Yes, we hid. From all the Border Drones.'

'Shush,' he whispered, his eyes betraying true terror.

'Did they come here?' she questioned, concerned he wasn't the right person to be doing this job if he was so scared.

'No, no, they can only go up and down the road. They can't veer from side to side. The sensors don't work, and they lose power.'

Ah, Harra thought, much of the previous advice about the railway line making sense now. Why no one had told her that reason, she wasn't sure. Neither was it entirely clear why the travellers weren't directed to follow the train line by default if there was the possibility of the Border Drones discovering them.

'Well then, they're gone. And my thanks for your help,' Harra tried to jar him back to the here and now, and not whatever fears stalked him as he mis-poured water from a jug so that it pooled onto the table.

Harra leapt up to get a cloth, while the man seemed entirely unaware of what he'd done.

The meal, for all that, was well cooked and tasty, if not a patch on Ted's cooking. All the same, she was pleased to seek her bed and shut her eyes the sooner to pass the time to her leaving the following day.

If she could have done, she'd have informed whoever ran the custodian service this particular gentleman was too apprehensive with his post. Perhaps he could have been moved, to somewhere the Border Drones didn't fly.

The thought allowed her to sleep, Jessy at her side.

CHAPTER 15
STAGE 13

'LEAVE AT PRECISELY 20:00 HOURS.'

SHE WAS WOKEN by a rough shake on her shoulder.

'You need to go,' the custodian whispered to her, his hands shaking violently, while Jessy whined unhappily beside Harra.

'Someone is coming, who can't see you here. Quickly. I only just got the word.'

Cursing softly, Harra reached for all of her possessions, pleased she'd removed only her clothes for the day from the backpack and nothing more valuable. Somehow she'd known this might happen.

'I don't know who put them onto you, but you need to go. And avoid the road. I'm sure I've heard the Border Drones flying low.'

Harra was listening to him with half an ear, the other trying to detect the click, click whirling noise of the Border Drones as he hastened her and Jessy to the door. Only at the last moment, did Harra let out a cry of worry and dash back to her room. She'd left the history book behind. She remembered now. It had fallen down the back of the bed as she'd nodded off to sleep.

Frantically her hand quested below the bed, not wanting to leave it behind, despite the custodian's obvious distress.

'Ah ha,' she cried with relief, dashing back to the door. The custodian was glaring at her now, especially when he saw what had sent her scurrying backwards.

'A damn book is worth more than my life,' he growled, but Harra was following him outside, where the moon was just about to sink low, and the sun was considering rising, a mass of pale pinks staining the distant horizon in the direction of the sea.

Harra didn't answer his vexed question, listening, rather than talking.

In the semi-grey of impending daylight, the building hulked against the ground ominously, as Harra sought the sight of the road so she could re-orientate herself. Only the custodian led her a different way.

'Go that way,' he commanded, pointing along a field stretching on forever into the distance. 'Stick to the hedge boundaries, and you'll find the railway line. It'll be up to you to determine when it's safe to make your way back to the Northern Road.'

Harra swallowed and nodded. It felt as though being out here was too big a risk. Surely she could have stayed in her bed, out of sight? Rubbing her eyes to wakefulness, Harra felt a package pressed into her arms.

'Food,' the custodian stated. 'Now go.' The urgency in his voice was impossible to ignore, and Harra's feet were moving before she'd half tied her backpack closed again. Harra could just detect a faint humming in the air, as the custodian dashed back the way she'd come, but there was no Border Drone sound. For a moment she paused, standing still, perplexed.

Was the custodian truly as worried as he implied, or did he just want her gone?

Intrigued, Harra crouched low and followed the path back toward the building she'd almost slept the night inside. She watched the scurrying figure of the custodian enter the building, and then nothing happened. Nothing at all. Annoyed, she lingered, while the sun rose around her, lighting the day.

The damn bastard, she thought uncharitably, crouching in the hedgerow, Jessy almost half asleep at her feet. Just as she was determined to bang on the door and seek re-admittance, Harra heard a new sound, and stooped lower, watching.

All she could see were boots from where she sheltered, belonging to ten people. Boots, making their way inside the door, without so much as a knock to gain admittance.

But the people moved in silence, apart from their footfalls. Only when she bobbed up to look did she genuinely appreciate these were people who would hurt her, for they carried shapes on their hips, that gleamed in the new light of day against the black of their uniforms, 'BORDER PATROL' glittering in red, capital letters on their backs.

Harra's breath faltered, but still, she waited, until they were all inside, and then she dashed back to the field and hedge the custodian had left her at. She half ran along the hedge, crouching as low as possible, dreading the shout of discovery, but it never came. Not that she stopped. Only when Harra stumbled across the railway line did she even consider ceasing her headlong dash, and she quickly reconsidered. Ahead, she could see a dark gaping shape, and she headed toward it, rather than relying on the dense hedgerows of ancient fields, so huge she couldn't see from one end to the other.

Her feet slipping on the metal struts of the railway line, Harra walked forward, not looking behind her, or to the side, until the well of blackness surrounded her. A tunnel. Only then did Harra pause, reaching for her water bottle and drinking deeply, before allowing Jessy to have her fill.

Harra coughed and retched as the water hit her stomach, her fear turning the earlier meal to a rolling mass of heat in her stomach she violently vomited down the side of the tunnel wall.

Jessy whined, and Harra reached for her, feeling weak all of a sudden.

'Come on, girl,' she encouraged. 'We can't stay here. The train might come. I've no idea how often the train line gets used.'

Flicking her torch on, Harra flashed it along the dark tunnel, but the light didn't penetrate deep enough. Neither did a tell-tale flash of daylight show from the furthest end.

'I've no idea how long this thing is,' she moaned, staggering on her wobbly legs. Jessy was immediately at her side, and it was her turn to encourage Harra onwards.

Harra wavered over the metal lines depicting the train line, trying not to slip, as she fought for breath against the rising tide of panic. After all her nights of travelling in the dark, she was distraught to find herself panicking inside the long, dark tunnel. Alone, she might have simply sat and cried, admitting defeat. But Jessy didn't allow it.

What felt like hours later, but was only forty minutes, because Harra had checked her watch display at the beginning when it read 11:03 and then when a chink of daylight appeared, as it showed 11:42, Harra almost ran toward the light, so pleased to see it. Jessy dashed on ahead, her nose close to the ground, a low whine coming from her lips when they were almost within touching distance of the end.

Jessy stopped so abruptly, her rear legs almost shot over the top of her front ones.

'What is it, girl?' Harra asked, just about aware enough to realise something was wrong.

Abruptly, a shape walked into the light of the tunnel exit,

and Harra shrieked with fear, the sound echoing back the way she'd come until it passed over her head once more. Harra clamped her hand over her mouth. The noise was terrible.

Some sort of animal blocked their path, causing Jessy to growl angrily, taking up a position of protection in front of Harra, her low snarl threatening.

Harra glanced back the way they'd come but knew she couldn't walk back. She couldn't endure the suffocating dark again, not when she was so close to the end. Firming her shoulders, Harra pushed Jessy to one side, even though the dog complained, as she made her way around her faithful ally.

'Come on,' she said softly. 'We can do this.'

Hesitantly, she began to walk forward, one small step, and then another, barely daring to breathe. Jessy followed behind, a low growl in her throat adding menace to their perilous situation.

Closer and closer, the number of steps forwards no more than five to exit the tunnel, Harra stopped and peered closer. The creature was still there, but somehow appeared smaller now, and far less intimidating. Even Jessy's growls had dropped away to soft whimpers.

Harra was sure she recognised the creature.

A thrum of a purr and Harra dashed forward to confirm what she thought she knew.

The cat let the pair of them pass into the daylight, without any problems, and then sank on its hind legs. Harra looked at it.

'Is it really you?' she asked, just to be sure, expecting no answer, but she got one all the same, as Jessy walked up to the straggly looking creature, and placed a wet tongue on the cat's nose in welcome. The cat responded by rubbing her body along Jessy's, and both then sat and looked at her expectantly.

'How did you get here?' Harra asked. 'They said you wouldn't survive in the better air outside the smog.' But the cat looked well and healthy, her coat gleaming in the sunlight, her belly much fuller than when Harra had left her behind.

'Have you been tracking me all this way?' Again, she received no answer, but the cat abruptly stood and walked away. Jessy followed, unsure what was happening.

To the side of the tunnel, mere metres from the railway line, there was a small outhouse, leaning precariously to one side, and only upright because it nestled against the tunnel wall. A cracked wooden door had been pushed closed, but the cat butted it open with her head and walked inside. Harra followed. Perplexed.

The hut filled with soft cries and Harra gasped, seeing not one cat, but four of them. They were small bundles of fluff, nestled tight against the wall and with a piece of ragged cloth on the ground.

'Are these your... kittens?' Harra asked, searching for the right word. 'Wow?' she exhaled, unable to believe what she was seeing. The stray cat had followed her footsteps all the way to this wild environment to raise her kittens. Had she known, or had she hoped Harra would lead her to somewhere safer and healthier for the animals?

Harra crouched on her knees, examining the kittens, wondering if she could be brave enough to touch one with their soft ginger colouring, interspersed with white, but the mother cat was unconcerned, instead entwining herself around Harra and arching her back to smell the backpack.

Harra quickly understood and reached for the parcel of food she'd been given. She had two now, one from Ted and one from the custodian. She had more than enough to share.

It was, she was unsurprised to find, Ted's parcel that attracted the most attention, as she pulled the bread aside, and fed chunks of meat to the cat and Jessy both. She also poured some water onto the bread, softening it up, so the kittens could try and eat some of the food, and when that failed, she simply made a well in the bread and poured on water so the mother cat could drink her fill, Jessy as well.

Harra watched the kittens intently. They were content with round, full bellies, and it was evident the mother cat was both healthier herself, and feeding the animals well. It was purely by chance that Harra had come across them, for the cat had evidently been in place for a good few days.

She had no idea what kittens looked like when just born, but Harra looked at the linen again and realised that the cat hadn't come here to birth her kittens. No, it seemed as though she'd bought them with her, tied in the linen, which she must have carried in her mouth.

'Clever girl,' Harra said, reaching out to run a finger over the cat's ears. The animal preened under the compliment.

'Are you staying here, now?' Harra asked, looking around, worried about the proximity of the railway line for the small animals.

Of course, she got no reply.

The mother cat accepted her caresses, and then curled herself around her kittens, and closed her eyes, while they climbed over her, feeding from her distended belly. Harra watched, wishing she could stay and see the kittens grow to full size. But that was impossible. She had somewhere to be.

With a heavy heart, she sorted through what food stores she had, leaving the chunks of meat for the adult cat, and keeping only the bread for herself. She knew she'd be fed by the next custodian, and the meat might help the mother cat.

A soft tear in her eye, Harra reached over to the sleeping cat.

'Goodbye,' she said, her voice cracking. Then she stood, a parting look of acceptance on the face of the mother cat, or so she imagined, just the one eye opening in farewell. And then she walked out of the cracked wooden doorway, leaving just enough of a gap so the mother cat would be able to open the door when she needed to go outside.

Outside, the sun shone on, and she needed to get moving.

'Come on Jessy,' she commanded. 'A few more miles yet.;

Once more she looked behind her as she left, but the mother cat didn't follow her as she walked along the side of the railway line, and for that, Harra was grateful. She couldn't take five cats with her, a dog as well. Bloody hell. They might not let Jessy through The Wall, let alone a cacophony of cats.

Her thoughts were sorrowful, as she continued her journey, yet for all that, the deserted countryside she walked through eventually made an impact on her.

Harra might well walk along the railway line, but to the east, the coastline was clearly visible in the bright daylight. The track rose and fell with the landscape, and was raised higher in places to the low-lying fields. It afforded her views she'd never expected to see. Ever.

To the east, the sea came in and out of view, a temptation to her soul, and to the west, a hilly range struck ever higher, those hills in the far distance seeming to be coated with white fluffy clouds.

Initially, she feared detection, but her fears fell away with the delight of all she could feast her eyes on.

To the east, an ancient building abruptly came into sight, and she gasped. Was this, perhaps, a castle, as well? It shared similar characteristics, certainly. Harra paused, absorbing the view. Pinkish stone reared up from the top of a hill, a long building running the entire length, dotted with what could be towers, and encircling a square building, or so it appeared, ancient and built from different stone. It was majestic and awe-inspiring, and her feet almost took her there without any conscious thought.

Only when she tripped over her feet, did she force her eyes to look where she was going, and away from the castle. Only then another ancient structure to come into view on the seascape. This one was further away, and as she held her hand over her eyes to squint at the shape, she gave a gasp of surprise. This building seemed to be on an island, set into the sea, and neither was it alone. Other specks of islands abruptly came into sight as well.

From where she stood, the building appeared as a pinnacle of a small hill, but she was sure she could see smoke rising high into the air, mingling with the fluffy clouds. It must also be inhabited.

She laughed, the sound too loud in the quiet day, and she clamped her hand over her mouth at Jessy's censorious look.

How much more she would have seen had she only been allowed to travel during the day. But, perhaps that was the point. Having met Ted, and seen all this land had to offer, the thought of leaving forever was no longer as appealing as it should have been.

No doubt that would have been frowned upon by the inhabitants of the Far North.

Full darkness had fallen by 17:47 as Harra walked ever northwards. Meeting the cat, and the beautiful countryside she walked through, had made her retrospective, and her calf muscles ached, as her mind was once more filled with the images of those she was abandoning.

Her life had been so constrained in York. Yet, it seemed it hadn't needed to be. Now she knew how much the rest of England could offer her, was she so keen to leave it all behind?

The thought disturbed her firm resolve to leave, and she blamed herself for forming attachments to many of the people she'd met on her journey.

When she'd met the first custodians, she'd thought them cold and lacking any emotional warmth, but now she understood their aloofness. Better to hold yourself apart, than like people you were never going to see again.

With her torch sweeping the railway line in front of her, Harra tried to determine how far she'd walked that day. But it was impossible. She'd run for some of the day, barely crawled for some of it, walked with her eyes on the views around her while the daylight lasted, and now traipsed with heavy feet. She might have been on the move for hours, but in that time she might have gone no more than a few miles.

Without the constant road signs she'd come to rely on, despite their often battered and broken state, she couldn't determine where she was or how far she'd travelled.

Every so often the railway line intersected with a roadway. All of them were broken and in need of repair. They all offered the chance of making her way back to the main road she should have been travelling along, and where her custodian would be waiting for her, in about seven hours.

The first few times it happened in the dark, Harra fought down the desire to leave the railway line. It was safer on the railway line. Enough people had told her that to make her appreciate it was probably true.

To the east, she still heard the rustle of the sea but knew the sound was carried on the gentle breeze. The sea was far away. But, if the road to the left led to the main road, then the one to her right must lead to the sea. Or so she thought, arguing with herself, and making her path stay true.

By the tenth such occurrence, her resolve had weakened, in light of her fatigue from a broken night's sleep. The call of the sea was strong, as was the conflicting hope of a comfortable bed and a warm meal.

At the next intersection, Harra stood, listening to the soft breeze, trying to argue she should walk onwards, and not explore the other options available to her.

Glancing at her watch display, which read 19:23, Harra knew she should, by rights, have time to head toward the sea, rather than risk arriving at the Northern Road too early. Yet still, she argued with herself.

Her feet hurt, her legs, back and shoulders as well. Really, she wanted to do nothing but sit down and rest for a while. Jessy seemed to have the same idea. Time and time again, Harra had found herself coaxing the dog to her feet.

She walked on, Jessy whining.

'I'm tired too,' Harra complained without looking back, almost faltering when Jessy's tap tapping failed to catch her ear.

At the next intersection, Harra knew they'd have to stop.

The moon had risen in the cloudless sky, casting a pale glow over the stark landscape. Harra could just make out a building up ahead. Her pace increased. It would be good to find some shelter, rather than sleeping under one of the hedgerows with all their prickly spikes, while they waited for it to be time for her to meet the custodian.

Even Jessy seemed buoyed by the sight of the building.

As they came closer, Harra noticed the high walls to either side of the railway line and made the decision to leave it and walk along what seemed to be designed for pedestrians.

'I bet this is a station as well,' she said softly. 'Just like in Alnwick.'

A door materialised before her torch, and Harra tried the antique handle. It didn't want to turn, as Harra applied pressure, but then abruptly it did. Ahe walked inside an old building, built of stone, and smelling of the cold, if dry for all that.

Running her torch over the walls, Harra saw discarded wooden benches, and a pile of leaves piled up in the far corner. Clearly, the door was not always as stubborn as it had just been.

Swinging the torch in a full circle, Harra made her mind up.

'We'll rest here,' she said to Jessy. 'Just for a few hours, and then we'll head out to the Northern Road.' Jessy sat, and then lay down immediately in the pile of crisp leaves, clearly to be preferred to the hard stone floor.

Harra eyed the wooden benches; sure they were wide enough for her to sleep on. She eased the door closed, although not quite all the way, and sat for only the second time that day. Exhaustion swamped her as she settled her backpack as a headrest, and her eyes might well have been closed before she fully lay down on the bench.

In moments, her body had stilled in sleep.

A noise startled her awake, of footsteps outside, and fear gripped her belly, as a flash of torchlight slowly made its way ever closer to the slit of the open door.

Harra didn't dare move, happy to feel the weight of the torch in her slack hand. She'd kept it there, in the hope when she woke it would still be in easy reach. It seemed she'd been right.

Jessy was immediately at her side, with no rustling sound of leaves, which made Harra think the dog had been aware of the torch beam for some time. Why hadn't she woken her sooner? Not that it was Jessy's fault. Harra shouldn't have allowed herself to sleep quite so deeply.

The footsteps grew louder, the light as well, and Harra screwed her eyes closed as though protecting herself by not being able to see. Perhaps they wouldn't see her if she couldn't see them.

Her heart beat so fast Harra could hear nothing above the rush of her own blood through her ears. As such it took her long minutes to realise the sound of footsteps and the torch had receded without anyone even trying the door to see if someone was inside.

'What?' she whispered to Jessy, but Jessy had no answer.

Still, Harra waited a few minutes longer, just to be sure. Then, convinced whoever it had been was gone, she stood and made her way to the door. She listened again and then winced as she pulled the door open. It screeched so loudly Harra ground her teeth in frustration, waiting to see if the light reappeared. When it didn't, she yanked the door fully open and peered up and down what she knew was a train station.

'Come on, girl,' she said, rushing to fit her backpack in place, before erupting into the fresh night air. She skipped along the raised concrete beside the train line, to the intersection with the small road, and then headed to where she hoped the Northern Road lay. With any luck, her custodian would be waiting for her now and would be able to provide her with shelter for the night where she might finally be free from discovery.

Her feet pelted the cracked tarmac of the almost entirely overgrown road, and Jessy puffed at her side, but neither of them stopped until they reached another intersection, replete with all of its signs, the most welcome sight of 'The North' Harra had ever seen.

So intent was both Harra and Jessy on striding out along the found Northern Road, that neither of them heard the echo of an old tractor engine on the still night air, or heard Ted cry out Jessy's name.

———

The custodian for the night found them at a little after 03:23.

'Ah, there you are,' a kindly voice offered. 'I thought you might be a bit earlier.'

Harra offered no explanation, but followed the woman inside the metal door, pleased when it slammed shut behind her. Harra finally relaxed for the first time in nearly twenty-four hours.

'A bit of an adventure,' the woman smiled, her old face devoid of smooth skin, where one wrinkle cascaded into another. Harra had no idea how old she was but knew one thing; she was far older than her own grandmother.

'Good food, and a night of sound sleep, oh, and I can do your washing as well, and then tomorrow night will be your last long walk. Mind. I hear the weather is coming in a bit nasty.' Harra sat at the chair indicated in the kitchen, Jessy at her side, enjoying being told what to do.

'Here, drink that,' the old woman said, both to her and Jessy, although she left the bowl of water for Jessy on the table so Harra could bend to place it between the dog's paws. Harra wasn't surprised. The custodian was ancient beyond imagining.

Jessy drank thirstily.

'Strange whispers,' the woman said, placing a bowl of food before Harra that steamed so much, Harra couldn't see what it was, not to begin with.

'Cautions, and worry, not that it concerns me. Why would it?'

'Because of me?' Harra asked, worried.

'No, because there just is, every so often. Someone trying to get a bit of political clout from pretending to give a damn about what happens up here. They'll be back in the south in no time at all, coughing on their own muck. Damn fools.'

Harra nodded, trying a chunk of the enticing meat and then having to breathe through her teeth and reach for her glass, to cool her burning tongue.

'It'll be hot,' the custodian said, a rueful smile on her lined face, as she busied herself preparing food for Jessy and placing the bowl beside Harra, leaving her hand outstretched as she did so.

Obediently, Harra bent and retrieved the empty water

bowl, handing it back, before offering Jessy her own plate of food. This was something different to Harra's meal.

'Proper food, for a proper little dog,' the woman said, although her back was to Harra. 'Shouldn't always feed a beastie like her your own food. Not good for them. I had a dog like her when I was a girl. Brown and white, instead of black and white. She was called Molly. I loved that dog.' Fondness rippled through those words. 'I still miss her whine and look for her in my bedroom before I sleep at night. Ah, the follies of the old and bereaved.' The words were reticent, said once more with a smile.

Harra tried the food again, this time managing to chew on a piece of meat that was just a bit too hot.

'What is this?' she asked, juggling the food from one side of her mouth to the other so she could keep eating, despite it still being too hot.

'Pork, from the pigs. It's good in a meal like that. When I was a girl, we'd have called it Chinese food, but I don't think you're allowed to do that any more. Sweet and sour. It was always my favourite.'

'It's delicious,' Harra agreed.

'Aye, I just wish my old teeth would let me enjoy it these days, but they don't like to chew. Damn things.'

The woman bustled around the kitchen, filling the washing machine with Harra's dirty clothes from her bag, having wrinkled her nose at Harra's outdoor aroma, and then spooning food from the cook pot into smaller bowls. Whatever the complaints about her age, Harra saw no sign she was failing, other than a desire not to bend.

'Eat up, then get some sleep. I'll be here for most of the day. I gave up sleeping some time ago. Waste of time. If I look like I'm asleep, don't tiptoe around me, because it annoys me. Just do as you would, and if I'm awake, you'll know soon enough.' Indeed, there was a comfortable looking seat to the side of the table, raised a bit higher than usual, Harra imagined, through choice and necessity.

'Room number three,' the woman cackled, removing Harra's empty bowl and waiting for her to hand up Jessy's as well. 'Room number three, bathroom at the end.'

'My thanks,' Harra offered, standing, but the woman made no answer, so Harra left her to whatever tasks she was busy about, yawning as she went, thinking only of a quick bath and clean sheets for the night.

CHAPTER 16
STAGE 14, 15 & 16

'LEAVE AT PRECISELY 20:00 HOURS. RETURN TO THE NORTHERN ROAD AND WALK NORTH FOR 10 MILES.'

HARRA SETTLED ON THE SAND, the sea a pleasant accompaniment to the bright blue sky, although the wind stung like ice on her exposed cheekbones, and she was glad to have her coat.

At her feet, Jessy had burrowed herself into the sand, out of the full onslaught of the wind, and Harra nodded with satisfaction, wishing she could do the same. But time, as ever, was short, and she wanted to savour this last moment, despite her shivering.

Day Fourteen. Now she had until 02:08 to reach the cave and be ready to begin the final phases, Stages 15 and 16, of her escape.

Casting her mind back over the people she'd met, and the situations she'd encountered during her travelling ever northwards, she struggled to find the core of who she'd once been. She'd been a child. Now she wasn't.

Hope had guided her steps, of a better future, but now she needed more than hope, and also less of it.

Her family had sacrificed themselves for her future. She'd understood that when leaving home, but she'd not understood why. Now she did, and the sorrow and anger were immense.

Stupid. All of it. It always had been. Built on lies none would question, it had simply become the truth.

She could well understand why so many were loath to see through the lies. There had been an attraction, but that was long gone. Buried under self-interest.

The truth had been very different.

The people she'd encountered had shown her how to cope in this strange new England. Some had prospered, while others had utterly failed.

No longer did she think of returning home to her family. Now she thought to free them, and not just them. She thought to release everyone.

Walls were built to keep people out, not in, of that she was sure. She would demand that The Wall came down. Demand it.

The sand was cold but a comfort beneath her fingers, as she trickled the grains through her fingers. Such a simple thing, a view of the sea, and yet how many had seen it in recent years? Not like this. Cold, harsh, stark, dark blue meeting the paler oval of the sky. The scud of white clouds overhead. The roar of white waves in front of her.

Something to be appreciated for its simplicity, and perhaps more importantly, for being her right to see. There was no cost for this view. None at all.

Her watch read 16:34 and she knew it was time to go. The final miles, across rough terrain, the jagged hills in the distance seeming to have lost their edges with the gentle sunset. Into them, the jaws of her future, she must walk.

But hesitation stayed her feet and her hand.

To see a sunset, over this land, just one final time. After all, she'd only seen her first a few days ago.

At her side, Jessy whined, as though able to read the softly glowing numbers on Harra's wrist.

'Soon girl, soon,' Harra promised. It wouldn't be long. In

her hand, she had her torch ready for when the sun disappeared, in her other, she held the set of instructions.

Last night's custodian had been clear. The middle-aged woman had been rudely efficient, but not unpleasant. Indeed, when Harra had asked, she'd directed her to this spot, to see the sea.

Still, Harra should not lose the instructions, that much was imperative. No matter what, Harra must take the directions with her. No one could find them on this side of The Wall. On that matter the woman had been the most adamant Harra had ever seen anyone. Not to protect her, the custodian had exclaimed, she didn't care, but the rest of the custodians needed to be protected. It would hardly be difficult to work out who did, and who didn't aid the escapees if the instructions were mislaid.

No one could know the truth.

Harra had assured the custodian she'd take the instructions with her, and now they weighed her down. Something else to add to the burdens she already carried.

Between one blink and the next, the sun was gone below the horizon, the pinks and oranges winking out to be replaced by a cool grey, and Harra struggled to her feet, sand pooling from her body, as she shivered. The wind was fierce. Perhaps it would calm as she journeyed in and.

The torch flickered on, showing her the way to go, into the darker recesses of the hilly countryside, as Jessy scampered to her paws.

The final part of her journey. She just wanted it over and done with, but there was no joy in that. The excitement of her earlier days was gone. Fierce resolve guided her steps now. Ever onwards.

In no time at all, they were back at the Northern Road, and then they were across it, following old and long abandoned roads, cracked and broken with vegetation, through villages that glowed faintly ghostly in the glare of her torch. There was no life here, only death, decay and abandonment.

Past old churches, where no one worshipped any more, along hedgerows long since restored to the wild, their reaching limbs, trip hazards wherever she walked, wildlife rustling deep inside them, frightened by the beam of yellow torchlight they were so unused to seeing. The wild was reclaiming what had once been civilised. As it should be, or so Harra thought.

She'd believed York was terrible, but here it was worse. In York people still lived and tried to work, but the last ten miles of her journey was through a dead land. No one could live there. Not so close to The Wall and the threat of the Border Drones.

Jessy padded quietly at her side, sensing the mood, the stark reality of the truth of The Wall.

A place of dead things, apart from wildlife, and trees, plants and flowers. They all grew with wild abandon, the problems of surviving against humankind mostly forgotten.

Harra sighed, tears falling from her eyes.

Such a waste. Always a waste.

She thought of her father, and his rages, written for her to see.

He had known. He had understood what the future would hold.

Perhaps they all had, in the end, but had been too stubborn to admit they were wrong.

A scuff of a footfall and Harra stopped, her ears straining. Had it been her or someone else?

Overhead, dark clouds swarmed, and Harra knew there would be rain to drench her and drown out all noise. The old custodian of two nights before had warned her rain was coming. She'd been a day out, nothing more.

Harra pressed on.

If anyone followed her, she couldn't hear him or her, and that meant they weren't truly there. Too many nights of late had been spent worrying about strange noises. No more. Harra welcomed the rain, even when it caused her torch to splinter its light, as though fingers covered the mechanism, making shadows where there were none.

When her watch display read 22:35, Harra came to the landmark mentioned in the instructions. An old building, built alone, on a rise, and highlighted by the moon, despite the heavy clouds and continuing rain. She smirked. It was illuminated better even than the arrow that had pointed her the right way on the first night travelling north.

Whoever had trodden this path before her, and laid down the 'Stages' that had to be followed, had been both very precise, and very smart. They hadn't chosen anything that a foot-weary soul would miss, no matter the weather.

The gate she needed to walk through appeared before her, the long struts of wood, covered in moss, barely on ancient hinges, that screeched open as she kicked it free, her gentle attempts at coaxing it with her hands and bum, having failed.

She winced, but the rain was relentless. If anyone heard the noise, then they'd have had to be breathing down her neck, and she'd heard nothing to suggest she was being followed. Not for a long time.

Peering upwards, Harra took the time to appreciate the moon-cast glow of the crumbling stone building. Turning slowly, she looked back the way she'd come, surprised to find how high up she must be. She'd not felt the burn of a steep climb in her calves. Even from here, the sea was illuminated, depicted in a rich shade of velvet by her second companion, the moon.

'Goodbye,' she whispered, kicking the gate closed, and checking her instructions in the glow of the torch.

As she thought.

She headed across the path of the old building, ever westwards, quickly losing sight of it as she was enveloped by hills.

'Not much further,' she comforted Jessy, but the dog remained silent.

Harra wondered what Jessy made of all this. Her unlooked for companion, and yet a stalwart all the same.

On and on she went. The ground squelched underfoot, and every so often, the slope downhill was so steep, she slipped and ran to the bottom, before beginning the journey back up the other side.

The moon slunk away, hidden by the hills, and Harra felt utterly alone in the moonless night. She could have been the only person alive in the world, and it wouldn't have surprised her.

Down another steep slope, and her hand hit something hard, and she winced, the pain of cold fingers jarring against wood. Yet, she ran them over the wooden post and then shone her torch on it. As expected, the sign she thought was on it, old, scarred, perhaps made of tin. 'The Scottish Border,' with a finger pointing back the way she'd come.

Now she just needed to find her cave, and shelter there until her watch, which read 00:04 flicked to 02:08 and she could begin.

Time was dragging. She'd thought it might. Yet she also needed to be alert.

Not that she crossed the path of the Border Drones, not yet, but, as had become clear, they didn't always stick to their flight paths.

Harra would have liked to pause, to view the area she must soon cross, but again, the custodian had made it clear once she was this close, she needed to reach the cave as soon as possible.

Head down, Harra followed the curve of the hill.

The grassy slopes had given way to rugged rocks, and

Harra slipped more than once on the uneven terrain, wincing with pain, but refusing to cry out. In front, Jessy skipped more freely, sniffing as she went, and Harra hoped she'd find the cave entrance soon.

To her right, the spectre of The Wall, was now a reality, out there, calling for her attention, but still, she ignored it. She must reach the cave before she did anything else.

A whine from in front and Harra choked off a gasp of horror as Jessy disappeared, only to reappear moments later, just her head showing.

At last. The end of almost the final stage of her journey.

'Good girl,' she whispered, thrusting her torch inside to check the cave was empty.

The stench of decay and rot reached her nostrils, and she all but gagged, before carefully reversing into the small hole. Jessy's doggy breath right in her face, and yet Harra preferred it to the stench of the cave.

'Good girl,' she said once more, lifting Jessy down the three rock built, steep steps to the floor of the cave. But before she followed her, Harra turned, forcing her head outside the cave to finally see The Wall.

It gleamed in the rain, as though made from marble, the stark white driving back the darkness as only a light normally could. Even with the moon almost hidden by the heavy clouds, The Wall glowed. There was no other word for it.

Harra had been expecting lights to illuminate The Wall, to show its length and height but there was no need. It was an impenetrable block of shimmery stone, towering into the sky, seemingly without a means through it.

Harra understood then that this Wall might just have been the greatest accomplishment of all. The final knife in the back from the Scottish to the English, who'd turned their back on all incomers to England.

She swallowed around the sorrow that brought her and then heard a strange whirring noise. She ducked, convinced a Border Drone flew close to her, perhaps wavering off course, but in fact, the Border Drone was close to The Wall, across the expanse of abandoned land, illuminated by its small red dot of light.

Harra shook her head, and forced herself away, to join Jessy on the hard, cave floor.

Jessy watched her expectantly, as Harra rustled through her backpack, searching for their final shared treat, wrapped in a piece of clean linen.

The dog had been much spoilt by the custodian, and inside, Harra uncovered thick sandwiches filled to overflowing, which Jessy sat and waited for, most patiently.

Harra fed her until she was sated, and then poured water onto her hand for her to lick. Only then did she consider her own comfort.

Her stomach rumbled, but she knew food was beyond her. Now here, in the final moments, she was nervous. She could not come so far, only to fail. It was inconceivable, and yet the area she needed to dash across seemed much broader than she'd imagined.

All those miles she'd walked in the preceding days, and this distance seemed the longest of them all.

To distract herself, she sorted through what she needed.

It had been a long time since she'd been injected with the gloopy liquid in the bags. She felt it had made her grow stronger, before, but it had also made her woozy and forgetful. Now, the sight of the gloopy bag she'd kept safe all this time, the clear tube, with the needle attached tormented Harra.

Why? Why take the risk?

But was it a risk?

But the gloopy contents had been in her possession for a

while now. Surely it wouldn't be good to inject it into her body? Surely she was asking only for trouble?

Annoyed, she left the items on the floor, and swung the torch into the cave again, searching the floor, hoping for some sign of those who'd come before.

Yet she found nothing, and that irked her. Having been told continuously to leave possessions behind on this final stage, Harra wanted to see what others had been forced to abandon. But there was nothing but the scent in the air. Perhaps that was enough. Death and decay. Did it come from the rocks and the ground, or from those who'd died here?

Returning to her collection of items, Harra shone the light against the entrance of the cave, noticing how the rain pooled into the cave, dropping down until it encountered the floor where she sat.

Grimacing, she lifted all of her items from the filling floor and found a stone shelf off the ground. Jessy quickly joined her.

Harra checked her watch.

01:08.

Still, an hour to go.

What could she do for another hour? How could she pass the time?

Jessy settled, her head on her lap, and Harra stroked the damp fur, amused by the contended rumble from the dog.

'Daft thing,' she laughed, the sound echoing too loudly so she clapped her hand over her mouth.

Sound, she'd been warned against. Sound and light.

A click, click, whirl from outside, heard over the rain, and Harra was reaching for the catch on the torch, plunging them into darkness, her hand over Jessy's mouth in warning.

The dog eyed her warily but kept quiet. She was too trusting. Jessy would do anything Harra asked of her.

The whirl grew ever louder, and then a spattering of red dots illuminated the interior of the cave, on the back wall. Harra was pleased now she'd moved, but still, she held her breath, hoping this was the extent of the machine's penetrations.

Harra heard a collection of beeping noises, and then the spots of red disappeared.

'Bloody hell,' she whispered to Jessy, her heart thudding so her legs felt deadened beneath her. 'I forgot,' she apologised to the dog, but Jessy, her own eyes calmed, seemed not to understand.

Harra settled again, the sound of the rain outside, lulling her to calmness, but not to sleep.

Not long now. Or so she told herself.

How quickly the time passed, with nothing to do but stroke Jessy and hope she made it across the abandoned land.

01:41

eventually came, and with it, Harra's legs began to jump of their own accord.

She gritted her teeth against the nerves, seeking solace from the steady downpour of the rain, resisting the urge to jump to her feet and make sure everything was in order in her backpack. She knew it was. It had been since she'd first arrived.

No, she sought her inner calm, happy memories that were not too sad as to make her wish to head back to her mother and grandmother. No, they were memories of her father, when she was a child, teaching her how to form her letters, read a book, so she could keep up with the other children, when she finally started school.

She banished the image of her father's drawn face as he

took her to school on that first day and the grey pallor infecting him when he'd come to pick her up, and thought only of his joy and delight, at her own glee at going to school.

Now, she realised, it had been a poor excuse of an education, but that didn't matter, not any more. It had been her father's wish, and she would have done anything for him, even then.

She smiled through her tears of memory. If only he could see her now, what would he think?

02:00

finally showed on her watch display. Harra sat quietly a little longer, listening, always listening for the strange whirling, clicking sound of the Border Drones.

The rain hadn't stopped, if anything, it had intensified, and she reminded herself of how difficult it had been to make her way over the tricky terrain. If the abandoned land before The Wall was the same, then she needed to be careful, and not just run, as she'd been advised. No, she'd need to be careful.

She made her way back toward her possessions, listening intently against the hum of the rain. Into her hands she placed the gloopy bag, hoping to warm it between her hands, a little numb from the damp, and now from sitting still for so long. Returning to Jessy, she sat rubbing the dog's belly, until she rolled over a little, and then she slipped the bag beneath her, cushioned by one of her jumpers. She knew Jessy wouldn't burst it.

She returned to her things, and grabbed the clear tubing and the needles, recalling everything she'd been taught by her aunt, uncle and mother. It wouldn't be easy, alone, but Jessy would help, if she could.

02:06.

Harra tickled Jessy until she returned the gloopy bag to her, and then settled herself beside the dog, out of sight of any prying eyes or the invasive red dots of the Border Drones.

'Here goes nothing,' Harra laughed, shakily. Her legs had stopped thrumming on the stone, but her voice caught in her throat. She was still nervous.

02:08.

Her sleeve already rolled up, Harra perforated the gloopy bag with the needle and then turned to her own arm. The swirling blood was already beginning to snake its way along the transparent tube. Quickly, she stabbed her arm, feeling the chill of the liquid entering her body.

She juddered, not from nerves, but with revulsion at what she was doing.

Tasting bile, she tried not to watch the procession into her arm and instead turned to watch the time advance on her watch.

Of all things, she wasn't prepared to miss the right time.

02:10.

The gloopy bag was empty, and Harra yanked the needle free with disgust and then moved down from her step with Jessy. The dog watched her with passive eyes, perhaps perplexed, or perhaps aware of what was happening.

Harra reached for the tube of glue to heal her tiny pinprick mark, and then she cleared away the final marks of her presence. She'd been told not to take the empty gloopy bag with her, but where to leave it so no one would find it?

A slither of plastic caught her eye, in a nook, just above where she'd been sitting. On tiptoe, she pushed her own bag there, not prepared to check if there were other needles already there. Indeed, she went to the trouble of thrusting both needles deep into the gloopy bag. She didn't want to hurt anyone should they come across her leavings.

'Come here girl,' she then called to Jessy, reaching for her backpack at the same time. 'We need to be ready, and we need to go together. You must stay with me,' she cautioned the dog, abruptly realising without Jessy she didn't think she'd go on. No, Jessy was her comfort now, and they'd be free, together.

With a final listen, Harra lifted Jessy onto the ledge they'd entered the cave by, up the three steep steps, cautioning her to stop with her hand on her head. Jessy hovered. Unsure whether to sit or leave, as Harra climbed to join her, torch in hand, although not turned on.

The only light came from the watch.

Green, it glowed.

02:13.

02:14.

02:15.

Harra turned the torch on quickly and swept it around the cave. Nothing. She had everything she was going to need.

02:16.

She forced her way through the slick cave entrance. Her front was drenched, even beneath her coat as she emerged into the gloomy night. The moon was fled, the rain making visibility almost nothing.

'Stay with me girl, please,' she begged, calling Jessy to her side. The dog came unwillingly, apparently having had enough of the rain.

'Run with me, now,' Harra gave the order, and set off, unable to look behind her to check her companion followed.

The last part of the slope was both slick and boggy with the rain. Harra feared for her boots, but she went on, ever northwards. The torch bounced in her hand, sending stray sparks of light all over the ground pockmarked with puddles.

The closer she got to the impenetrable menace of The Wall, she splashed through more and more puddles. It had seemed huge from the distance of the cave, now it reared before her as a behemoth that would stamp on her and grind her into insignificance.

On she ran, fearing to hear the whirring click click of the Border Drones.

Jessy rushed just in front of her, and Harra laughed at her enthusiasm as she streaked through the abandoned land. On and on they went. She glanced at her watch.

02:17.

She was amazed no more than a minute had gone by.

Jessy's legs flew in and out of the torchlight, where it focused on a stretch of The Wall before them, a part that had looked indistinguishable from any of the others, but into which she'd been instructed to run. Only now did Harra notice it seemed to expand over the abandoned land, perhaps twice as far out as the marble of the rest of The Wall.

'Come on, girl,' she gasped, pointing toward the part of The Wall she wanted to go toward, even though Jessy couldn't possibly understand.

As she swerved, just a little, to ensure her path was correct, Jessy dipped out of the torch's beam.

'Jessy,' she cried, unheeding of the warning she must be quiet.

'Jessy,' Harra called again when the dog didn't immediately reappear in the right place.

02:18.

She had but moments. Where was Jessy? Where was her friend?

She ran on, hoping Jessy would come to her. 'Jessy,' she called again, coming to an abrupt stop just before The Wall, and the place she'd been instructed to put her hand on.

'Jessy,' she cried, sagging to her knees, her breath little more than a whisper, not carrying on the sodden air at all.

'Jessy,' she swept the torch over the path she'd just trodden, but still it didn't pick up Jessy's swishing tail and bright eyes.

'Jessy,' her watch displayed

02:19

and she was out of time. She stood, eyeing the flashing panel before her with distrust. She knew what needed to be done.

'Jessy,' she bellowed once more, as a small compartment opened and pricked her fingers viciously. The tablet glowed red.

'No access.'

She turned once more, hoping for a sight of Jessy.

The whirling and click of a Border Drone reached her ears, the red probe of its sensors sneaking their way along The Wall toward her.

'Jessy,' she cried, no longer caring if she was detected.

Beside her, the tablet abruptly flickered to green, words pooling across the screen that she could hardly read.

'Legal agreement.'

'Term and conditions.'

'Please acknowledge and accept.'

A wet dog landed in her arms, just after she pressed the 'accept' button and a door opened behind her, the red dot of the Border Drone highlighted on the interior beyond.

'Get in,' a voice coughed, shock rippling through it, as an ear piercing alarm enveloped them, the sound almost enough to arrest all movement.

'Get inside.' A command now.

Harra did just that, falling to her back, Jessy in her arms, as the door closed in front of her.

CHAPTER 17
IT ENDS AT THE WALL

A HAND on her arm caused her to scream, unsure what was happening, as the loud wailing noise ceased on the closure of the small door.

Squinting in the light that was suddenly too bright, Harra tried to decipher what was happening.

One moment she'd been calling for Jessy, waiting for the light on display to turn green, and the next she'd been the focus of a Border Drone, trying to focus its weapon range on her. Was she safe, or not?

Around her feet, Jessy wound, first one way and then the next, as unsure as Harra was, both of them dripping wet, the water pooling from their bodies onto the white floor beneath them. Harra wasn't sure she'd ever been so wet in all her life, and she'd been caught out a few times on the journey.

'Welcome,' a deep voice gave her something fresh to focus on, and she turned to meet the sparkling eyes, and there truly was no other word than sparkling, of a young woman and a slightly older man.

They seemed to be wearing some sort of uniform, as their clothes matched. Both wore heavy-duty black boots, and their clothes were navy blue. Harra blinked and then squinted at them.

'He, hello,' she managed to say. Above her head, there was strip lighting that accounted for the brightness, although the stark white corridor didn't help.

'Follow us, we'll take you through,' the man said, his voice filled with joy.

'Oh, okay,' Harra said, she wasn't sure what she'd been expecting, but knew it wasn't this. Not at all.

'You're Rhiannon's first,' the male voice continued. 'She's just as excited as you are. I'm Bruce, by the way.'

'My dog's called Jessy,' Harra said, on safer ground. And then, faced with such friendliness from both of them, as they walked down the short corridor continued. 'I'm Harra.'

'Welcome to Scotland,' Rhiannon trilled. She truly did sound excited.

'Thank, thank you,' Harra tripped over her words again. She was mystified. The instructions had stopped with her hand pressed against the keypad. What happened next was unknown, but, in all the times she'd considered it, this hadn't been what she'd thought would happen next.

The man pushed open a door and gestured her inside.

There was someone else sat at a large desk, a welcoming expression on his or her face as well.

'Margaret will help you with everything that needs to be done,' Rhiannon explained, bending to stroke Jessy.

'Your dog's lovely,' she offered and then turned to leave.

'Good luck,' the pair chorused as the door swung closed behind them.

Margaret observed Harra, and in light of her smart navy suit, Harra felt dirty and messy.

'Don't worry, just a few questions, and then you can go through, and we'll sort you out with everything you need. I know you've already been welcomed by the border guards, but I too would welcome you to Scotland. I take it the journey was hard going, but everything will be okay from now on.'

Harra tried to smile but was struggling to process the array of emotions she felt.

As though sensing her confusion Margaret smiled once more.

'Give yourself time. It'll all become more normal to you than what you're used to. Now, did you say your name was Harra?'

'Yes, yes I did, and my dog is Jessy.'

'Hello Jessy,' Margaret said, leaning around the table to look at Jessy who seemed to be coping with the abrupt change far better than Harra.

'We'll have a vet check her over, but she seems healthy enough to me. A fine breed. I have a spaniel myself.'

Spaniel? The word was unknown to Harra, but she nodded all the same.

'Harra, do you know your date of birth? This is just to enter you into the system, you know so those who need to know can work out how many people make it through The Wall and how old everyone is. It's nothing to worry about.'

'I was born on June 26th 2032,' Harra said. 'In York, or so I understand it to be.'

'Do you have the names of your parents, just so we can add them as well?'

'Yes, yes, my mother is called Rebecca and my father was called Harry.'

'So your mother yet lives,' Margaret asked, not unkindly.

'Yes, she does, and my aunt and uncle. My grandmother as well.'

'But they didn't come with you?'

'No, no, they could only afford to send my cousin and me.'

Something like fury swept over Margaret's face, but her questions remained gentle.

•

'Did your cousin already make it? If you have his name, I can ensure he knows you're here?'

'William,' Harra blurted without thought, but Margaret smiled.

'Oh yes, I processed him too. I must say, you look much better than he did when he first crossed The Wall. I can assure you he's fit and well, and already making decisions about his studies for the future. He's been relocated to Edinburgh, not far from here. I seem to remember he mentioned you when he first arrived, but he was exhausted and confused. Poor boy.' Genuine sympathy marked the woman's words.

Harra remained silent. This was all far too pleasant. She'd expected to face sanctions when she arrived, not be accepted in such a way.

Margaret was watching her again, as though waiting for the inevitable question.

'We're always keen to welcome new members to Scotland. Of course, you can go anywhere you want now you've made it to The Wall, but we do always hope people will stay here and build new lives.'

'Are we not a burden to your society? Are we not sent back if we're caught?'

'Why would we do that?' Margaret asked, her forehead furrowed in thought. 'There's much you must learn, to begin your new life, but I'll tell you this, while your new documents are processed. Much of what you know, and what you've been told, is a lie. The biggest lie of all you've been told is that The Wall was built by Scotland.'

Harra's mouth dropped open in shock.

'Yes,' Margaret said. 'It strikes most people that way. The English, on the instructions of their politicians, built The Wall. It wasn't built to keep you out of Scotland by the Scottish, no, no, it was built by the English, to keep you in.'

Harra shook her head in denial.

'Then why the secrecy, the need to pay, the need to change our blood?'

Margaret was shaking her head.

'There's no need. None at all. All are welcome. Regardless of their political inclinations. I believe the instructions are a way for the unscrupulous to benefit from the misery of those desperate to escape. They charge exorbitant sums to provide what they do.'

Harra was speechless, shaking her head quickly in denial.

'But,' she said, again. And then 'but' once more.

'I have, I have this journal, I was supposed to leave it behind, but I couldn't bring myself to. It tells me all about the building of The Wall.' As she spoke, Harra reached into her bag and pulled out her father's journal. It was tatty and frayed after its long journey, but still intact.

Margaret looked at it at first in surprise, and then with intrigue.

'May I look?' she asked, holding her hand out. Harra, although unsure, eventually handed over the journal fearing that if she didn't, she'd be sent back through The Wall.

Turning the first page, Margaret's face softened.

'You look very much like her,' she offered, before lapsing into silence, turning page after page. Harra was alert to her every move and saw a flurry of emotions engulf the woman's face. As she turned to the back page, Margaret met Harra's eyes.

'This is filled with the lies of your government at the time The Wall was built. It's a priceless thing for you, I understand that, but there are historians of The Wall who would learn much from studying your journal. And they could teach you a great deal as well. If you wanted,' Margaret finished, handing the journal back into Harra's keen hand. 'We know little of what happens in England now. It's a secretive Government that has control.' She paused, as though considering what else to do.

'You'll learn much more, in time, but for now what you need to know is this. It's your own Border Drones patrolling the land before your side of The Wall. They do so on the orders of your politicians, who built The Wall to keep the English inside. It's they who don't want you to leave England, who'll kill you to prevent you from leaving. They must preserve their population as best they can, and they do it through lies and threats.'

Harra nodded as though she understood, but she didn't, not really.

'Your father's scrapbook would enable people here to help those beyond The Wall. But it's your choice if you wish to share it with them.'

Again, Harra heard the words but didn't understand them.

'How?' Harra asked, but Margaret shook her head.

'It's not for me to explain such complicated legal matters, but there are some who will, in time.'

There was a low buzzing noise as Margaret finished speaking, and she looked down and then moved to pick something up.

'Here you go,' Margaret said, offering Harra a random selection of items.

'The wrist band should always be worn. It has all of your details on it. As you find somewhere to live and choose a profession, it'll be automatically updated. There's a keypad for you as well. You can ask it anything you want, or you can type on it. It'll be your guide during the next few days. And last, but not least, you have a new passport and birth certificate. We still make them from paper, but the information is also stored in your wrist band.'

Margaret stood then, and Harra rushed to do the same.

Margaret held out her hand to Harra and Harra hurried to grasp it.

'I'd like to officially welcome you to Scotland, and I wish you all the best for your future.'

With that, a door opened on the opposite wall to the one she'd first entered, and another smiling face greeted her.

'Hello, Harra. If you follow me, I'll take you where you need to go and get you sorted. No doubt you're hungry. I'll sort food as well. Thank you, Margaret.' Harra did as instructed, walking from the plain white room, and outside. She'd assumed it would be another corridor, but instead, Harra stepped onto rolling green grass, and into bright daylight.

The woman handed her sunglasses, to shield her eyes from the too bright light, but Harra wanted to see the sun and the sky and the soft white clouds unfiltered for the first time in this strange new land.

Water streaming from her eyes, Harra took one step, then two and then three, Jessy running free from her side, barking with raucous delight.

This was it. All the lies she'd been told had ended at The Wall.

Now, she was truly free to discover the truth. All of it.

CHAPTER 18
2017
32 YEARS EARLIER

'SHOULD WE BE DOING THIS?' a voice called out in the dark.

'Just shut up and get on with it,' was the snapped reply. 'You signed up, remember? NO questions, no answers, just get on with it.'

The shuffle of paper on paper filled the air. There were many of them there. All working in silence, under minimal light, so none could truly see what they did or who they did it with.

With three bags filled, he moved them into the waiting back of the large van. Unconvinced the truck would reach capacity, he worked quickly all the same. The sooner the floor was clear of all the pieces of paper, the sooner it would be time to move on to the next part of his bizarre night's work.

On the other side of the hall, another door was open, another van also being loaded, only with different papers. People were patrolling the area between the two piles of paper, and he was desperate to know what they did and why there was segregation.

A long time passed, in utter silence, many, many sacks

filled with the small flyers, and only then, when he was scurrying around on his hands and knees, did he feel able to read what he was picking up.

Confusion knit his brow as he looked at what he held.

'What the?'

He, of course, knew what he held, but why did they want the papers packaged in such a way? His experience told him such things were kept for a year before being destroyed. This, though, felt very different.

Yet, he held his tongue, reaching for another ballot paper and then another, as many as he could, quickly scanning them all before he placed them in his sack. All of them, without fail, had a cross against the 'Leave the European Union' question.

'Are we done?' a harsh voice called across the hall.

'Yep, all done here,' was the firm reply.

'Then we'll be leaving. Have you arranged for someone to lock up?'

'Yes, yes, I have. I'll wait for them and then leave.'

'No problem.'

He followed that voice to the truck, where the doors were slammed shut and secured.

'You drive,' the other demanded, and he strode for the driver's side door.

He was a trucker and had been all his life. For some reason, his company had been employed to transport this vehicle to Edinburgh. He wasn't sure why unless there was a vast recycling plant there.

Turning the key in the ignition, the vehicle leapt to life, and he carefully drove free from the building and joined the A1 Northbound on the odd little junction that never quite gave enough warning to drivers joining the dual carriageway. It would be a pain of a journey until they reached the Scottish Border, most of the road just a single carriageway. But it was still dark, very early morning, and he looked forward to watching the sunrise over the stunning coastline as he drove.

At his side, the person who accompanied him slunk into their seat and was quickly snoring. He turned the radio up just enough to drown out the noise and then concentrated on his driving and the view. He expected the other vehicle to be close behind, but he never saw it and quickly realised it must have gone a different way.

He was curious, trying not to consider the implications but doing so all the same.

A year since the EU Referendum, and all was shit and crappy politics. He tried not to listen to the arguing politicians. Didn't they have anything better to do?

When they arrived on the outskirts of Edinburgh, he turned the volume on the radio up sharply, keen to wake his sleeping passenger.

The passenger grunted and groaned and then reached for a piece of paper. Directions. He barked them out, and the driver obeyed, growing even more and more confused when they pulled up, not outside a recycling facility or shredding facility, but rather a building that looked more like a laboratory.

'We just need to wait until they get here, and then we can unload, and head back.'

He nodded, turning the truck off and sitting in the warm cab as his stomach slowly rumbled. Driving always made him hungry.

It didn't take long before men and women in white lab coats swarmed to the truck.

'Stay inside,' he was told. 'Your job here is just to be the driver.'

Yet, he watched all the same as sack after sack was carried inside. What were they doing with the ballot papers?

He'd been paid a lot for such a simple driving task. He'd

jumped at the chance at the time, but now he felt uneasy. What were they doing?

'Come on then, back we go,' his passenger said, already giving instructions to return to the by-pass that would take them, eventually, to the A1 Southbound.

As he drove off, he caught a glimpse of the building in his side mirrors, and men and women pouring from fancy-looking cars, a bit like on the TV when royalty or politicians visited places.

'Just drive,' his passenger instructed, and he did as told.

———

Inside the building, the task of stacking the papers began. It was not easy, but neither was it hard. Fiddly was perhaps the best word.

She worked quickly and concisely, one of those funny orange rubber stamps on her finger to help her promptly sort the papers without having to lick her finger continually.

She grimaced at what she was being forced to touch. The papers smelt stale from being stored in a dry environment, and she wasn't the only one to keep sneezing.

This wasn't really her task, and yet she wanted to at least say she'd been involved before her work turned into the most crucial task.

She'd initially been perplexed and confused when they'd come to her with their questions. But now she had a greater understanding and respect for what they hoped to achieve. That they were also paying a tremendous amount for this task wasn't to be ignored either.

She could only hope it worked, as she'd promised.

Taking her pile of ballot papers to the machine, she lined them up carefully with the intake feed. It would be unfortunate if the machine snagged immediately, although she did foresee problems with the particularly scrunched-up ballot papers. She'd already set up a staging place where those ballots could be processed by hand. It was another cost 'they' would have to meet.

With a swift prayer and a steady hand, she spooled the machine to begin and looked at the touch screen before her. It was busy, flashing with each ballot paper, as a photo of it was taken and then sent to the next computer to process. This one was much faster, and she watched as the programme she'd written quickly identified a few key elements from the ballot paper, hunting for fingerprints as it did so.

They'd been adamant about this. There'd be many fingerprints on each ballot paper, not just the person who'd cast a vote. They wanted to exclude the poll clerks, the counters, and any other person who might have legitimately touched the paper, including the printers. They wanted the principal fingerprint, perhaps closest to the crossed mark and more than likely, on the back of the paper as well. These would be the fingerprints of the voter.

Why they wanted the fingerprints of those who'd voted to leave the EU, she wasn't sure, but she had an inkling, especially with the shit storm taking place around the whole Brexit fiasco.

She was Scottish. She cared only for Scotland and always would. The English? Well. They didn't think as she did and she pitied them.

On a third machine, her colleague was watching as more and more information was fed into it. This machine was the master one. It would pool all the available data and sort it via an algorithm into a usable programme to quickly identify everyone using their fingerprints.

She swallowed heavily as the first results began to come through.

This was it. It was a travesty of the rules governing the

voting electorate of the United Kingdom which stipulated all votes should be kept secret and destroyed 12 months after the election. Yet it excited her to be witnessing such an event, and to know that she'd manage to produce what she'd promised to 'them.'

This then would forever mark people for what they'd done.

She shivered at the thought.

For those who'd voted to leave the EU, there would be no hiding from the decision made on that fateful day. Not for them. And not for their descendants, who'd forever be marked by the fingerprints and DNA of those who'd cast their votes.

2030, 19 YEARS EARLIER

THEY GATHERED LIKE HOUNDS, scenting their prey.

Few would meet the eyes of the other, but they knew all the same what they were about to set in motion.

Was it self-interest or greed? Perhaps interchangeable. Or were some probably assured their dogma was the only way forward?

Together, or not at all.

They had the tools at their fingertips, ready to set loose, should they choose to, and they would. They all knew that.

Still, there must be one final agreement—another act of unity so none could ever blame the other.

Their blame game was old and tired, their victims too bamboozled by it all to truly understand the extent to which they'd been betrayed by these men and women who, in their own interests, had become the overseers of all that was right and wrong. All that could happen and all that could not.

None dared to even think of how their actions mirrored other despots in the past and of how those regimes had tumbled.

It would not happen this time. It could not. This was the

United Kingdom. Once THE only superpower the world had known, an Empire stretching all around the globe.

Yet one of them must speak. Say the words.

All of them looked one from the other, not wanting to be 'the one' to set in motion the long years of planning, haphazard on occasion, totally spontaneous at others. All supported through thick and thin by their 'own' kind.

The moment dragged, the tension rising around the conference table. Perhaps it should have been round, as legend told of King Arthur and his knights. But no, it was an elongated sphere. Not quite equal, but almost.

Before them, some flicked a final time through the document they read, the words before them giving them a brief pause for thought but nothing more.

They'd lied and schemed, lied some more, and then they'd done worse when the lies had been discovered. They'd made up their own truths. Anything, anything, could be used as the weapon they needed to get their way.

They wouldn't be laughed at or ridiculed for their false ideas. They'd not allow another to say a word that doubted what they'd promised. No, they'd promised it, and they would do it. As democratically voted for.

This final act was to be the ultimate betrayal, and their argument would always be that it was what 'the people' had democratically voted for.

'It's agreed then?' a lone voice, brokering no argument although the words were a question.

'We must all say it out loud,' the voice reiterated. 'Around the table, one at a time. I'll begin. I agree.' The face looked expectantly at the person next to it.

'I agree.'

'I agree.'

'I agree.'

And so it went on.

'I agree.'
'I agree.'
'I agree.'

Some voices were firm; others broke a little, showing the sign of strain.

'I agree.'
'I agree.'
'I agree.'

And then the final two. Of them, would either refuse? It had to be unanimous, or they wouldn't proceed.

'I agree.'
'I agree.'

The last rushed as though a relief to finally be asked.

'Then we can commence,' the first voice said, pressing a button before her and sending the command to the AI Drone Storage centre, far north of them. So far away they knew they'd never see it. They would never have to know what happened as part of their orders.

Now, it was done.

England was sealed and isolated from their neighbours, as it had been 'voted' for, 'democratically' and despite all logic, reason, and the truth being contrary.

ABOUT THE AUTHOR

Lissy Porter is a pseudonym for an author who usually writes in a very different genre.

Follow Lissy on Instagram, Amazon or BlueSky.

www.throneofash.com

    instagram.com/lissyporterauthor
    bsky.app/profile/lissyporterauthor.bsky.social

Printed in Dunstable, United Kingdom